I0663094

Cowboys of Cavern County

RIHANNA'S RANCHER

BELLA SETTARRA

Rihanna's Rancher
ISBN # 978-1-80250-972-4
©Copyright Bella Settarra 2022
Cover Art by Claire Siemaszkiewicz ©Copyright August 2022
Interior text design by Claire Siemaszkiewicz
Totally Bound Publishing

Published in 2022 by Totally Bound Publishing, United Kingdom.

RIHANNA'S RANCHER

Dedication

To all my readers, with eternal gratitude x

Chapter One

Rihanna frowned at the figures on the screen. It was going to take a while to get her bank balance to look anything like healthy again. In her job, that wasn't a good thing—the bank manager with the humungous overdraft!

Her wedding dress hadn't fetched half what she'd paid for it, and the fancy hotel had refused to refund her a single penny for the canceled reception, despite the fact that they'd gotten months to find another couple to take their place. She wished now that she hadn't been so keen to pay it all off early. Had she paid in monthly installments, she'd have saved over a thousand dollars on the cost of the venue, but she could never bear to be in debt. *"Never a borrower or a lender be,"* her dad had instilled into her from an early age, and she'd lived her whole life by the motto.

Phil Cartwright had been the love of her life—and now he was the bane of it.

"At least he didn't jilt you at the altar," Mum had said, sympathetically.

Rihanna half-wished he had. At least then everyone would see for themselves what a cruel, heartless bastard he was. And she'd have gotten the chance to wear that gorgeous dress and show off her new figure. But the humiliation of him turning her down in front of everyone — or, worse still, not turning up — would have been insufferable. Almost as bad as having to return all the gifts and explain to everyone that the wedding was off.

Of course, they'd all been sorry for her, which just compounded the situation. She hated pity about as much as she hated Phil Cartwright right now. That sorrowful expression of his haunted her dreams, as well as every waking moment.

"I'm really sorry, but it's just not going to work," he'd told her softly.

Oddly enough, he'd omitted to mention that it wasn't going to work out with her because he already had someone else waiting on the sidelines — someone much richer and more sophisticated than Rihanna could ever hope to be. That much didn't become apparent until way after he'd moved out and left her to deal with the fallout. *Bastard.* She'd spent weeks believing it was her own fault, that she hadn't been good enough for him. She'd even begged him to give her another chance, for God's sake!

This promotion couldn't have come at a better time. She'd moved all her belongings into storage, packed a bag and headed out into the middle of nowhere to begin a new life — not where she wanted to be, of course, but at least she was away from Phil Cartwright and all her sympathetic, well-meaning friends and family.

She looked around the hotel room the company had put her up in. It was nice enough — clean, with high ceilings and dark wooden furniture. Not quite as good as she'd have had in New Moldington, but then, she was no longer in the city. Far from it...literally. This was Almondine in Cavern County. It had been described on the net as 'a busy town with everything a person could need'. Yeah, right. She wouldn't count on that.

The new job was in a place called Pelican's Heath, a few miles down the road. She'd been told it was more rural there and had been highlighted as 'a small up-and-coming town with lots of potential'. Yet it didn't even have a decent hotel for the bank to accommodate her in! Not that she'd want to stay too close to where she worked, anyway — not in her position. She was the boss and needed to be seen as such at all times, not be caught socializing with staff and customers during her downtime.

Talking of her new position, she noticed the clock by the bed as she checked that her hair was neatly tucked into a bun. Only a quarter to seven? That couldn't be right, surely? She went over to the coffee table where she'd left her cell charging. Half past eight? *Shit!* She was about to be late for her first day. What sort of impression would that give everyone?

She threw her laptop into its case, grabbed her phone and handbag and charged out of the door. She'd complain to reception later about the damn clock.

* * * *

The country roads were narrow and bumpy, jostling her about like a baby's rattle. She wondered why she'd even bothered to spend so long on her hair this morning. It was bound to be a hot mess by the time she got to work. At least her makeup looked good today, and she was pleased with her choice of skirted suit.

The roads became progressively worse as she neared Pelican's Heath, and it was nearly impossible to maintain a decent speed. She dreaded to think how filthy her car would be by now and considered whether the bank would be likely to pay her extra for wear and tear of her vehicle.

As she rounded a tight bend, she screamed and swerved the car right off the road. A massive horse reared up in front of her, its rider holding on for dear life as he steered the beast away from her car and steadied it a short way farther along.

Rihanna's heart beat wildly. She put her head in her hands, slumping over the steering wheel in relief and shock. She didn't dare imagine the damage an animal of that size could have done to her precious car — and she'd have a hard time claiming against her insurance. Furthermore, it could have killed her!

The thought riled her, and she looked over to see that a guy in a cowboy hat was strutting toward her. He'd secured the horse to a tree, a little way from the road.

She quickly got out of the car to await his apology — which would have to be good.

"Well, I see you're all right, then," the guy fired at her.

She stared at him. "I'm not so sure about my car, though," she snapped.

"Your *car*? That heap of metal? What about my poor living, breathing *horse*?"

"That lump of meat shouldn't have been on the road!" she yelled. "Roads are for cars. That's why I was driving on it."

"Where the hell are you from, lady?" He gawped at her in disbelief. "Firstly, horses used the roads long before cars were invented, and secondly, you do realize you're in Cavern County, don't you?"

"Oh, I'm well aware of where I am, thank you," she scorned. "In the back of beyond with a stupid redneck who thinks he and his livestock own the fucking road."

He looked slightly taken aback, then furious. He clenched his jaw tightly, making cute dimples appear in his cheeks.

Her whole body heated as she took in his appearance for the first time. He sure was handsome, even if he was a cowboy. He had dark eyes and, from what she could see around his hat, very dark, wavy hair. He was clean-shaven and had a full mouth with perfect teeth. Not exactly what she'd expected from a local.

"What makes you think I don't own this road?" he asked, his eyes flashing at her.

She swallowed hard. It was just possible that he did. After all, the land around here could conceivably be owned by the farmers and ranchers rather than a local council. "Well, if you do, I'd like to have a word with you about the dire state of it," she replied, sticking her nose in the air. "It's clearly not signed as private property, which means you'll be liable for the damage all the loose stones and potholes have caused my car. If you'd just give me your name, I'll be getting my lawyers to contact you."

He gaped at her. "You've got to be kidding me?"

"Do I look like I'm joking? I've got every right to sue for the damage caused by your lack of maintenance of the road."

He shook his head. "You really are something, lady."

"And you're delaying me from getting to work." She suddenly remembered the tearing hurry she was in.

A huge grin covered his face, making him look even more handsome. He waved a hand to indicate the horse and her car. "Are you sure all this wasn't just a ruse for you to ask my name?"

Her face flushed as anger and embarrassment mingled to what she knew would probably be a bright hue of scarlet.

"What?" she demanded, not quite as assertively as she'd hoped.

"Ace Blenheim," he replied, grinning even more as he studied her. "And you are...?"

"Late." She quickly got back into her car, knowing full well that he was amused at her blushes. Not that it had been any kind of trick, of course, but there was no way of explaining that to him.

He was still chuckling as she started the engine, and she seethed as she drove gingerly past him and into Pelican's Heath. She'd had enough of being humiliated.

By the time she'd reached the bank, she'd already planned all the ways she could exact revenge on the smarmy redneck. At least she had his name. All she had to do was check to see if he had applied for an account at the new bank in town. She hoped so. It would give her great pleasure to turn him down.

Rihanna was embarrassed to find two people in smart clothes waiting by the door. She'd really hoped to arrive before the staff, today of all days. A large sign was plastered across the window of the bank proclaiming 'Opening Today'.

"Good morning. I'm Rihanna Richards," she told them politely, taking the key from her purse and unlocking the large door.

"I'm Sarah, and this is Paul," the woman said officiously.

Rihanna stood back to let them enter first. They were both quite a bit older than she was, assuming Paul to be in his fifties, while Sarah was possibly mid-forties. She wondered whether they might have a problem working with someone as young as she was. Still, there was nothing she could do about it now. They'd been hired without her input and would all just have to make the best of the situation.

She was pleasantly surprised at the light, airy building, with modern equipment and blonde wood furnishings. It had occurred to her that a place like Pelican's Heath might be full of musty old buildings and dark wood fixtures. It probably was, she surmised — just not in here.

She locked the door behind them while Sarah drew up the blinds and Paul took his seat behind the counter. Rihanna had read their résumés and knew they were both experienced tellers, so at least she wouldn't have to get involved in staff training and suchlike.

A door marked 'Manager' stood to the side of the room, while the staff room was behind the counter, down a short corridor.

She went straight into her office and was immediately greeted by the smell of rose-scented polish. Like the rest of the building, her fittings were all blonde wood, including the large desk that dominated the room.

After putting her purse in her bottom desk drawer, she went back out to see how her staff was faring.

"Is it okay to open?" Sarah asked, walking toward the front door.

"I'll do it." She cut her off and went straight back to unlock the door they had just entered through.

She took a deep breath for a second. This was her very own branch and, although it wasn't exactly in the location she'd have preferred, it still carried some kudos.

"Good morning." She greeted a couple of men who were waiting outside.

One of them checked his watch. She narrowed her eyes. Although she was supposed to encourage as many of the locals as possible to open accounts here, there were one or two whom she already had serious doubts about. Here was number two.

She watched them go up to the counter. Mr. Williamson, the area manager, had ensured that the new staff had been briefed, and he'd already gone through all their duties with them when he'd hired them.

"Morning, Geoff." Paul was local and would obviously know some of the customers already.

Sarah was a little more quiet, having recently moved to Pelican's Heath. She seemed efficient enough, however, and Rihanna guessed she'd probably be friendlier once she got to know a few people.

She, on the other hand, had no intention of getting acquainted with the locals of Cavern County, except on a professional level. This was not her home, and as far as she was concerned, it would never be.

The sooner she made her mark and proved to Mr. Williamson that she was more than capable of running her own branch, the better. He'd promised to consider her for a bigger branch in the city, and that was the job she really wanted. Pelican's Heath was merely a steppingstone.

She smirked as she heard the time-conscious customer ask Sarah for an application form to open a new account. He turned back to look at her, and

Rihanna guessed that Sarah had just informed him that she was the manager and the person who needed to sanction his request. His face fell. Maybe she *would* enjoy working here, after all.

The leather swivel-chair in her office was sumptuous, and she raised the seat a little to adjust it to her liking. At five foot four, she wasn't especially tall and didn't want customers to look down on her when they sat in the chair opposite hers.

A big pile of mail had been heaped onto her desk, presumably by the cleaner, and she started to sort through it. Most of it would be application forms for new accounts, and she knew that hundreds of people had already transferred theirs here from Almondine. Having a bank at Pelican's Heath was a novelty to the community, and she could see they were keen to exploit it.

Her phone rang and she smiled. As she'd thought, it was Sarah.

"Hi, Miss Richards, I've got a gentleman here who needs to open a new account with us as soon as possible. He has completed his form. Would you be free to consider it now, please?"

Rihanna quickly opened a drawer and stuffed the pile of mail inside. She didn't want to look disorganized in front of Mr. What-time-do-you-call-this?

"Of course, send him straight through, would you, Sarah?"

She smiled, looking forward to seeing his expression when he realized how much power she had around here. Her supercilious grin was soon wiped from her face, however, when a certain dark-haired cowboy opened her door.

Chapter Two

His face looked as stunned as hers must, although his was still as devilishly handsome as it had been earlier.

"Come in," she said, noticing that he hadn't even knocked.

He narrowed his eyes as he walked over to the desk. "*You're* the new bank manager?"

"That's right, Mr. Blenheim. Was there something you wanted my help with?"

He swallowed hard. "I didn't realize."

"Why would you?"

He huffed, sitting down, and put his hat on her desk. She stared at it, pointedly.

"The horse is fine, by the way," he told her.

"I'm not so sure about my car." She kept her voice calm and polite, though she felt anything but.

"He didn't touch your car, ma'am," he reminded her.

"I'm well aware of what happened, Mr. Blenheim. I was practically run off the road while trying to avoid hitting your horse."

"Welcome to Cavern County." A twinkle glinted in his eye.

She sniffed. "Thank you."

"Well, Miss Richards, the reason I'm here is to get this here bank account opened," he told her, handing over the form. "I've put all the details on there, but the lady outside said you need to sign the bottom."

She took it from him, impressed at his neat handwriting. "That's correct, Mr. Blenheim. I need to consider each application on its own merits and decide whether or not to allow the account to be opened here."

He frowned. "*Allow* it? Why the hell *wouldn't* you allow it? You do *want* folks to use the bank, don'tcha?"

She sat a little straighter, enjoying having the upper hand. "Of course, Mr. Blenheim, we want customers to make use of the bank and to open their accounts here. However, we can't just allow *anyone* to associate with the branch. We have a selection procedure to follow."

His frown became deeper, marring his gorgeous looks. "What kind of *selection* procedure?"

"One that involves background checks," she told him, slowly. "We have to ensure our clients are worthy of an account. I'm sure you must understand that. We're entering into a business agreement, and we can't do that lightheartedly now, can we?"

He pursed his lips. "But how long will that take?"

She glanced at his form. "It depends."

He huffed, and she delighted in his apparent annoyance. "Depends on what, exactly?"

"A number of factors."

"Yeah, I'll bet."

She smiled. "I've got your number, Mr. Blenheim. I'll get one of the staff to call you once a decision has been made." She put the form on the table and clasped her hands together.

"Is that it? You can't just sign it so I can get my wages paid in?" He looked incredulous.

"For now." She nodded.

"But usually you just fill in a form and open an account. You don't have to wait around for *background* checks."

"Maybe not where you come from, Mr. Blenheim, but this is business. Everything has to be done by the book." She gave him a dismissive look. "Was there anything else you needed from me?" Her smile was even sicklier than before. She was enjoying this.

"Nope. That was it." He got up, shaking his head. "Well, thank you for your time, Miss Richards. I appreciate it." He leaned forward to shake her hand.

She stood and held hers out to him, surprised by how small it looked there. His long, warm fingers wrapped around her hand, and something lurched in her stomach. Glancing up into his face, she saw him smiling at her and her insides melted. He sure was a handsome cowboy.

"You're welcome," she whispered, having suddenly lost the ability to speak.

His smile turned into a shit-eating grin before he turned and left the room.

She sat down as her legs turned to Jell-O. Right up until the last minute she'd thought she had the upper hand. Now, though, she wasn't so sure.

* * * *

The day was really busy, with several new customers coming in to ask for an account. It wasn't usually a long process, but they were clearly as surprised as Ace Blenheim that she couldn't just sanction them on the spot.

The pile of mail in her drawer eventually got smaller, and she was pleasantly surprised that several successful businesses seemed eager to transfer their accounts to Pelican's Heath. It would provide welcome relief to the already-overstretched Almondine branch, which, although bigger, didn't appear to have enough staff to cope with the work demand.

It seemed that Pelican's Heath had grown exponentially over the past year, with more businesses moving to the area, and hence, the bank had been forced to open another branch.

She went through to help on the counter while Sarah and Paul took turns to take their lunch breaks. Luckily it was a very busy period, as trying to make conversation with both her members of staff was like attempting to get blood from a stone.

"How long have you lived around here?" she asked Paul.

"Ages."

"Do you like it in Pelican's Heath?"

"Yes."

That was how each conversation went. She didn't know why, but they seemed to speak quite freely between themselves, but when it came to her, one-word answers were all she got.

Rihanna was pleased to get back to the sanctity of her own office when the lunch breaks were over. She took her purse from the drawer and locked her door on her way out.

"I'm just going to get something to eat," she told Sarah, as Paul was serving an old lady.

"What if anyone wants to speak to you?" Sarah looked astonished.

"They'll have to wait. I won't be long." Rihanna hadn't meant to snap but was appalled at the woman's attitude. She'd just spent the past two hours covering so the staff could eat their meals, and now Sarah was questioning whether her boss should leave the premises long enough to fetch a sandwich from the café across the road?

Sarah looked taken aback, but Rihanna didn't care. She was the boss around here, and if the staff had a problem with that, then they could take it up with Mr. Williamson.

She stalked out of the bank and walked headlong into a familiar cowboy, who, it turned out, had an enticingly ripped chest.

"I'm sorry." She flushed, looking up into his dark eyes. "Oh, it's you."

His shirt was undone, and she could see a sheen of sweat across his torso. He smelled divine, a sort of musky, spicy scent mixed with the smell of sheer hard work.

"Apparently so."

"Look… I'm sorry. I'm just in a hurry."

"Again? Would that be because you need to get back and sanction all those account applications?" he asked, with a pointed expression.

"Yes, actually. I've been working hard all morning, and now all I want is to grab something to eat so I can get back to it. Is that okay with you?" she snapped, partly from embarrassment. There was something about this guy that really affected her in ways no other man did—or should.

"Is everything all right, lady?" A scruffy-looking man with uneven teeth came up behind her, making her jump.

Ace huffed, irritably.

"Yes...thank you," she mumbled.

"Good, 'cause if this man's giving you any trouble —"

"No, not at all. It was my fault. I just bumped into him." She was rambling, but there was nothing she could do about it now.

The guy nodded, and Rihanna offered Ace an apologetic look before scurrying across the road to the café.

The food didn't look very appetizing, but she settled on a ham and salad sandwich and headed back to her office, praying that she didn't see Ace again.

Sarah gave her a disparaging look as soon as she returned to the bank.

"Someone wanted to see you," she informed Rihanna, as soon as she arrived.

"Who?"

"Mr. Shearer. He owns the big ranch around the back of town."

"I'll call him," she said, firmly.

Sarah didn't seem pleased, but Rihanna ignored her look of disdain and dived into her office.

The Shearer Ranch was very successful and had a good reputation, according to the Internet, when she'd looked it up. It seemed Mr. Matthew Shearer had made some good investments and his property had expanded and flourished over the past year or so.

Rihanna was impressed. She'd imagined the locals to be a load of uneducated rednecks with no idea about business at all. She'd envisaged them all being farmers with insular attitudes and no interest in progress. It seemed she'd been wrong.

"Hello, is this Mr. Shearer?" she asked, phoning him up a short while later.

"Yes, it is. But which one is it you're after, ma'am?" a guy asked, politely.

"Oh. I hadn't realized. Um… *Matthew* Shearer," she said quickly.

"That's me. What can I do for you?"

"I'm Rihanna Richards from the bank in Pelican's Heath," she explained. "I had a message that you wanted to speak to me."

"Oh." He sounded surprised. "You're the new bank manager?"

"That's right, sir."

"Well now, it's very nice to hear from you. The reason I popped into the bank was to ask about an account for one of my staff. You see, he's new to the job, and I need to set up the payments for his wages."

"I see."

"Good, 'cause that's pretty impossible with no bank account to pay them into," he said.

"I understand, Mr. Shearer. Perhaps if you'd ask your employee to come and fill in an application form, I could see what I can do."

"Thank you, ma'am, but he has actually already done that…and spoken to you. But he said it's going to take a while to get it all sorted. And, as you can imagine, when it comes to a man's wages, we can't afford to waste time."

A sinking feeling hit her stomach. "What is the name of your employee?" she asked, though she could guess the answer. "Maybe I could see if there's any way I could speed up the process a little."

"Well now, that would be real nice of you, ma'am. I appreciate that. His name's Ace Blenheim."

Of course it is.

"Oh yes, I was just working on that one," she lied. "I'll get back to it right now and see if we can expedite the application."

"Thank you, ma'am. That's real kind of you."

She put the receiver down with a sigh. Shearers had an account here at the branch and there was no way she could afford to upset them. *Damn!* She'd rather enjoyed winding up Ace Blenheim this morning.

Digging the form out of her drawer, she set to work on it straight away. She'd have to find another way of getting one over on the handsome cowboy, but he wasn't worth losing the Shearer account for — especially not on her first day!

The afternoon flew by, and she managed to get through several of the account applications. Tomorrow she would contact the customers and let them know the good news. She yawned, ready to go home.

Paul and Sarah were already in their coats, waiting for her to unlock the door again when she left her office.

"Thanks for all your hard work today," she said, smiling.

They both looked at her incredulously.

"Have a nice night," she added as they parted company on the street.

They both mumbled something incoherent, and she sighed as she locked up and went over to her car.

"Oh no!" Her whole, tired, body sagged as she gaped at the muddy truck that had parked so close to her trunk that there was no way she could maneuver it out of its space.

"Are you okay, miss?" It was the guy from earlier with the wonky teeth.

"Yes, thank you. It's just that someone's hemmed me in." She gestured to her car.

"Selfish bastards, they are," he cursed. "No thought for anyone but themselves. Want me to call the sheriff?"

"No, no, honestly, it's not that important," she assured him. "I'll just go get a coffee over the road and watch out for them to come back and move the truck."

"Well, if you're sure?"

"Positive. Thank you, though."

"Just lookin' out for a neighbor." He doffed a hat he wasn't wearing.

"I appreciate it." She smiled before heading over the road, praying that he didn't follow her.

The guy was very nice to look out for her like this but he smelled a bit funky, and she was pleased to think that she was, in no way, his neighbor.

"Hey, I haven't seen you here before." A pretty girl with long, dark, wavy hair pulled up a chair next to her. "I'm Carla." She gave her a wide smile.

"Hi, Carla. I'm Rihanna. I've just taken over as the bank manager across the road." She was glad to see a friendly face.

"I heard they'd opened up," Carla said, her eyes shining. "How's it going?"

"Good. Busy," she replied before taking a sip of her coffee.

"Well, I guess that's a good thing," Carla replied. "I work part-time at the grocery store, when I'm not helping out at my husbands' ranch."

"I'll probably see quite a lot of you, in that case." Rihanna smiled. She'd been afraid she wouldn't make any friends here, but, yet again, it seemed she'd been wrong.

"So, do you live around here?" Carla asked.

"No. I'm staying at a hotel in Almondine for the time being," she replied.

"Phew, I'll bet that's expensive." Carla shook her head, making her dark waves bounce around her face.

"The bank's paying for it," Rihanna confided. "Just for a little while."

"So, are you looking for somewhere local?" Carla asked, before taking another sip of her coffee.

"I'm not sure," Rihanna confessed. "I thought I'd wait and see how things went, what with the new job and all." She didn't like to confess that she didn't want to stick around and was only waiting for a better job opportunity with a city bank.

Carla nodded. "That makes sense. It's good of your company to be so understanding."

"Yeah, they're a great bank." She forced a smile, trying not to think about the conversation she'd had with Mr. Williamson, who wanted her to move into her own place as soon as she possibly could, to save the bank some money. She knew it made financial sense from his point of view, but it was a lot of hassle for a job she wasn't expecting to stay in for long.

"Well, I'm really pleased I ran into you," Carla said, standing up. "Looks like my ride's here." She gestured through the window to a good-looking cowboy who had just crossed the street.

Rihanna gawped. "Ace Blenheim?"

"Yeah, do you know him?" Carla gestured that she was on her way, and Ace went over to the truck that was parked behind Rihanna's car.

"Is that *his* truck?" she seethed.

"Sure is. Can we offer you a ride?" Carla smiled as they left the café.

"No thanks. That's my car right there. I couldn't get it out of its spot with that truck parked so close behind." She spoke through gritted teeth, loud enough for Ace to hear.

"Oh." Carla put her hand to her mouth.

"That's *your* car?" Ace clarified when they caught up to him.

"Yes. I couldn't get it out with yours practically parked in my trunk," Rihanna replied, tight-lipped.

"So, what, you had to wait a while?" He frowned.

"Yes, I did. I was hoping it wouldn't be all night." Her voice was clipped.

"Yeah, that wouldn't have been much fun," he said, thoughtfully. "Having to wait around for things is always such a pain in the ass, don't you think?"

She opened her mouth, ready to speak when she caught his expression. The twitch around his mouth told her he knew darn well it was her car. He'd have recognized it from this morning's encounter.

He nodded politely before getting into his truck. "Touché, Miss Richards."

Chapter Three

Rihanna made sure to be at the bank early the following day, despite driving a little more cautiously than she had the day before. No way could she afford repairs to her car, should anything untoward happen. It was a good thing the bank was paying some of her living expenses, as she'd never have been able to support herself otherwise.

She unlocked the bank and sighed with relief. She took the opportunity to have a good look around while it was empty and was impressed that the clerks had plenty of space behind the counter and their chairs were of good quality. Everything was neat and tidy, as she'd expected, which was good as, apparently, they only had a cleaner in twice a week.

She removed her jacket and fired up her computer before going into the staff room to make herself a cup of coffee. It had been a little disappointing yesterday to find that Sarah and Paul made each other drinks throughout their shift but never offered her one.

There was a knock at the front door a short while later, and she took her drink with her as she went to unlock the door for the staff.

"Good morning," she chirped, as they both filed in.

"Morning," they mumbled back at her.

"How are you both?" she asked, trying to sound cheerful.

"Fine," Sarah replied, with a surprised expression.

Paul just looked at her as though she were stupid — but said nothing.

"I've just put the coffee on," she went on. "Would you like some?"

She ignored their bewildered expressions as she went back to the staff room and poured their drinks.

"Milk and sugar?" she asked as they followed her in to put their things in their lockers.

"Three sugars and milk," Paul mumbled.

"Coming up. What about you, Sarah?"

"Just milk, thanks."

"Great. You're the same as me. Sweet enough, eh?" she joked.

Sarah said nothing as she took the cup from her.

"We didn't get much time to get to know each other yesterday," Rihanna went on, just as Paul turned his back to leave the room. "So I thought it would be good to make more of an effort today. I mean, I know we're all busy, which is great, but I think it's important to look out for each other, too, don't you?"

Clearly not, if their expressions were anything to go by.

"I'm staying in Almondine for the time being. Do you both live in Pelican's Heath?" She knew the answer from their résumés but thought it polite to ask.

"Yeah. Lived here all my life," Paul said, turning back around to face her.

"And you're married, aren't you, Paul?"

He huffed. "Yeah. Nearly twenty years."

She nodded. He was quite broad with short, dark hair that was graying at the temples. His face was clean-shaven but had a rugged appearance, like someone who spent a lot of time outdoors. *Unusual for a banker,* she thought.

"And what about you?" she asked Sarah with a smile.

"No, I'm divorced. No kids or anything." Sarah seemed a little reticent to talk about herself, which Rihanna felt was fair enough. "I think it's time to open," Sarah added quickly.

Rihanna nodded and went back to the front door while the other two sat behind the counter.

"Let's hope for another good day." Rihanna was determined to keep cheerful, despite their reluctance to reciprocate.

She unlocked the door, surprised to see a man standing outside.

"Good morning. Miss Richards? I'm Sheriff Dyson Shearer. Do you mind if I have a word with you?"

"Of course not. Come in, Sheriff. Can I get you a coffee?"

"No, thank you, ma'am." He followed her into her office, where she closed the door after him.

"Is everything all right?" She frowned as she gestured for him to sit down.

"Nothing to worry about, ma'am," he assured her, removing his hat and placing it on the empty chair next to him. "I wanted to introduce myself, anyhow, but just thought I'd check on something while I'm here."

She narrowed her eyes. "Did you say your surname was Shearer? As in the Shearer Ranch?"

He nodded with a smile that lit up his whole face. "You've done your homework, I see."

"It's just that I spoke with Matthew Shearer yesterday." She smiled.

"My brother. *Twin* brother, actually. Yeah, he runs the ranch while I run the town." He chuckled.

She took a sip of her coffee. "Well, it's very nice of you to come by and say hello, Sheriff."

He sat forward in his seat, treating her to a waft of his spicy aftershave. He really was a handsome guy, clean-shaven with really dark hair that was cut short. Even from here she could see that he was fairly muscular under that gray shirt of his, and she noticed his big hands.

"I spoke to Ace Blenheim yesterday," he said slowly. "I believe you've met him?"

Her eyes widened as she studied his expression. Had Ace complained to the sheriff about her? Had he accused her of dangerous driving, maybe? Her whole body tensed, and she sat a little straighter.

"Yes, I've met Mr. Blenheim," she concurred.

"He works on the ranch with my brother, Matt," Dyson clarified.

"So I understand." For a second she wondered if he'd been recruited to try to persuade her to rush through Ace's bank account application.

"Ace told me that he spoke to you yesterday and that you were interrupted by an older guy." Dyson spoke slowly.

She narrowed her eyes. "Yes. The gentleman was concerned that Mr. Blenheim was bothering me." She took another sip of coffee.

Dyson licked his lips, thoughtfully. "And *was* Ace Blenheim bothering you, Miss Richards?"

She shook her head. "No." *Not that time, anyhow.* "I'd just bumped into him in the street, literally," she clarified. "I was hurrying to go fetch some lunch while the bank was quiet, and we just...sort of...collided."

Dyson nodded.

"Is there a problem?" She wondered what version of events Ace Blenheim had given him.

He shook his head. "No, not really." He chewed his lip. "It was just that Ace mentioned the guy who spoke to you—an older guy in a red checked shirt and Levi's with a general unkempt appearance and light-brown hair." He was reading from his notebook now.

"What of it?" She shrugged.

"Do you know the guy?"

"No. Why would I?" She frowned.

"He doesn't sound familiar. Did he open a bank account here, do you know?"

"No, not that I know of. I'm still processing all the applications, but it would be impossible to check without a name." She shook her head. "Is he important to you?"

Dyson smiled, putting his notebook back into his breast pocket. "No, not really. He just seems to be new in town." He sat back in his chair. "Here at Pelican's Heath we're always a little wary of strangers, that's all."

She stared at him. "Like me, you mean, Sheriff?" She hadn't intended to sound quite so snappy.

He shook his head with a grin. "Not exactly."

"But *I'm* new around here. Have you gone around asking people about me?"

He chuckled. "No, nothing like that. Besides, we know who you are."

"We?"

He nodded, seemingly surprised at her concern. "The townsfolk. We're a close-knit community, Miss Richards. Everyone knows everyone's business, if you know what I mean?"

She narrowed her eyes, seething. "Really?"

"It's nothing sinister," he assured her. "It's just the way it is in a small place like this. You'll get used to it." He stood up. "Anyhow, if you find out who this guy is, I'd be obliged if you'd give me a call at the office." He handed her his business card before retrieving his hat from the other chair.

"Why? Has he done something wrong?" She stood and followed him to the door.

He turned back to face her. "Not that we know of. But we can never be really sure until we find out who he is. It's just for the safety of the town, you understand?"

"I think I'm beginning to." She spoke through gritted teeth.

He chuckled. "Wait till you've been here a while. This sort of thing will all become second nature to you." She watched his pert ass as he swaggered out of the office and into the melee of the busy bank.

It was as much as she could do not to slam the door behind him. There was no way she'd get used to all this nosiness—and it was just another reason she wasn't planning on hanging around this place.

* * * *

Ace Blenheim was having a great day. Matt Shearer had been really impressed with the way he'd dealt with a problem with the feed delivery, and the guys he was working with seemed to like him.

He'd met Carla, the pretty brunette who was married to both Shearer brothers, and she'd even given him breakfast, being as he'd arrived so early for work today.

Truth was, he hadn't been able to sleep without dreaming about a certain blonde bank manager all night, and he was eager to get out there and see her again.

He noticed the sheriff's car pulling into the drive of the ranch house and went over to see if he'd had any news. Dyson had been mighty interested in the guy who'd so rudely interrupted his conversation with Rihanna the day before and was going to see what he could find out. Being new to Pelican's Heath, Ace hadn't realized the guy was also a stranger, but Matt had noticed them talking when he and the boss had popped into town for a few supplies in the afternoon and had asked about him.

"Morning, Sheriff." Ace nodded as the guy got out of his car.

"Ace, I was hoping to see you. I've just been into the bank to ask if Miss Richards knew that guy you spoke to yesterday. She doesn't know anything about him, but she'll let us know if he crops up on their records. All we need now is a name."

"I guess I could've asked him at the time, but I didn't think anything of it." Ace pursed his lips.

"And why would you? It's probably nothing." Dyson shrugged. "We're just always on our guard around here, that's all. Once we know who he is and what he's doing in Pelican's Heath, we can forget about him. It's just a precaution."

Matt came out of the house just then, smiling. "Hey, bro."

"Hey, yourself. I was just saying we haven't found out anything about that stranger yet," Dyson told him.

The guys were identical, so it was helpful that Dyson wore a uniform. Ace wasn't sure he'd ever be able to tell them apart otherwise. Their only other distinguishing feature was that right now Dyson was clean-shaven, where Matt had left a little stubble to grow on his face. It seemed to suit their personalities.

"Damn. We'll just keep our ear to the ground," Matt offered. "But I got some good news. That new manager down at the bank just rang to say Ace's account's been sanctioned." He turned to Ace. "Seems like you *will* be getting paid this week, after all." He grinned, just as Carla came up behind him.

"Well, that's a relief." Ace smiled. Although he knew it was just a formality to get the account up and running, he wouldn't have put it past Rihanna to have delayed things a little longer. He hoped that she'd got the message after their encounter the previous night.

"Seems like you got your point across," Carla said, beaming.

She sure was cute, and he could certainly see why the twins loved her so much.

"I'd like to think it had something to do with it." Ace smirked.

"So, you don't think it was my phone call that did it?" Matt feigned shock, putting an arm around Carla.

"Well, maybe that, too," she conceded with a giggle. "The poor girl didn't seem to have any choice with the both of you ganging up on her like that."

"*Poor girl?* She almost ran into my horse." Ace raised his eyes in mock astonishment.

"Hey, buddy, I've seen Trident. That horse of yours would have done a darn sight more damage to her pretty little car than she'd have done to him," Matt pointed out.

"She *was* a little concerned about the mud on it," Ace conceded.

"She sure is a townie," Dyson added. "Got quite upset at the thought of everyone knowing her business." He pursed his lips.

"You think she's got something to hide?" Matt asked, narrowing his eyes at his brother.

"Only time will tell." Dyson shook his head.

"Maybe she just likes to keep to herself. After all, her life's no one's business but her own, ain't it?" Ace hadn't meant to jump to her defense so blatantly, but he could see by the smirks on his bosses' faces that he'd been quite obvious.

"Of course." Dyson put his palms up in a pacifying manner. "No one's trying to invade anyone's privacy. Just doing my job." He grinned.

Ace rolled his eyes. "Well, I hope you don't go digging into my business. That's all I'm saying." He pointed at the sheriff as he joked.

"Oh no. You never know what you might find in there," Matt added with a chuckle.

"Hmm, that's what worries me," Dyson said with a laugh. "Think I might consider a career change, after all."

"What? And not find out all the juicy gossip around here?" Carla shook her head. "You'd hate it."

"Talking of which, you looked quite cozy with Miss Richards when I rocked up yesterday." Ace grinned. He'd tried to wheedle some information out of her as he'd driven her home last night, but Carla wasn't giving much away.

"You've met her?" Dyson raised his eyebrows at his wife.

"Just in passing." Carla nodded, her dark curls bouncing around her shoulders. "I saw her in the coffee shop, so I stopped to say hi."

"That was very neighborly of you," Ace pointed out.

"I can tell you haven't lived around Pelican's Heath for long," Carla replied. "We always try to make strangers feel welcome."

"Unless they look a bit shifty," Matt cut in. "Something about that guy didn't look right to me."

"That's good enough for me, bro. I'll be looking out for him from here on in. Don't you worry about that."

Ace could tell he wasn't going to be able to wangle any more information out of Carla, so he just grinned. "I'd best get back to work."

He'd planned to go into town for some lunch later, so he'd look out for Rihanna while he was there — and the guy in the red checked shirt. Matt had been right about him. Something wasn't right. And the fact that he'd spoken to Rihanna was even more reason to dislike him.

Chapter Four

Ace worked hard all morning, deliberately keeping busy so he wouldn't have to think about the gorgeous new bank manager. It didn't work. He couldn't keep her off his mind. She was just so pretty, with her beautiful blonde hair, which he longed to unpin from that bun she kept it tied in. He liked that it was clearly fine, as it didn't keep in place too well, and strands of it hung loose around her face and shoulders. He'd love to run his fingers through her golden locks.

She sure was feisty, too, which he loved. He felt that he was one up on her for now, having persuaded her to open his bank account, but he guessed she'd already be scheming to get her own back. He grinned.

"You look happy," Tom, one of the hands, remarked, as they finished mending a fence panel on the bottom field.

"Just enjoying my job," he replied.

"Yeah, right. I know that look. I guess there's a pretty girl behind it somewhere." Tom was a good guy and a hard worker. He was married and lived in

Pelican's Heath with his wife and two children. He was also a shrewd judge of character, and Ace guessed nothing would get by him.

"There might be," he replied with a lopsided grin.

"Come on, bro. Spill. Maybe she's someone I know," Tom teased.

"She's new in town," Ace told him, thoughtfully. "Her name's Rihanna Richards."

Tom raised his eyebrows. "That name sounds familiar. Isn't she the new bank manager?"

"You know her?" Ace frowned.

Tom shook his head. "My wife went in there yesterday to bank a check. She didn't get to speak to her, but it sounds like it was just as well. She's not too popular, by all accounts."

Ace picked up his tools, putting them into his leather bag. He stopped suddenly and stared at his colleague.

"Why ever not?"

Tom shrugged. "She spoke to the guy on the counter, and he was quite scathing, apparently. Said she was a stuck-up townie and wouldn't last five minutes in Pelican's Heath. Not only was she late for work on her first day, but she seemed to have an air about her—like she was looking down her nose at everyone and everything."

"Really?"

"I think it didn't help that she was so young. He kinda felt she was *too* young to be running the bank."

"Let me guess. He'd do a much better job himself, I suppose?" Ace shook his head.

Tom shrugged. "It's just what I heard."

Ace seethed, wondering how many more of the locals had been given the guy's poor opinion of her. She'd only been there a day, for Christ's sake.

"It's a shame when locals don't take kindly to strangers," he said with a sigh.

"You had any problems like that?" Tom frowned.

"Not really. I love it here on the ranch, and everyone's been so friendly. Sometimes it's hard when you come in as a new foreman, as it's always possible the staff will begrudge your authority. I can imagine how hard it must be for a young girl, though—especially one with a responsible position like that—with staff who resent her for her age."

Tom smirked. "You're welcome to take on the hassle around here," he assured him. "Some of us don't want the extra weight on our shoulders. I, for one, have got enough to contend with without all that, thanks very much."

"I wish the staff down at the bank were of the same opinion."

"Maybe they'll warm to her once they get to know her." Tom put his hands up in submission. "It was just his first impression."

Ace huffed, gathering up his tools. He had to admit that *his* first impression of Rihanna hadn't exactly been favorable. She had been pretty pissed when she'd nearly collided with his horse, Titan. And she hadn't been able to hide her annoyance when he'd deliberately parked his truck so close to her car that she couldn't move it, but it still wasn't any reason to dislike her. In fact, he'd seen her attitude as a challenge—and one he was more than happy to accept.

"I'm going to take an early lunch," he said, throwing his tools into the back of the pickup. "Want a lift back?"

Tom grinned. "No, I want a word with Derek, who's over in the next field. I'll grab a ride with him, thanks."

Ace nodded and climbed into the truck.

He wasn't all that hungry after the large breakfast Carla had treated him to, but he was hoping to catch a glimpse of Rihanna. Part of him wanted to make sure she was okay, having heard what the staff thought of her. She must be having a hard time.

He loved the short drive into town. The Shearer Ranch had clearly been built quite near to Pelican's Heath originally, but it seemed, over the years, it had grown as the guys bought more land, and it now stretched quite a way beyond.

Ace was pleased to have found such a good job with great people. Heck, he'd never had the boss's wife cook him breakfast before. The people around here sure seemed to care about one another.

He saw Rihanna's little red car parked in the street outside the bank and grinned. He'd relished the look on her pretty face last night when she'd realized he was the one who had hemmed her in. He purposely parked on the opposite side of the road today.

As he got out of the truck, he almost bumped into a young guy in a dirty gray work shirt.

"Sorry, buddy." Ace smiled at him.

The guy grunted and went on his way.

Disappointed at his demeanor, Ace watched him stroll up the street and was surprised to see him meet up with the guy in the red checked shirt from the day before. *Doesn't that guy have any other clothes?*

Ace backed into the doorway of a shop to watch the guys as they went into the café opposite the bank. He followed them in, desperate to know what the heck they were up to.

"Do you know those guys?" He kept his voice low as he quizzed the lady behind the counter.

She looked over to them and shook her head. They'd taken their cups outside to sit at one of the tables by the street.

"I think the one in red was in here the other day," she said with a shrug, "but I've never seen his friend."

Ace nodded with a smile. "Right. I thought one of them looked a little familiar, that's all. Must have been some other guy." He took his coffee and a sandwich and went to sit near the window.

The café was getting quite busy, and he was disappointed not to be able to hear what was being said at the outside table. Although the door was generally kept open, every now and then it would get closed after a customer went through, and it was impossible to hear a word.

He took out his phone and surreptitiously took a picture of them both. He couldn't get a good look at red-shirt guy, but the other one was facing his way. They were muttering to each other, and occasionally looked up at the bank opposite.

Ace felt a lurch in his stomach. Why were they interested in the damn bank? He had to remind himself that the building just happened to be opposite them, so it was natural to look up at it from time to time, and he was just being paranoid.

His protective instincts had kicked in as soon as Tom had told him that the staff wasn't very supportive of their new boss, and he couldn't help feeling sorry for her.

He knew only too well how uncomfortable it felt being somewhere where people had taken a disliking to you. His last girlfriend, Alice Springer, had been a really popular member of the community over in Wells End. Her family had lived there for years and were well-known for all the charitable work they did over that way. Her father was a lawyer and on the local council, and her brother's business had provided good employment for a number of the locals. When Alice had announced after two years of them living together that she was leaving him, he'd been shocked.

Their relationship had been a little rocky for a while, but he'd thought it was stable enough to weather the storm. He had a good job at a ranch a short way from the town, and she worked in her dad's legal firm, doing secretarial duties. Some days it meant they didn't see each other for long, when work was unusually busy, but he'd regarded it as just taking the rough with the smooth.

As if it weren't bad enough, suddenly the whole town had to know their business, as it seemed Alice had no qualms about divulging details of their break-up to anyone who'd listen—which was practically everyone in a tight community like Wells End. He received the cold shoulder from all Alice's family, whom he'd come to regard as friends. Her father seemed to think it was his fault that his daughter was unhappy, and it wasn't long before the rest of the town had started to agree with him.

Ace had no idea what Alice had been saying about him, but it was clear that he was getting the blame for their split. He knew that it had been difficult with their work schedules, especially as he was looking for promotion, so had put in some extremely long hours to impress his boss.

Alice loved her job and thought nothing of going out for a drink with her colleagues after a long day.

It was all circumstantial, and something they'd talked about on several occasions. He had no idea Alice had felt this badly about the situation, though, and couldn't help wondering if the handsome new lawyer who'd recently joined the family's firm hadn't had something to do with her change of heart.

It had soon become unbearable living in a place where he'd suddenly become public enemy number one, and he was glad for the opportunity to move to Pelican's Heath as foreman of the Shearer Ranch.

Looking back, he questioned whether he and Alice had really been in love in the first place. He'd thought they had been, but with hindsight, it certainly didn't seem that way.

The door opened and he heard the guys outside mumbling to each other.

"Wouldn't be hard," Red Shirt said.

The door closed again but he watched Gray Shirt's reaction. He nodded, then smirked before they both got up and walked down the street.

What the heck was that all about?

Ace shook his head, laughing to himself. He was getting as jumpy as the sheriff! Why would he view every stranger as a potential threat? They were just a couple of guys, probably catching up after not seeing each other for a while. There was no law against that.

He finished his drink and went over to the bank. It was quite busy, being lunchtime, and he was surprised to see the woman behind the desk go out back and reappear a few seconds later with her coat and bag.

There were mumbles from the customers who were waiting in one long line, ready to be served.

Rihanna came out of her office a few moments later, smiling as she glanced around the room. She quickly took the woman's seat behind the counter and began serving.

Ace joined the line. He watched the guy behind the counter smirk and murmur to some of the clients and was desperate to know just what he was saying. As it turned out, it was Rihanna who was free when Ace reached the front of the line, and she looked taken aback to see him.

"Hi. I just dropped by to thank you for sanctioning my account here," he told her with a big grin.

"You're welcome, Mr. Blenheim." She looked a little unsure of herself and tucked some stray hair behind her ear.

"Matt Shearer wants to pay my wages in this week, and I wondered if there would be any delay in me being able to access my money?" He tried to sound polite.

She huffed a little. "No, Mr. Blenheim, there shouldn't be any problem."

He snickered. "Well now, that's good to know. Thank you, Miss Richards. I won't keep you, as I can see how busy you are."

"I appreciate that, Mr. Blenheim. Thank you."

"Thank *you*, ma'am." He nodded and left the counter.

The bank was just as busy when he left, and he couldn't help thinking it might have been better if the staff had their lunch breaks staggered a little better. He made his way back to his truck and was surprised to see the two guys from earlier standing farther down the road. They were just chatting there, but Ace had an odd feeling about them.

He climbed into his truck and headed back toward the ranch. It had been nice to see Rihanna today. She looked as pretty as she had the day before, with a dark red shift dress and jacket, high heels and her hair tied in a bun. The memory of their interaction would keep him smiling for the rest of the day.

* * * *

Rihanna pasted on a smile and tried to keep cheerful as she served the customers. It had already been a long morning, as she'd been trying to sanction as many of the new accounts as she could, but some needed to be thoroughly checked, which took longer than she'd have liked.

She couldn't believe that Mr. Williamson had given her staff permission to each take their lunch break during the busiest period for the bank, and she planned to speak to him about it when she had the chance. It meant she had no choice but to spend two hours covering the counter, instead of dealing with her mountain of paperwork, or, better still, offering better customer service to the clients.

It had been a nice surprise to see Ace Blenheim today, though she knew she should still be mad at him. She'd been proud of how officious she'd been, while the sight of him had made her insides flutter in a way no customer should affect their bank manager. He sure was a handsome guy, there was no disputing that, but there was something about him that made her smile.

His prank with the car yesterday had annoyed her at the time, but once she'd gotten back to the hotel and relaxed in her PJs, she'd realized that she had probably deserved it. She shouldn't have even considered delaying the sanctioning of his account — but that didn't mean she wouldn't find another way to get back at him. After all, with the horse and now the car, she figured he was still two-one up on her. *Not for long.*

Between customers, she tried to converse with Paul, but he was really hard to talk to. It seemed he could talk quite easily with the customers — even have a joke with one or two — but he seemed reluctant to speak to her.

Sarah wasn't much easier to get along with, when she came to relieve Paul. She was a nice-looking lady with short, dark hair and glasses. She was quite portly, but she carried it well and looked good in the simple shift dresses she seemed to favor. They hadn't been issued with uniforms yet, and she just hoped that there wouldn't be any complaints from the staff when they were.

"Did you have a nice lunch?" Rihanna asked her, as she waited for an elderly lady to make her way to the counter.

Sarah looked surprised. "Yes, thanks."

There wasn't time to elaborate as Sarah immediately made herself ultra-busy talking with her next customer.

Rihanna sighed. It was going to be much harder to fit in here than she'd thought. Maybe it was just as well she wasn't planning to stick around for long.

Chapter Five

The next few days passed slowly for Rihanna, despite how busy she was with work. She soon became despondent about trying to be friendly to Sarah and Paul, who clearly didn't want to know her. She just wished she knew why. She'd never felt so unpopular. It didn't help that she didn't have any other friends to talk to, having retreated to her hotel room every night in favor of sticking around town to get to know the locals.

There didn't seem much point in making new friends, she'd told herself, as she wouldn't be here long enough to get too close to anyone. Her stomach lurched at the thought.

Ace Blenheim had been the only person to put a smile on her face, and she was still trying very hard to think of a way of exacting revenge on the gorgeous cowboy.

Although he didn't come in the bank every day, he'd be in the café when she went to grab lunch or in the street when she was going home. She had bumped into him in the little grocery store one evening when she'd popped in for some much-needed candy. He was good for her diet, though, as seeing him only strengthened her resolve, and she bought a healthy cereal bar instead. Carla had been pleased to see her, too, and she could imagine her being a lovely friend.

Mr. Williamson, the area manager, came to see her on Friday afternoon, to see how her first week had gone. She had expected him at two-thirty, so had finished covering for the staff's lunch breaks and forgone her own to get ready for his arrival. By three o'clock she hadn't received a call from Sarah or Paul to say that her visitor had arrived, so she popped her head out of the door to see how busy the bank was, fearful that they were keeping him waiting if there was a long line of customers.

To her dismay, the bank was empty, save for her visitor, who was chatting and laughing with both staff at the counter.

"Mr. Williamson, have you been waiting long?" She forced a smile, walking forward, her hand outstretched.

"Hi, Rihanna. No, we were just catching up on how things have been going around here." He was still chortling from a joke he seemed to have been sharing with Paul. Funny how her teller had never made *her* laugh. In fact, she noticed that both he and Sarah looked quite relaxed in the company of the boss.

"Of course, would you like to come through to the office?" she offered.

"Why not?" He smiled as he picked up his case from the floor and led the way. "See you guys later," he threw to the cashiers as he left them.

Rihanna felt more than a little perturbed at how familiar he seemed with them, and she couldn't help wondering if there was something she didn't know about her boss and fellow employees.

"Sarah, would you mind making us some coffees please, while it's quiet?"

The older lady glared at her, and she knew that if looks could kill she'd be six feet underground by now. Rihanna straightened her back, daring the woman to object, but nothing was said before she followed Mr. Williamson into her office.

"She won't like that," he said, sitting opposite the desk.

Rihanna walked around to take her seat. "I don't think it's unreasonable to ask someone to make coffee for two senior members of the staff, is it?" She frowned. "After all, it's not like they're busy out there, are they?" She pulled her chair forward a little, jutting out her chin.

"How are you getting on with those two?" A curious expression crossed his face as he narrowed his eyes.

Rihanna swallowed hard, wondering just what they'd been discussing before she joined them. "Well, it's early days," she said, candidly.

Williamson laughed, just as the door opened and Sarah came in carrying two mugs of coffee.

"Your drinks," she announced curtly before placing them both on the table.

Rihanna tightened her lips in annoyance. Not only would she have preferred that Sarah had used cups and saucers instead of mugs for the occasion, but she hadn't bothered to knock and had just put two wet cups on top of her paperwork.

"Thanks, sweetheart." Williamson lifted his with a smile, which the older lady reciprocated.

"Thank you."

Sarah didn't reply to Rihanna before leaving the room.

"She's lovely, isn't she?" Williamson chuckled as the door closed.

Rihanna was tempted to tell him exactly what she thought of Sarah as well as Paul, but thought better of it. If she was seen to be whining about them, it might be seen as a weakness on her part. Besides, it would be bound to get back to them that she'd been berating them. The sheriff had warned her that, in a small town like Pelican's Heath, everyone got to know everyone's business.

"They're both very efficient," she replied.

He raised his eyebrows. "Efficient?"

"Yes." She nodded slowly. "They seem very well experienced in the job."

He frowned, leaning forward slightly. "And?"

Rihanna wasn't sure where this was going, and couldn't quite read the expression on his face. Was he amused? Confused? Certainly surprised by her reply, that much was certain.

"They're both very well qualified," she went on, "and punctual."

He looked taken aback. "Well, yes, they're good at their jobs, but what do you think of them personally? How are you getting along? Any problems?"

She gathered that he was expecting her to say something derogatory, but she wasn't about to give him that pleasure. Not that she particularly liked the staff's attitudes, of course, but he didn't need to know that.

"No problems at all," she assured him. "Of course, we don't know each other personally, but then, it wouldn't be professional to be too familiar with the staff, would it?"

He swallowed hard, sitting back in his chair a little, and she knew he'd taken the hint. "Well, I suppose not. But it's nice to have a good working relationship with your colleagues, don't you think?"

"Absolutely." Her mind whirled. Something was off. It was as though he wanted her to be having trouble with the staff. Did he really want her to fail at this job? Just what was his intention in placing her here?

"Any luck finding somewhere to live?" he asked, changing the subject after a long sip of his drink.

"Not yet. I haven't even been here a week, and as I've been working all day and every day, there hasn't been the time for me to look around. Hopefully I'll get over to the real estate agent tomorrow. I just hope it's not too expensive to rent around here."

Williamson's jaw tightened. "I don't think it'll be a problem on your salary. Besides, you don't need anything too big, do you? You could just rent a room or something until you find your feet."

She shook her head. "I think that would be false economy, don't you, Mr. Williamson? Better to get somewhere permanent organized the first time around than waste time and money flitting from one place to the next. I need to find somewhere with some longevity, if I'm going to stay here, don't I?"

His look of discomfort indicated that perhaps he hadn't expected her to want to stay in the position long-term. *Perhaps that's his game,* she wondered.

"Well, I'm afraid the bank can't keep paying your hotel bills while you pick and choose, Miss Richards," he replied, a little irritably. "You need to find somewhere straight away if you don't want to be out on the streets."

She shook her head. "Now that wouldn't be a good look for the local bank manager, would it?" She gave a wry smile. "Made homeless because of the bank that was employing her. I'm sure my contract states that accommodation will be provided until such time as I can secure my own."

His face reddened. "Yes, it does, Miss Richards, but it also states that you will be accommodated for a 'reasonable period', not 'indefinitely'."

He was riled. Good. That meant he'd gotten the message loud and clear. Although he was now looking as pompous as he sounded, she knew that she had the upper hand.

"Don't worry, Mr. Williamson. I'm not planning to stay at the hotel any longer than I need to—after all, it's hardly the Beverly Hilton, now, is it?" She gave a smile which was bordering on a smirk.

His eyes widened and his nostrils flared. "Well, I think it suffices for your needs, don't you?" he countered.

"For now," she replied with a shrug, noticing that he'd started to get up. "But, actually, there was another matter I wanted to run past you."

He resumed his seat, frowning. "Really?"

She nodded. "As it stands, the staff schedule isn't working as efficiently as I'd like."

He raised his eyebrows. "Oh?"

"It's just the lunch period," she went on, matter-of-factly, taking a chart from her drawer. "It's one of our busiest times. Look." She showed him the graph outlining the number of customers throughout the day.

"Well, what would you expect?" His condescending tone irritated the hell out of her, but she wasn't about to let on.

"Exactly." She rolled her eyes. "I knew you'd understand."

He shifted in his chair, an uneasy expression on his overly tanned face. He wasn't a bad-looking guy, probably in his late forties, with gray hair and pale-blue eyes. *He'd look much more handsome if he didn't scowl quite so much, though,* she thought.

"Banks are always busiest during lunch periods." He spoke evenly, his eyes narrowed as he was clearly trying to figure her point.

She took out the staff schedule and showed him. "Well, someone obviously didn't realize that when they made out the schedule," she said, shaking her head incredulously. "Look at this. They've put both tellers on lunch breaks right over the busiest period. I'm having to cover each of them, taking me out of my office at the busiest time of day — not to mention not giving me a proper break myself — and you know how much the company prides itself on looking after the welfare of its staff."

His eyes widened and she knew full well that it would have been he who had organized the staff timetable.

"Anyway," she went on, "I raised my concern with Sarah and Paul, and they seemed to think it was their right to take their lunch breaks at these times as they'd been agreed at their interviews. I doubt that very much, Mr. Williamson. As you can see as well as I can that it would be ludicrous for them to continue with this rotation, and, besides, I thought *I* was in charge of this branch?" She stared at him expectantly and watched him swallow hard before replying.

"Yes, of course. Although, I think any big decisions should still be passed through me — given your inexperience, of course."

"Absolutely. But I'm sure someone in your position has much better things to worry about than what time my staff takes their lunch breaks, surely?" She chuckled, shaking her head.

"Well…yes…of course." He sat a little straighter. "Is there anything else you need any help with, Miss Richards?" An officious air overcame him, and she realized the power of flattery.

"No, that's it, thank you," she said, with an equally officious tone. "I just wanted to ensure we were both singing from the same hymn-sheet, as it were." She smiled, slowly standing up. "Well, thanks for coming in, Mr. Williamson. It was very nice to see you again." She held a hand out, and he shook it a little unsurely.

She followed him out into the bank, which was a little busier than it had been previously.

"Thank you again, Mr. Williamson." Her voice was a little louder than usual, but she was sure that she'd gotten her message across. He'd been dismissed, so there was no reason for him to hang around chatting idly to her staff anymore, was there?

After watching him leave, she went back to her office and studied the rosters again. She knew the staff wouldn't be happy with her new arrangements, but there wasn't much she could do about that.

Seeing how chatty they'd been with Williamson had given her an uneasy feeling — one that had intensified when he'd spoken to her in that supercilious tone of his. Perhaps it was her imagination, but she'd gotten the distinct impression that he was expecting—or hoping—that she'd be unhappy in her new role. Had he given it to her with an ulterior motive? Or perhaps it wasn't *his* decision to give her the promotion in the first place. Could the order have come from the hierarchy?

Whatever the reason she'd been offered the role, she wasn't about to give anyone the pleasure of seeing her fail in it. She'd tried the nice approach with her staff, who had clearly tried to undermine her. Williamson had shown her little respect by not reporting for their meeting on time and by chitchatting with her staff.

When she'd worked as a teller in their New Moldington branch, she wouldn't have dared chat casually with the area manager, especially less than a week into her employment. Neither would she ever contemplate not calling her manager as soon as a visitor had turned up for a meeting.

It was clear that things worked a little differently out here in the country. But she was still working for the same company. Surely she owed it to her employers to ensure that standards weren't allowed to slide? After all, if any of the management from New Moldington came out here, they'd be mighty shocked to find the place in a mess, especially after she'd made such a good start with new accounts this week.

She looked at the dirty coffee mugs on her desk and the even dirtier rings they'd made on the papers they'd been plunked on. Shaking her head, she picked them up and headed toward the little kitchen to wash them.

Paul and Sarah were grumbling behind the counter. She couldn't make out their words, but it was clear they were unhappy about something. Well, so was she. The only difference was, *she* was about to do something about it.

It was time for a few changes around here.

Chapter Six

First thing Saturday morning Rihanna went down to the real estate office in Almondine to check out some properties. She hadn't planned to look for somewhere else to live quite so soon but couldn't help wondering if Mr. Williamson was likely to move her to somewhere less salubrious than the local hotel. He seemed to think she could manage in one room, so maybe he was considering a local B&B for her accommodation. He sure seemed to have something up his sleeve.

Gillian, the lady on the counter, was very helpful and friendly, but Rihanna couldn't hide her disappointment at the cost of the local rentals.

"I'll take the details and have a think about them," she told her, forcing a smile. In any other circumstances, these prices wouldn't be a problem on a bank manager's salary, but Rihanna was only too well aware of the debts she had to pay before she could think of any luxuries for herself—not that a roof over her head should be considered a luxury, but that's just the way it was.

She was perusing the property details as she left the office and almost bumped into a cowboy who was passing.

"Sorry," she mumbled, still deep in thought.

"Don't be."

His reaction startled her, and she looked up into the dark eyes of Ace Blenheim.

She gasped. "I didn't realize it was you." Not only had she not expected to see him in Almondine, but she also hadn't expected him to look so darn gorgeous. He was clearly not working today, as he wore clean Levi's and a shirt, along with his usual boots and hat. There was something very relaxed and clean about him today—not that he was usually dirty as such. He just looked...different.

He grinned. "Looks to me like you were too busy to notice anything." He nodded at the papers in her hand. "Planning on moving somewhere a little more permanent, I take it?"

She frowned. "Well...I'm not sure."

His face fell slightly. "Wanna grab a coffee?"

"You're not working?"

He shook his head. "Not today. I'm as free as a bird."

She followed him down the street a short way to the nearest coffeehouse and welcomed the warmth as they went inside. She'd worn jeans and boots today, with a thick jumper and her coat, but she still felt the chill in the air.

"Anything there worth considering?" He looked over at the papers, which she'd placed on the table in front of her. As he sat opposite, she wasn't sure how well he could see the properties, and she wasn't entirely sure she wanted to include him in her decision, anyway.

"I don't really think so," she replied, pursing her lips as the waitress arrived with their coffees.

"Well, what is it you're looking for?"

"I'm not really sure."

He frowned at the top page. "You're looking at Almondine. It's way more expensive over this way, with it being the bigger town and all. If you try Pelican's Heath, you can save on your rent as well as your traveling expenses for work."

He took a sip of his drink as she stared at him.

"What makes you think money's a factor?"

He put his cup down, an incredulous expression spreading across his face. "Well now, I didn't mean to offend you." He put his hands up in submission, clearly realizing how that could have sounded. "I merely meant that there's no point in throwing money away. I'm sure you're on a good salary, being a manager and all, but I'm also sure you know the value of the dollar, and someone in your position would know how to look after their assets. You don't seem the type to throw your cash down the drain, if you don't mind me saying." He gave a chuckle, picking up his cup again. "Being in your job, I'm sure you know how to make the most of your money."

She took a deep breath, feeling a little less affronted. "Indeed," she agreed.

He looked slightly surprised, and she realized she probably sounded quite formal, but she really wasn't sure how to take him.

"I'm sure Carla will be able to help you," he said, thoughtfully. "Folks often put those cards in the shop with details about places they're renting out. It's cheaper than going through the real estate agent, and it's often easier to cut out the middleman, if you catch my drift?"

She was beginning to. He clearly expected her to move to Pelican's Heath.

"Do they include properties all the way out here, though?" she asked, as airily as she could manage. "I would have thought that sort of thing would be reserved for the locals."

He narrowed his eyes. "You really wanna stay over here, in Almondine?"

She took a long sip of her coffee before replying. "Why not? It seems like a nice area, and it's not too far from work...but far enough."

He raised his eyebrows. "Why wouldn't you want to live near your work? I'd have thought it was more convenient that way — and less expensive, of course."

She sat back in her chair. "Ace, I'm not from around here. I haven't been brought up in the kind of community where everyone knows everyone and their business."

"You prefer your privacy, is that it?"

She nodded. "Is there something wrong with that?"

He chewed his cheek. "I suppose not. Must get pretty lonely, though."

"Why?" A lurch in her gut reminded her that he was right on the money. She was lonely as hell out here all on her own with no friends, but she could hardly admit that to him now, could she?

He sighed. "Don't you *want* to make friends?"

She shrugged. "I'm not here for that. I'm just here to do my job."

Staring at her, he took a moment before replying. "But you've also just moved to the area. You're looking at getting yourself a home here." He nodded at her papers. "Why wouldn't you want to make a proper life for yourself? Make friends, have a social life. Have fun."

She swallowed hard. Instantly she imagined doing all those things with him. He seemed so easy-going that it would be fun to hang out with him. But she couldn't. It wouldn't work.

"You clearly don't know me," she said with a supercilious look. "I don't need to go out drinking in order to enjoy myself. And I don't need to hang out with a bunch of rednecks, either."

His jaw tightened. "So, what are you gonna do? 'Cause I don't see none of them city slickers you're clearly used to around here." There was an edge to his voice that irked her. How dare he be mad at her?

"Who said anything about staying here?" She raised her eyebrows.

He gaped. "But you just got here." He spoke slowly, deliberately. "And I thought you were looking to settle down." He eyed the property papers again.

She shook her head. "Mr. Blenheim, I rather think you've made a few assumptions about me." She tried to sound officious to hide the way she'd started to tremble. She daren't allow herself to even contemplate a future here...with him.

He carefully put his cup back on the table.

"You're right, Miss Richards. I believe I have." He threw some notes on the table and walked out of the coffee shop.

Rihanna just stared after him, stunned. If she'd been hoping he'd try to convince her to stay, she was sorely disappointed. The hurt look in his eyes haunted her as she continued to finish her drink. No way was she about to follow him outside. She had no idea what she'd say to him, anyhow.

As she looked down at the property pages in front of her, she became aware of a big wet tear suddenly smudging some of the print, as her vision went a little blurry. She quickly rubbed the back of her hand over her face, cleared her throat and stood up.

Leaving and walking back up the street on her own, she suddenly felt like the world was closing in on her. She was running out of options, and she seemed to be burning bridges everywhere she went. No one liked her at work. She had no friends and no hope of making any, either. She'd convinced herself that it didn't matter. She wasn't going to be staying here for long, anyway, so what was the point in becoming attached to anyone?

But as she stared at the crowds who were jostling her on the sidewalk, the truth dawned on her like a suffocating cloak of doom. Ace was right. She was lonely. And it looked like she'd just alienated the nearest thing to a friend she'd found.

* * * *

Ace felt the cold bite him as soon as he strutted out of the coffeehouse and up the street. It was always busy on a Saturday in Almondine — one of the reasons he rarely ventured there at the weekend. Crowds weren't his thing, which was probably why he felt so at home here in Cavern County. There was plenty of wide-open space, and living in Pelican's Heath with its quaint little shops and businesses, as opposed to these monstrous industrialized buildings, was much more preferable than anywhere he'd been before.

He made his way back to his truck and sat behind the steering wheel, contemplating his next move. His hope had been that he'd bump into Rihanna and they could spend the rest of the day together, but that certainly wasn't happening.

She couldn't have made it clearer that she wasn't interested in spending time with him or sticking around the area for long. It seemed ludicrous that she'd just got a managerial job and yet she wasn't planning on staying. It was unusual for businesses in Pelican's Heath to take on temporary staff, and the bank had only just opened. Having only been here a week, surely it was too soon for her to decide she didn't like the position?

He'd parked in the street and was idly watching people bustling around. They were always much busier here than back at Pelican's Heath, and he was glad it was much more relaxed back home. Even the cowboys didn't seem as laid-back, and he figured their jobs must be much more intense than his own. He felt sorry for them in that respect.

The shops here were much bigger — some of them chain stores — and people were carrying big bags of shopping. With a sigh, he reached for his seatbelt and caught sight of something — or rather some*one* — out of the corner of his eye.

Rihanna was strolling slowly down the street, darting her eyes at all the people and shops that surrounded her. Being a city girl, this must have seemed really quiet to her, but she didn't look too happy about it. In fact, the way she wiped her hand over her face suggested that she may have been crying.

He abandoned the seatbelt in favor of watching the pretty, fair-haired girl. She seemed quite aimless, and he wondered what she would do all day in a place like this, alone. It was no wonder she was looking for somewhere to live, even if just temporarily, as staying at that hotel must be really boring, not to mention lonely. He imagined her just reading books—or probably working, knowing Rihanna—in her room with maybe just a radio for company. He shook his head as she got a little nearer. His heart lurched at how sad she seemed. Lost, almost.

Quickly climbing out of the truck, he went over to her. She didn't appear to recognize him at first. She wasn't really looking directly at him, just in his vague direction as that was the way she was heading.

"Rihanna."

She almost walked right past him. Stopping suddenly, she blinked hard before realizing who he was. Frowning, she gave a big sniff.

"I thought you'd gone."

He nodded. "I had—from the coffee shop, anyhow."

She swallowed hard. "I noticed."

"You would."

She sighed. "I assumed you'd gone home or about your business—or whatever it is you do on a Saturday."

He put an arm out, ushering her toward his truck when people jostled her as they hurried past. "What do *you* usually do on a Saturday?"

She bit her lip. "Well, if I were back in the city, I'd probably be visiting friends or maybe doing a little shopping." She suddenly remembered how good it was to actually have enough money to go shopping.

"Do you need to do any shopping today?"

She shook her head. "No. I have most of my meals at the hotel, and I have enough clothes to last a while."

"So, what are you planning to do? Got any friends to go visit?"

He regretted the question as soon as he saw the tears pool in her eyes, and she quickly looked away. "I'm sorry. I didn't mean to upset you."

He put a hand on her arm and realized she was trembling.

With her free hand she hurriedly wiped her face. "You didn't."

He smacked his lips together. She was a proud woman and clearly hated that he'd seen her looking so vulnerable. It was a shame she felt that way, and he sure was ashamed for making her feel like it.

"Have you ever been riding?"

Her eyes widened. "Not in years. I learned to ride when I was really small, then we moved to the city."

Ace grinned. "So, you haven't always been a city girl, then?"

She shook her head. "I was brought up in the country for my first ten years or so. I really loved it at the time."

"How about we take a couple of the horses for a trek? It's cold, but the view over the foothills is beautiful. I think you'd enjoy it." He looked at her clothes. "You might need a thicker coat, mind you."

She looked at her attire. "It's the only coat I have."

His stomach lurched at the thought that he may have offended her. "That's fine. We can borrow one up at the ranch. That is a lovely coat, though I just think that for riding—"

"That would be really nice, if you're sure?" She sniffed again, gazing up at him. "It would be good to blow away the cobwebs a little."

He grinned. "Hop in."

He felt a sense of relief as he drove them back to Pelican's Heath. The thought of Rihanna spending the weekend on her own, cooped up in her hotel room, just didn't sit well with him.

"So, this job at the bank," he started, a little warily. "Are you enjoying it?"

She seemed a little reluctant to reply and bit her lip.

"Hey, it's okay. I won't tell your boss if you say no." He leaned over a little closer to her, speaking conspiratorially.

Rihanna sniggered. "I've only been there a week, so it's probably a little early to judge."

He nodded, chewing the inside of his cheek. "How are you getting along with the staff?"

"Okay, I guess."

Her expression told a different story. Ace was tempted to press her for more details but didn't want to upset her again. Besides, it was the weekend, and he was taking her out to forget about work.

The Shearer Ranch was up a long drive and situated just outside of town. Evergreens lined the road, and shaded parts of the ground were still frosty.

"It sure is pretty out here," she remarked.

Ace looked over at her with a smile. She was sitting back in her seat, looking way more relaxed than earlier. Her face wasn't so tense, though her tears had wiped off what little makeup she'd had on when he'd first seen her. His heart ached at the thought that he'd been the one to upset her, and he wondered just what was going on in her head to make her so defensive. He had to concede that it probably was none of his business, but it didn't stop him worrying.

"I think so," he agreed. "Certainly the most beautiful place I've ever lived."

"Have you been here long?"

He shook his head. "Nearly a month now. It sure is a lot different from anywhere else I've lived. The people here are lovely, too."

She nodded.

He eyed her a little warily. "Did you know that Carla is in a ménage with both Matt and Dyson Shearer?"

Rihanna's eyes widened. "Really?" She seemed more surprised than shocked.

He grinned. "I gather it's pretty common out here."

She pursed her lips. "Well, each to their own, I guess. I'm not sure I could cope with two guys, but if it works for her, then that's great."

Ace chuckled, slightly relieved.

He pulled up and switched off the engine. "Let's go see if Carla's been baking again."

Rihanna smiled as she climbed down, and he slung a warm arm around her as he led her inside the large ranch house.

Sure enough, the smell of chocolate cake greeted them into the kitchen, and Rihanna sighed as they went through.

"Hey, Carla, I've brought you a visitor," Ace announced as she turned from the stove to smile at them.

Her smile widened even more at the sight of Rihanna, and she immediately came over to give her a welcoming hug. "It's lovely to see you, Rihanna. What brings you all the way out here on your day off?"

"I did, actually," Ace replied for her. "I thought we could take a couple of the horses for a trek. Rihanna hasn't ridden in years, and it'll be a lovely way to show her the county from the hills."

Carla nodded. "It sure is pretty up there, Rihanna. You're gonna love it." She pulled out a chair at the large breakfast table. "But first I need a taster for my new chocolate brownie recipe. Think you'd be up for that?"

Ace noticed Rihanna's face light up and she quickly sat down, removing her coat and putting it on the back of the wooden chair. "Anything to help out." She grinned.

Ace chuckled and removed his coat, hanging it on the back of the kitchen door before joining the girls at the table.

Carla had placed three hot mugs of coffee and a plate of brownies in front of them. "Now, I want your honest opinions," she told them, handing around some plates. "Is this, or is it not, a little too chocolatey?"

As Rihanna took her first bite of the cake, a little moan escaped her throat. "You can never have too much chocolate," she assured Carla. "And these are delicious. How did you get the inside to be so chewy? Mine never come out like this."

"You bake?" Ace couldn't hide his surprise — or his delight.

"Of course." Rihanna gave an indignant look.

"Hey, maybe we could do some baking together? I can show you how to time the brownies just right to get the center like that. In fact, if you're free tomorrow, I could sure use some help?" Carla beamed.

Rihanna nodded. "You've got a deal."

Ace grinned. He'd already been racking his brain to think of a way to encourage Rihanna not to be on her own for the rest of the weekend, and it looked like the answer had been handed to him on a plate...literally.

Chapter Seven

Rihanna was grateful that Ace had chosen a really placid horse for her to ride up into the foothills. She'd forgotten how rusty she was at riding, but she very much enjoyed getting back into her stride.

The horse was a dream, obeying her every command and showing much more patience than she felt she deserved. Ace was great, too, never once making her feel silly or that she was going too slowly.

She'd swapped her coat for a thick Carhartt jacket that must have belonged to one of the men, as it was huge, but she was more than grateful for its warmth and comfort as the air was still frosty on the higher ground.

"What do you think?" Ace grinned at her as they stopped at the top of a hill and looked out over the county.

Most of the land was green, with fields spreading for miles across the landscape. Pelican's Heath looked tiny beneath them, and she was surprised at how rural even the town looked from up there. Almondine was a little farther to the east, and, although it was clearly a larger town with more industrialized buildings, from there it still settled comfortably into the countryside.

"It's lovely." She smiled as her whole body relaxed. It had been years since she'd been for a trip out into the country, and to feel the cold, wintry air on her cheeks was a delight she'd forgotten. "The air's so fresh up here," she added, taking in deep breaths, "and I just love how quiet it is."

Ace nodded. "I wouldn't want to be anywhere else," he admitted. "I know you're a city girl and I don't mean any offense, but for me, you can't beat the stillness of the air and the peace you feel when you're in the heart of the country."

She nodded, remembering long summer days spent on country walks with her parents when she was growing up. They'd go out in all weathers, either tramping on leaves, stomping through snow or just enjoying the ease of the warmer months. Until now she hadn't realized just how much she missed all that. Everything had changed once she'd moved to the city, and she had been teased at school for the way she'd dressed, her accent and her simple view on life. The only way to fit in had been to comply with their ideas, so she'd forced herself to become just like them. Her education had become more important than nature and spending time outdoors, and she'd done really well with her studies.

When she'd landed a financial job in the city, her parents had been so proud of her, and that had made her feel even better about herself, too. A bank manager's job was a dream come true, and she couldn't wait to tell her folks about her promotion. Of course, they'd been over the moon. The only problem was that the job was all the way out here in Cavern County, so she wouldn't be able to visit them as often as she was used to, but when everything had gone wrong with her marriage plans, she'd been grateful for the lifeline.

"Hey, are you, okay?" Ace was suddenly alongside her, offering her a handkerchief, and it was only then that she noticed large tears rolling down her frozen cheeks.

"Yeah. Must be the cold." She took his hanky and wiped her face.

"In that case, I think we'd best be getting back," he said, decisively. "I don't want you catching your death out here."

Rihanna took one more look at the gorgeous view before turning her horse around and following Ace back down the hill and toward the ranch. Her heart ached as sweet memories of her childhood when she would go trekking with the riding school filled her mind, and she wondered if she'd actually done the right thing in sticking to the city. Of course, she'd had no choice when she was young and her parents had moved with Dad's job, but once she'd been old enough, there had been nothing stopping her from returning to her roots.

She supposed she'd just gone with the flow and hadn't wanted to stray too far from her parents. That was one of the things Phil had held against her when they'd been making plans for their future together.

A lump formed in her throat as she recalled all the wonderful things she and Phil had planned to do together once they'd been married. He wanted to travel, and she'd agreed it would be good, as long as they weren't away from her parents for too long. Dad had had a heart attack a few years before and had subsequently left his job. It was felt that the stress of his work had finally taken its toll, and he'd taken early retirement. Mom worked part-time at the local library, and they seemed quite happy in their new routine. It didn't stop Rihanna from worrying, though.

Phil had felt that she was mollycoddled by her parents and was still tied to her mom's apron strings. It had been the cause of their first real row. It didn't help that he was very independent and hadn't been to visit his parents for years. She knew he could never fully understand how she'd felt but had hoped it wouldn't become an issue. Unfortunately, it had.

When she'd started earning more money than her fiancé, it hadn't helped matters, either. At first, he'd been reluctant to let her pay for anything, saying that he was the man and therefore it was his duty to provide for them both. However, as the bills started stacking up for the wedding, he'd conceded that it made sense for her to pay toward it, and she'd ended up paying the lion's share.

"Wow, that cold wind's really gotten to you, hasn't it?" Ace offered her a sympathetic smile as they dismounted outside the stables.

It took a moment for Rihanna to realize what he'd meant, and she reluctantly put her hand to her face to discover that tears had been pouring down as she'd been riding along, thinking. She wiped her eyes yet again with his handkerchief, just as a couple of stable hands came over to them.

"We'll take care of these," one of them offered, taking the reins from her hand. "You get your girl into the warm. She looks perished."

"Thanks, guys, I'll do just that." Ace gave over the reins to the other guy and put an arm around her, leading her back toward the ranch house. "You okay?" he asked, just before they went inside.

She nodded with a sniff that belied her claim that it was the cold making her eyes stream.

"Let's go see if Carla's got any of them brownies left." He took her inside, where the heat hit them as soon as they opened the door.

Ace helped her out of the large coat, which he replaced on the hook at the back of the door before removing his own.

"Come on in," Carla called over from the sink. "I was just gonna make more coffee. The guys are on their way."

Rihanna suddenly felt nervous at the idea of more people seeing her red, tear-stained face and immediately excused herself for the bathroom.

"It's just through there." Ace pointed it out to her, and she went as quickly as she could, hoping she wouldn't bump into anyone on her way down the long corridor.

Once behind the locked door, she took a deep breath and gaped at her reflection in the mirror. Her face was bright red, which could have been partly attributed to the cold air on the hills, but there was no denying that the swollen eyes and tearstains were exactly as they appeared. *Damn!*

She splashed copious handfuls of cold water onto her face, slightly annoyed that the makeup she'd applied this morning had disappeared already. In the city she used to wear plenty of it, as did all the other women. Here, though, it seemed most of the women didn't bother with it. Even Carla only seemed to wear a little mascara and lip gloss, and she looked beautiful.

After freshening up, Rihanna gave herself a good talking to. "This is ridiculous," she scolded herself in a whisper, staring at her face in the mirror. "You've had a lovely time out with Ace in the fresh air, chatting and enjoying yourself, so why get all weepy now? Things were never going to work with Phil Cartwright. It just took you too long to realize it. He's out of your life now, thank goodness, so how about making that new start you promised yourself? You're being offered new friendships here, and all you can do is mope about the past. Come on, girl. Get a grip."

She blew her nose one more time, then forced herself to smile at her reflection. She'd been really lucky to meet Ace and Carla, and she was determined not to mess it up.

Loud voices were heard as she made her way back toward the kitchen — then raucous laughter.

"There you are," Carla said, looking up as she joined them. "Come and have some lunch. You must be starving." Her easy smile was infectious, and Rihanna beamed back at her.

"Have you met Matt and Dyson?" Ace asked as she took the seat next to him.

Rihanna swallowed hard, remembering her previous encounter with the sheriff. He wasn't in uniform today and looked very relaxed as he passed around a basket of warm bread rolls.

"I saw you at the bank the other day," Dyson reminded her. "I was asking about a stranger in town." He smiled at her.

"That's right, Sheriff," she replied, a little warily. She hadn't exactly been polite to him, and she wondered if he was going to mention it.

"I think we spoke on the phone," Matt piped up with an easy grin. "You very kindly sorted out a wage account for me."

"I did." She managed a returning smile but felt a knot in her stomach, remembering how that had come about.

"How are you getting along at the bank?" Carla asked.

"Fine."

"Well, I have to say it's real convenient having the bank right on our doorstep," Matt said, taking some salad from a large bowl in the middle of the table. "And you seem to be running it efficiently. It's so much easier than having to trek over to Almondine all the time."

Rihanna nodded. "We've opened a lot of new accounts here this week."

Ace offered her a plate of cheeses, and she took a few slices with a smile.

"You've got that guy working there — Paul Smithson, I believe?" Dyson frowned. "How's it going with him? I know he's a local. Quite opinionated, I believe?"

Rihanna's jaw tensed a little. "I've only known him a week, but I haven't had any trouble."

"Well, that's good." Dyson actually looked relieved. "He's got a lot of friends around here, but I think it's mainly because of all his contacts. Got some influential family, I believe. It tends to open all sorts of doors for him, I've heard."

Rihanna's face went hot. That would certainly explain Paul's laid-back attitude. "He hasn't worked in finance all that long," she thought aloud, recalling his résumé.

"Really?" Dyson raised an eyebrow, which was actually quite a sexy look, though she doubted he'd realize it. Both he and his twin were handsome guys, with dark hair and dark eyes. Matt had a little stubble around his chin, which was probably the only way to tell them apart, she surmised.

Ace had piled some salad and meat onto her plate, and she started to eat, suddenly realizing how famished she was. It must have been all that fresh air.

She nodded. "I noticed his hands were quite rough and calloused," she said. "So I checked out his HR records. It seems he only came to the job about a year ago. There's not much there about his history and nothing about past jobs. I was quite surprised, actually, as you usually have to provide a lot more past information when you take a bank job, but I assume head office must have all that. I haven't got much of a résumé on Sarah, either, although it does say she's got lots of experience. I've got no details about her past employment, however. I can only assume they're both well qualified to be given jobs in a brand-new branch."

She was suddenly aware that they were all staring at her and wondered for a second if she had lettuce in her teeth or something. She flushed.

"I would have thought, as their manager, you'd have all the information you needed," Matt pointed out.

"Maybe they think it *is* all I need." She shrugged.

"But you're in charge of the whole branch," Carla pointed out. "Surely you should have *all* their records. What use are they to your head office when the staff are working here in Pelican's Heath with you?"

Rihanna rolled her eyes. She'd thought the exact same thing herself. "When I was offered the job, I understood that I'd be the manager of my own branch," she explained, after taking a long drink just in case she'd been right about the lettuce. "But once I got here, it became apparent that I wasn't really in charge. I've got this area manager, Mr. Williamson, who had already hired the staff before I arrived. He seems to think he needs to keep an eye on me. I guess it's because I'm new to the job, but it doesn't make my life any easier. He'd even drawn up their work roster, allowing both Sarah and Paul to take their lunch breaks right at the busiest times." As soon as she'd said it, she regretted admitting that she wasn't really in charge of her own bank. These people were her customers, after all. She was relieved, however, to see that they looked more appalled than supercilious.

Dyson frowned. "I'd have thought it safer, as well as more efficient, to have you all there when the place is at its busiest. It's easier for you to keep an eye on things if you're not stuck behind the counter, too."

"That's what I thought." She sighed. "Anyway, I've spoken to Mr. Williamson about it and, starting Monday, I'm making a few changes."

"Good for you." Ace patted her arm proudly, which gave her an unexpectedly warm feeling.

"Williamson?" Dyson looked quizzical. "I don't think I know him."

Rihanna shook her head. "I don't think he's all that local."

"Have you seen much of that other guy I was asking you about?" Dyson asked, raising his eyebrows.

She shook her head, feeling guilty for the way she'd spoken to him the day he'd come in. She could see now that he was actually a really nice guy who was only doing his job. He obviously took his role very seriously. "He hasn't been in the branch as far as I know — though, of course, I don't mind the front desk usually, so he could have been. I've certainly not had any dealings with him. I've seen him hanging about in the street a few times, though, like many of the other locals."

"He and that friend of his like to hang around the café," Matt interjected.

"Hmm. I've yet to figure them out," Dyson replied, pursing his lips thoughtfully.

"Anyway, enough shop talk. How was it up in the hills this morning?" Carla asked, gathering up the dirty plates. "Were you warm enough?"

Rihanna smiled with a nod. "Yes, thanks. That jacket sure did the trick."

"Good. I was afraid you'd be perished up there in this weather." Carla started to take the dishes over to the sink, and Rihanna got up to help.

"The air seems so much cleaner up there," Rihanna said cheerfully as she gathered up more plates and followed her.

"Hey, you don't have to do that. You're our guest." Carla's eyes were wide as she turned to see Rihanna helping out.

"I'm happy to do it. Believe me. I get so bored at that hotel — everyone doing everything for me all the time. I'd rather be at home doing normal stuff, to be honest." She meant it, too.

"Well, you can come over and help out here anytime," Carla assured her with a giggle. "There's always something to do at this place."

"I'd love that." The words tumbled out of Rihanna's mouth before she had time to stop them, and she wondered afterward if Carla had actually been serious or not.

"How long are you staying over in Almondine?" Carla asked, without batting an eyelid. "If you move over this way, we can see each other all the time. And it'll be fun baking together." She beamed.

Rihanna's heart lifted. She *was* serious. Carla clearly wanted to be a proper friend to her. And, boy, did Rihanna need a friend right now — not that she'd ever admit that out loud, of course.

"She was actually looking for somewhere this morning," Ace piped up from the table.

"Really?" Carla raised her eyebrows. "There are a couple of apartments going above the shops in town."

Rihanna gaped at her. "Seriously?"

"I told you Carla would know," Ace interjected, as the girls brought fresh coffee and another plate of chocolate brownies over to the table.

"It's amazing what you pick up at the local shop," Carla replied with a grin. "I only do a few hours every week, but I sure find out a lot of stuff."

"By 'stuff' she means gossip," Matt said, taking Carla's hand and kissing it with a grin.

"Hey, don't you knock it, bro. Carla's tip-offs have come in handy on more than one occasion, don't forget." Dyson put an arm around the brunette and pulled her head down for a kiss.

Matt put his hands up in submission. "I didn't say there was anything wrong in it. I was just clarifying the situation, that's all."

Rihanna giggled, taking her seat next to Ace again. It was good to see the easy-going way they all reacted with each other, and the relaxed atmosphere was a real tonic. She envied Carla being in such a loving a relationship with two such hunky guys, and it was clear how much they doted on her.

Ace caught her eye and grinned. He really was handsome and fit in here perfectly. She wondered if she'd ever be accepted as one of the locals. Although it was the last thing she'd originally wanted, she was beginning to have second thoughts. How wonderful would it feel to be surrounded by such lovely people and live in a laid-back fashion, instead of always rushing around worrying about work and money and stuff?

"That was a big sigh," Ace remarked, offering her the plate of cakes.

Rihanna smiled. She hadn't even noticed herself sigh, but she *did* notice that, along with the brownies, there were some slices of angel food cake on the plate. She took a slice and straight away registered how light it was. Carla sure was a good cook.

"I was just thinking how lovely this is. Being here, I mean," she admitted.

Ace feigned a look of shock. "You mean, you actually like being here in Pelican's Heath? Does this mean you might consider staying for a while?"

"Oh, I thought you were here permanently," Carla piped up with a concerned frown.

Rihanna's stomach churned. She'd been so adamant this morning that she wasn't going to stick around, but somehow that had all changed now.

"I wasn't sure how long I'd be here," she admitted. "But now I'm really hoping to stay a while. If I can find somewhere to live, I think life would be much easier."

"Well, the shop's holding the keys to those two apartments I mentioned," Carla replied, her eyes shining. "Why don't we finish up here and we can go into town and take a look? No obligation, of course, but it might be good to see what's available around here."

Rihanna couldn't stop the beam that spread over her face. "Could we? I mean, that would be lovely."

Ace's face lit up. "You'd consider moving to Pelican's Heath?"

"Why wouldn't she?" Carla frowned. "It makes much more sense than being all the way out at Almondine, especially as she works here."

"You'll find it much easier to make friends," Matt piped up. "There's a couple of bars here, and folks are real friendly."

"Great." A warmth spread through Rihanna's stomach, and she knew it wasn't just down to the coffee. These people actually wanted her here, and that was a feeling she hadn't had for a long time.

Chapter Eight

Ace drove Rihanna and Carla into town after lunch. It was much quieter than it had been over at Almondine, and Rihanna embraced the peacefulness. Having spent some time in these guys' company had left her feeling much more relaxed and hopeful about her future. Perhaps she had been rather blinkered before, thinking that she wasn't going to stay long and therefore she had no reason to make friends. It had already led to loneliness and regret and given her far too much time to think about things she'd rather forget.

The first apartment they checked out was above the hairdressers' shop at the bottom end of the main street. Rihanna was surprised at how light and airy it was, given that it was rather tiny. It had one bedroom with an ensuite bathroom and the rest was open-plan. The kitchen area was very small, but it didn't matter as it led straight onto the dining and living areas.

"It's a bit cramped," Ace muttered as soon as they went inside.

"It's only for me," Rihanna pointed out. She'd seen the cost of the rental and it had surprised her that here was somewhere she could actually afford. It would take a large chunk of her wages, of course, but not as large as the places she'd found in Almondine. Perhaps it was time she set her sights a little lower. After all, she wasn't as affluent as she used to be. It seemed crazy, having got the promotion and a higher wage, to have to be so strict about her budget, but it was the only way she was going to drag herself out of the wedding debt that her ex had left her with.

"The bedroom's through here," Carla pointed out.

Rihanna had to admit that it was rather tiny. But she wasn't expecting company in there, so it shouldn't matter.

"You're not claustrophobic, are you?" Ace asked in a jokey tone as he peered around the doorway.

Rihanna glared at him, and he looked quite taken aback.

"Well, it's small and compact," Carla said with a nod, clearly sensing the tension in the air. "But, as you say, it's only for one person. And it's going to save a fortune on traveling expenses. It should be quite warm, too, with the hairdressers' downstairs."

Rihanna was glad of Carla's tact and even more pleased that Ace seemed to have gotten the message and had left the room. "That's true."

"Well, you don't have to decide right away, and there's still the one above the grocery store to look at next. I'm sure that one's a bit bigger than this." Carla sounded cheerful.

"It'll cost more, too, though, won't it?" Rihanna kept her voice quiet, not wanting Ace to overhear.

"Are things really bad?" Carla put an arm around her and Rihanna sighed into her friend's warmth.

She nodded. "I'm in so much debt," she whispered.

"Oh, hon." Carla squeezed her tight, and Rihanna felt tears prick the edges of her eyes. She was determined not to cry again, though.

"It's only temporary," Rihanna said, forcing a smile. It was the mantra she kept repeating to herself whenever she started worrying about her finances. She had a schedule all worked out to pay what she owed, and if she stuck to it the way she was hoping to, she'd have everything repaid, including the bank loan, within a couple of years.

Carla smiled back at her. "Why don't we go take a look at the other property then go back to the ranch for a good girly gossip?"

Rihanna nodded. It would be good to confide in Carla about what had happened. She hadn't really opened up to anyone about it, although, of course, her family all knew. They had no idea how much it had affected her self-esteem, though, or the added pressure she'd felt to repay the debts. Heck, her parents would have a fit if they'd any idea how much she'd spent on the wedding.

Ace was staring out of the front window when they went through. "You've got a good view of the street," he said, helpfully. "You'll be able to sit up here and watch the world go by if you want to."

Rihanna appreciated that he was trying to make up for his earlier negativity and smiled. "Well, that's another tick in the box. We're going to check out the other one now."

"Great."

They piled out of the building and pulled their coats tighter as they headed up the street to where the grocery store stood.

"It doesn't get too busy, so I don't think you'll have a problem with noise," Carla pointed out, going up to the counter to fetch the key.

"Is this temporary, too?" Ace asked, looking a little wary.

Rihanna swallowed hard. He must have heard what she'd said to Carla and had assumed she was talking about the apartment. He looked so handsome, and she was sorely tempted to tell him she wanted to stay in Pelican's Heath if only to be nearer to him, but she couldn't. Instead, she just shrugged. "I don't know."

"Come on." Carla called them over to a side door and they headed up the carpeted stairs. "Would you like to do the honors?" She offered Rihanna the key.

Her heart beat with excitement as she unlocked the door and was welcomed with warm, scented air. All the walls had been painted white and the kitchen units gleamed.

She noticed that Ace held back this time, and she went in first. It was certainly much bigger than the place they'd just seen. There was a kitchenette with a little dining table and a largish living room. The bedroom was bigger than she'd expected, and the bathroom was a separate room. *Better for guests*, she thought.

Ace immediately went over to the window and looked out. Double-glazing blocked out the noise of the street outside, and the thick carpets offered warmth and quietness to the whole place.

"This is lovely," Rihanna said, looking around. She tried to quell her excitement. It was bound to be more expensive than the smaller property, and she'd really need to weigh up whether she could justify spending the extra money on accommodation just for her.

"Could you see yourself living here?" Carla grinned, as though she had already guessed the answer.

Rihanna nodded. "If I could afford it, I'd love to."

"I believe the cost is up for negotiation," Carla replied with a secretive smile. "And don't forget, having someone live above the shop is better for the insurance. They figure it's more secure with a tenant up here."

"I don't know about that." Rihanna grimaced. "I think if anyone was going to rob the place, I'd be more likely to hide under the bed until they'd gone." She giggled.

"And Dyson would applaud you for it," Carla assured her. "Too many people get hurt trying to defend material things, and it's just not worth the risk. Things are replaceable. People aren't."

"Don't tell the landlord that, though, will you?" Rihanna said with a giggle. "If it'll get the rent down, I'd let him think I was a black belt at karate or something."

They both chuckled, and even Ace smiled. She was aware that he hadn't commented since they'd arrived and wondered if he was sore at the thought of her only being here temporarily. Not that it would affect him, of course, but she'd noticed he seemed to favor stability over anything else. The thought took her back to her childhood, when she'd always thought nothing would ever change. How wrong she'd been.

"What do you think, Ace?" she asked.

He looked around. "It's really nice." He nodded.

"Think she should live here?" Carla asked, giving him a playful nudge. "She'd have me for company in the evenings and the odd weekend. Shouldn't that clinch the deal?"

Ace laughed. "Oh no, in that case she should *definitely* get the rent reduced."

"*What?*" Carla gave him a pretend swat and they all laughed.

Rihanna took one last look around the apartment before they left and headed back to the ranch. It was getting dark already.

"Are you still up for some baking tomorrow?" Carla asked.

"Of course. I'm looking forward to it." Rihanna beamed.

It would be fun to spend some quality time with Carla, and it had been months since she'd done any baking. It was something she'd enjoyed ever since she had been very young, and she'd always baked at least once a week until her relationship had fallen apart. After that, it had become an effort to do anything fun, and she knew if she baked a cake she'd probably eat the whole thing herself. She'd thought she'd had lots of friends, but once Phil had left her, they'd all seemed to peter off. Maybe they'd liked him better than her — or maybe they just didn't know how to treat her, knowing she'd been jilted at the last minute. Whatever the reason, it made her realize that they couldn't have been good friends after all.

"Let's go see if there are any brownies left," Carla said as they clambered out of the truck. "I'll bet Matt's been eating them."

"He'll blame you for being such a good cook," Ace piped up with a smile. "He always does."

Carla giggled. "Well, I can hardly argue with that, now, can I?"

She led them inside and they immediately felt the warmth. Carla went straight over to the coffee pot. "Looks like they're still working," she said, looking around the empty kitchen.

"Does Dyson work on the ranch, too?" Rihanna asked.

"Sometimes," Carla replied with a smile as they all removed their coats. "He likes to keep his hand in, but he can't do too much."

Rihanna nodded, desperate to ask why, but realized there was probably a medical problem stopping him from exerting himself, so she said nothing.

As they sat around the kitchen table drinking more coffee and nibbling at the seemingly endless supply of brownies, the subject of the apartments came up again.

"I think we can all agree that the second one was the best, can't we?" Carla chirped up.

"It was certainly bigger." Rihanna nodded.

"And airier. More spacious. Warmer. Had thicker carpets and nicer furniture," Carla added. "You agree, don't you, Ace?"

He bit his lip thoughtfully. "It depends what you want...or need."

Both girls stared at him.

"If it's just somewhere to sleep and maybe eat the odd meal, then either would be fine. The cheaper the better, I'd say. But if you wanted to make it your home — somewhere you were planning on spending some time — then clearly the second one would be the nicer."

Carla raised her eyebrows. "You've certainly thought this through."

Ace shrugged. "Just being practical. You need to weigh up the pros and cons as well as deciding what you're really looking for."

Rihanna nodded. He was right. The only trouble was that she wasn't really sure *what* she was looking for.

After finishing his coffee, Ace got up. "I'm just going to check on a couple of things for the morning," he announced. "I've got an early start tomorrow, and I want to make sure everything's ready."

Rihanna guessed he was very helpfully giving them some time to talk. Poor Ace must have heard them whispering in the bedroom earlier and felt like a third wheel.

Carla poured more coffee before taking her seat again, as the door slammed shut. "So, what are your thoughts?"

Rihanna took a sip of her drink. "About what? The apartment?"

Carla nodded slowly. "Yes, and everything else. I mean, you've got to admit Ace Blenheim's a gorgeous guy. Even *I* think so, and I've got two handsome hunks of my own." She giggled.

Rihanna nodded. "He's very easy on the eyes."

"What?" Carla raised her voice in surprise. "Easy on the eyes? Is that all you can say? Come on, girl. You've seen him. The guy's a walking sex-god!"

Rihanna chuckled. "Okay. He *is* very handsome," she conceded.

"Now we're getting somewhere." Carla gave a nod of satisfaction. "And he's clearly got the hots for you — so where's the problem?" She narrowed her eyes.

Rihanna gaped at her. "What?"

"You like him, and he likes you, so what's the obstacle here?"

"I'm not so sure he likes me in that way," Rihanna protested.

"In what way? Did he not come to Almondine looking for you this morning? And did he not then bring you up here and take you horse-riding in the hills?"

"Well...yes."

"And would he really have done any of that if he hadn't liked you and wanted to spend the day with you?"

"He *is* lovely." Rihanna put her cup on the table in front of her. "And it was really good of him to take me riding *and* to take me apartment-hunting today."

"But?"

Rihanna winced. "Well, I don't really *know* him, do I?"

"Don't you?"

She shook her head. "And, besides, I don't know that I want a relationship at the moment." Even as she said the words, she felt tears burn the backs of her eyes and that sinking feeling returned to her stomach.

Carla's eyes widened as Rihanna's became more blurry. "Oh, hon, I'm so sorry. It never occurred to me. I'm such a dumbass. Have you got someone? Is it serious? I don't know why I just assumed you were on your own. You just seem so...alone."

That was it. The floodgates opened and Rihanna sobbed hard into her hands. Carla immediately grabbed a box of tissues and put them in front of her before taking her in her arms.

"Go on, girl. Have a good cry. I think it's what you need," she cooed, surrounding Rihanna with her warmth.

It seemed to take ages for Rihanna to recover herself, and when she did, she just knew her eyes were red and puffy and there would be more tearstains down her cheeks. "I'm sorry," she managed with a large sniff.

"Don't be. Hey, we've all got a past, hon," Carla assured her.

"I was getting married," Rihanna blurted out. "I'd paid most of the wedding costs myself and it was all going to be so perfect. Phil had big ideas about what he wanted for the big day, and I just went along with them. Then he dumped me just days before we were due to walk down the aisle." She sniffed again, wiping her eyes with a tissue. "I had to explain to everyone and return all the wedding presents."

Carla squeezed her tight. "Oh, hon, that must have been awful!"

Rihanna nodded. "He'd found someone else. He didn't admit it at the time, of course, but he had." She sniffed again. "I was just too stupid to see it. I blamed myself, of course. He said it just wouldn't have worked, and I took it to mean that was because of me." She shook her head. "But it wasn't me. It was him."

"It sure was." Carla stroked Rihanna's arm gently. "And he left you with the tab?"

Rihanna nodded. "He soon realized that he could get a better deal by paying non-refundable deposits and paying for stuff early. Unfortunately, it was mostly with *my* money, which, of course, I couldn't get back afterward. I was on a decent wage — better than him, in fact — but I had to take out a large bank loan to cover it all. He said we'd pay it off together after the wedding, but, of course, that went down the pan when he left me. I've no idea where he is, even if I *wanted* to chase him for his share."

"Maybe you should?" Carla looked thoughtful. "A private investigator could find him. I'm sure Dyson would help. You could find him and demand that he pay his half."

Rihanna shook her head. "It would mean more costs — getting someone to find him, then taking him to court. I'm in enough debt as it is, Carla. I just can't manage any more. Besides, he'd find a way to wriggle out of it. And, to be honest, I never want to see him again."

"So you're planning to just carry on and pay it all back yourself? That could take years." Carla frowned.

"Three years and four months, if I can stick to my budget," Rihanna replied. "And providing the interest rate doesn't rise in that time, of course."

Carla sighed. "That's a long time."

Rihanna nodded. "I was so lucky to get this promotion. If I was on my previous wage, it would take even longer to pay it back."

"So, it was good timing, getting the new bank?" Carla looked thoughtful.

Rihanna nodded. "I couldn't believe my luck. I didn't realize it was going to be all the way out here, but I'm kinda glad of it now. A complete new start...and somewhere I can't bump into Phil Cartwright."

"Yeah, I know how that feels," Carla said with a little smile. "The main thing is you're safe here and you've got friends. You don't have to be alone."

Rihanna offered her a grateful smile. "Thanks, Carla. It's really good to know."

Carla gave her another hug before returning to her seat. "I'll have a word with my boss about the rent on that apartment, too," she said, decisively. "See what he can come up with. I take it you would prefer the grocery store to the hairdressers'?"

Rihanna nodded. "It *was* pretty small down there, wasn't it?"

Carla grinned. "Just a bit."

They both giggled.

"I'd best go wash my face," Rihanna said, standing up.

"Good idea. Ace should be back soon to take you back to Almondine."

She went down to the bathroom and splashed cold water over her flushed and swollen face yet again. "You really need to stop all this crying," she told her reflection, but she had to admit that deep down she felt much better for it.

She heard whispering as she neared the kitchen door, and stopped, not wanting to intrude.

"Oh, no." It was Ace's voice, and it wasn't a whisper.

Just what had Carla been telling him? Surely she wouldn't betray her confidence? With a loud sniff, she opened the door and went in.

"Ace, you're back?" She raised her eyebrows, trying to look surprised.

"Yeah, are you okay?"

She looked from him to Carla then back again. "Of course. Why wouldn't I be?"

Ace offered her a kind smile. "You've had a busy day. I thought you might be tired. Need a ride home? Well, back to the hotel, anyway."

"Sure. Thanks."

She pulled on her coat and gave Carla a big hug. "You won't tell anyone, will you?" she whispered into her friend's ear. Immediately she felt Carla's body tense. *Too late?*

Chapter Nine

"Did you have a good day?" Ace sounded quite guarded as he drove her back to Almondine.

Rihanna had mixed feelings. She'd had a lovely time with him when they went riding, and it had been good to take a look at the apartments in Pelican's Heath — especially the one above the grocer's store. The idea of moving nearer to her friends had grown on her, but now she wasn't so sure.

"Yes, thank you. I especially enjoyed the riding." She forced a smile.

He looked back at her, his face partly shadowed by the night. "I enjoyed it, too. We could do it again sometime, if you like?"

She knew she'd really love to, but wasn't so sure it was a good idea...not now.

"Perhaps."

His jaw tightened. "Rihanna, is something wrong?" His voice was deep and his tone kind.

She almost felt like crying all over again. He seemed like such a nice guy, and she'd been flattered that Carla thought he liked her. But he knew too much, and that would mean that any feelings he might have had for her would now be marred with pity and sympathy.

"No, I'm just tired."

"Are you sure that's all it is?"

"Of course."

He sighed, slowing the truck down a little. "Look... I'm really sorry for being so negative about that first apartment we looked at. I should have kept my opinions to myself. I'm afraid it's one of my worse traits, speaking before I've fully engaged my brain."

"You're entitled to your own opinion."

"I'm not entitled to blurt it out when it's not wanted, though. I'm sorry if I sounded really down on the place."

"You didn't like it."

He sniggered. "Aw, come on. You saw it. It was tiny, even for one person. The other one was much nicer."

"In your opinion."

He gaped at her. "Yours, too, if my ears didn't deceive me."

"Yeah, well, it was the better option, space-wise," she conceded.

He grinned. "So, are you going for it?"

"I'm not sure."

"I'm sure it won't cost too much more than the first one, and you'll be much happier there."

She narrowed her eyes at him. "Another of your opinions, I suppose?" She tried hard to keep the edge from her voice but was getting quite irked by his assumptions.

"Exactly." He nodded, frowning a little.

"Well, thanks for that. I'll bear it in mind." She glanced out of the window into the darkness.

He huffed. "I've said the wrong thing again, haven't I?"

She swallowed hard. "You're allowed to say whatever you like."

"But I know I've annoyed you. Don't you *want* to live over the grocery store?"

She turned back to face him. "I don't even know if I want to live in Pelican's Heath."

His face fell. "What? But I thought you'd warmed to the idea, especially as it means you'll be able to make more friends. And if you got the bigger place you'd even be able to invite them back to yours. Carla was really excited at the idea, I thought you were, too."

Rihanna pursed her lips. "Look… I'll sleep on it, okay?"

He nodded. "Well, don't leave it too late. I guess that property won't be vacant for long."

"Thank you. I'll bear that in mind."

He pulled up in the hotel parking lot and thumped his steering wheel. "Rihanna, why won't you talk to me?"

She gaped at him, surprised at how angry he looked.

"What do you think we've been doing all the way here?" She frowned.

"You know what I mean. Something's upset you, and I wanna know what it is. I've a feeling it's me, but I don't know what I've done. Can't you help me out here?"

Rihanna's stomach churned as she realized it was frustration, not anger, that she saw in his handsome face — and a little sadness, too.

"You haven't done anything wrong." She purposely kept her voice soft. "I've just got a lot to think about, okay? I'm sure things will look much different in the morning."

His face relaxed a little and he nodded, placing a hand on her arm. "I really enjoyed spending time with you today."

She smiled back at him. "I had a great time, too. Thank you."

"Shall I pick you up in the morning?"

Her mind whirled for a second before she remembered that she'd promised to help Carla out with the baking. She'd looked forward to it when she'd agreed, but now she wasn't quite so sure. "It's fine. I don't know what time I'll be going up there, and I know you've got work to do, so I'll drive myself."

Ace couldn't hide his disappointment. "If you're sure?"

"Positive. Thanks, though. I appreciate the offer."

He nodded.

"Right, well, I'd best let you get home. I'll probably see you tomorrow. Thanks again, Ace." She quickly opened the door and jumped out of the truck before he could say anything more.

It was a relief to get back to her hotel room in a way. There was no one here to speak to, but that was a good thing right now. Company was the last thing she wanted. It had been hard enough to keep making polite conversation with Ace all the way there, and she'd wished more than once that she'd taken her own car so he wouldn't have had to drive her back.

It wasn't that she didn't like him — far from it. It was just that the dynamic had changed now. Carla had betrayed her. She'd clearly told Ace about her past.

Now all she'd get from them was sympathy, not the friendship she'd hoped for.

Lying on her bed, she let the tears run down her cheeks once more. Why had she been so stupid? It had felt cathartic telling Carla about Phil Cartwright, but the last thing she'd expected was for her to tell Ace.

That was the problem with small towns. Everyone knew everyone else's business. How would it look now, when all her customers knew that she'd been jilted just before her wedding? She'd never live it down. They'd give her sympathetic looks and snigger behind her back. She could just see it now. And Paul and Sarah would lap it up.

The whole day flashed before her eyes. At the time she'd thought she was making friends, chatting about work and confiding in Carla about her past. Now it looked as though she'd said way too much. Soon the whole of Pelican's Heath would know that she wasn't *really* in charge of the bank, and that she was only there to escape the embarrassment of being dumped by her fiancé. Would they also hear that she was broke? Was she likely to lose her job when the whole town discovered that the bank manager was up to her eyes in debt? There was no way the bank—or she—could save face once that secret was out. At least she wouldn't have to worry about finding somewhere to live, as, without a job, there was nothing to keep her in Cavern County anymore. The thought hurt her more than she'd expected.

* * * *

The following morning Rihanna didn't really want to get out of bed, which was unusual for her. Most days she'd be up as soon as the sun started to stream though the open drapes, but today she just rolled over and tried to go back to sleep. She simply couldn't face the day — or the people, or the world, to be honest.

She'd had nightmares about being laughed out of town, of having to go back home and tell her parents she'd been fired because of her debts — debts they weren't even aware of. The thought of facing Phil Cartwright with his new girlfriend churned her stomach. Not because she wanted him back — far from it — but because she could just imagine their smug expressions as they swanned about, looking down their noses at her.

"I'm not going to cry today," she promised herself, as she finally pried the pillow from her face and slowly crawled out of bed. "I'm a bank manager, for goodness' sake. I need to act like one, even if I'm not in the job for long."

She took a hot shower while giving herself a pep talk about how strong she was and how she could overcome anything she had to.

She pulled on her Levi's and a pretty sweater before fixing her hair with a sparkly clasp and putting on the makeup she normally kept for work. There was no denying she felt a lot better as she looked into the mirror to see a confident, determined woman smiling back at her.

It seemed pretty cold outside, the wind blowing litter down the empty street, so she grabbed her boots before heading downstairs for breakfast.

She wasn't all that hungry but was glad of the coffee, as well as the thinking time it bought her. Although she wasn't really looking forward to going to see Carla today, she'd made a promise, and she certainly wasn't one to renege on them — even if Phil Cartwright was.

With a clear head, she decided that the best thing to do was ask Carla about what she'd said to Ace Blenheim. Perhaps she'd been worrying too much? What if it was just coincidence that Ace had given her a knowing look and that Carla had tensed when she'd asked her not to tell anyone her business? Okay, she knew it was highly unlikely, but she wasn't about to make a fool of herself without knowing exactly what had happened. It was all too easy to go off half-cocked, and she prided herself that it certainly wasn't her style.

That, she had to admit, was probably why she'd been so shocked when Phil had dumped her. She just hadn't seen it coming. With hindsight, all the signs had been there, of course, but she had been too focused on their future to notice what was going on around her. She didn't intend to make that mistake again, but she was darned if she'd let it turn her into a jaded, bitter woman who trusted no one. Phil just wasn't worth it.

Which was why she'd decided to go speak to Carla properly before allowing herself to fall into a pit of despair, as she'd almost done the previous night. She shook her head. She'd always had a methodical mind, which was probably why she was so good at math, but every now and then her emotions took over and ran wild.

She went upstairs to fetch her coat and bag, as well as a warm scarf, and headed for Pelican's Heath. It was the same route she'd taken every day the past week to get to work, but without the rush, she was able to appreciate the beautiful scenery that surrounded her. It was still frosty, and as she left the large town of Almondine and drove toward the country, she enjoyed seeing the scenery painted in white glitter, glistening as the hazy sun swept over it.

The road was quiet, and she took her time, grateful for the hush that seemed to smother the countryside, slowing her heartbeat and granting her the peace she so dearly needed.

The Shearer Ranch was just outside of the town, and she sensed movement as she meandered up the drive. Pulling up outside the ranch house, she could see horses being led out of the stable, and a couple of them already being put through their paces in the large training paddock. She didn't recognize any of the staff, but they all looked quite cheerful as they went about their work, and she was sure Ace and the Shearers would be around somewhere.

The door opened before she'd even reached it and Carla stood smiling at her with open arms. "I was hoping it was you." She gave Rihanna a hug before ushering her into the warm kitchen. "I'm so glad you came. I was afraid…" She bit her lip.

Rihanna hung her coat and scarf on the back of door then looked back to see Carla almost in tears. Her heart went out to her. She knew she wouldn't hurt her on purpose and went over to put an arm around her.

"I'm sorry." Carla sniffed. "I was afraid you'd think I'd told Ace about what you'd said."

Rihanna frowned, not wanting to admit that was *exactly* what she had thought. "You wouldn't betray a confidence," she replied, studying Carla's tensed face. Something about the girl told her that Carla wasn't the type to blab anyone's business about the place. She inwardly cursed herself for even considering it in the first place.

Carla managed a smile, sniffing back tears. "Absolutely. I had enough secrets of my own when I first arrived in Cavern County, so there's no way I would disclose anyone else's."

Rihanna's eyes widened. Carla seemed to have her life all sorted. She lived here with her two handsome men and looked after everyone in this place, including the staff. Ace had told her that, on occasions, Carla had even given him a hearty breakfast when he'd arrived early for work, and she was always ready with a smile and hot drink, not to mention something tasty from her baking repertoire. "I didn't know," she said as they sat at the kitchen table. "You seem to be so together."

Carla smiled. "I am now, but it wasn't always like this. Anyway, enough about me. I just wanted to let you know that when Ace came in last night, he asked me if he'd upset you. I said I thought he might have, and he was real sorry. I said he needed to be more careful about what he said, as he could be trampling on your feelings without realizing it."

Rihanna stared at her. "That was it? That's all you said?"

Carla nodded. "I hope that was all right. I saw how you'd reacted when he'd been so negative about the first apartment and thought he needed to be aware, that's all — not just for your sake, but for his, too. Ace is a good-hearted guy, and he wouldn't upset anyone for the world, but sometimes he just doesn't think."

Rihanna smiled, recalling the conversation she'd had with him last night. "I think we're all guilty of that sometimes."

Carla nodded, pouring some coffees from the pot on the table. "Of course, we're only human. But I thought, as he'd asked the question, it was only fair to tell him the truth. He was genuinely worried about it."

"He was just giving his opinion, I know, but he was a bit negative about the whole thing, wasn't he?"

"You can say that again." Carla rolled her eyes, then chuckled, and Rihanna joined in.

"So, what are we making today?" Rihanna picked up an old recipe book that sat on the table and started leafing through.

"I need to fill the freezer," Carla explained. "We often get cut off when the snow gets heavy, and I want to make sure we don't run out of anything. Sometimes the power goes, too, and I can't use the stove, so I want to have enough for snacks, even if I can't cook."

"That sounds horrendous." Rihanna suddenly remembered harsh winters when she was growing up, when the power would go out and they'd have to make do with candles, while only eating sandwiches. It had actually been quite an adventure when she was small.

Carla shook her head. "No, it's fine, really. We have a back-up generator that automatically switches to the freezer, so nothing gets ruined, and it's really cozy up here with just the fires for warmth. I feel sorry for the guys outside, though, but they have another generator to keep their staff area warm and keep the coffee going."

"Sounds like your boys have thought of everything." Rihanna smiled.

"Oh yeah. They're well used to this sort of thing," Carla assured her. "They've been ranching all their lives."

"What about you?" Rihanna asked.

"I only came to Pelican's Heath a few years ago," Carla replied with a wistful smile. "Though it feels like

I've lived here forever. It's that sort of place, I reckon. It gets into your blood. No one ever wants to leave once they settle here."

Rihanna took a sip of her coffee, wondering if her friend was right. When she was here at the ranch, she felt at home. The place, the people, the whole atmosphere enveloped her like a warm blanket. Could this really be where she belonged, after all?

Chapter Ten

Ace had been up since before dawn today, unable to sleep the past night. His mind whirled with the events of the previous day, and he couldn't fathom why he felt so bad about it. The way he'd left Rihanna at the hotel rankled. It was as though she couldn't get away from him fast enough. Had he really upset her that much?

"Penny for them?" Matt Shearer caught him gazing across the countryside while in the middle of mending a fence.

"Sorry, boss. I was just thinking." He quickly tightened a piece of rope he'd used to keep the post in position.

Matt winced. "Don't hurt your head."

"Very funny." Ace rolled his eyes, used to the guy's banter.

Matt stood next to him. "It looked serious, buddy. Is everything all right?"

Ace grimaced. "To be honest, I'm not sure."

"This wouldn't have anything to do with a certain fair-haired beauty with bright green eyes, now, would it? The one who's currently baking in our kitchen?"

Ace widened his eyes. "Really? She's here?"

Matt nodded. "Yup. Last I heard, she and Carla were giggling like a couple of schoolgirls." He grinned. "I haven't seen Carla looking so happy in a while. I think she really likes that girl of yours."

"Hey, now, I wouldn't call her that." Ace put his hands up in submission. "I wouldn't complain, of course, but I'm just not sure she's that into me, you know?"

"Carla seems to think she is." Matt raised his eyebrows. "Didn't stop talking about you guys last night. She's real intuitive, that wife of mine. Can sense a vibe a mile off."

Ace gaped at his boss. "Did she say anything about me upsetting Rihanna yesterday? I kinda put my big foot in it, I reckon."

"She'd sensed some tension between you guys, but then, she said that seems to be how you two roll. Something about you blocking in her car the other day, just to get a reaction. And I'm dang sure there wasn't really a problem with you opening up a new bank account down there. I get it. Some people have a different way of showing their feelings toward one another. Nothing wrong with that, in my book." Now it was *his* turn to hold his palms up.

Ace chuckled. "Yeah, well, that *was* kinda fun."

"There you go. There's definitely a connection there. It just might not be as obvious as with some folk. We're all different, ain't we?" He grinned.

"Hmm-m." Ace narrowed his eyes in thought. Carla wasn't the only one who was quite perceptive. It seemed at least one of her husbands picked up on a lot more than he let on. "Thanks, boss."

"No problem. Don't forget to take your break as soon as you're ready. By my reckoning, the next batch of gooey butter cake should be coming out of the oven in about twenty minutes."

Ace sniggered, watching his boss go back to his horse and head back down toward the ranch. He took a heavy mallet and cheerfully hammered the stake into the hard ground. At the rate he was going, he'd be finished here and well on his way back to the ranch house in time for warm cake. His heart warmed at the idea, too.

* * * *

Rihanna hadn't laughed so much in ages. Carla really was great company, as well as a talented cook. The kitchen was strewn with cooling trays with various cakes and cookies, and the smell was heavenly.

She couldn't believe what a rough time her friend had had before coming to Cavern County and berated herself for thinking *she'd* had it hard. Carla seemed convinced that Pelican's Heath was the place to make everyone's dreams come true, though, and even told her a little about some of her friends who lived here. She couldn't wait to meet them all—especially the famous fashion model, Isla Gillingham. Rihanna had no idea that there were any celebrities living out here, and it raised her impression of the place ten-fold.

"Phew! It's getting warm." Carla opened another window, allowing the cold air to condense with the heat of the kitchen.

"Everyone'll think we're on fire in here," Rihanna remarked with a giggle, as steam flowed out into the wintery cold.

"Ha. It'll be a good excuse for them to come in and taste some of these." Carla chuckled as she placed some chocolate brownies into a plastic container.

"You don't think all this is going to get into the freezer then?" Rihanna grinned.

"Why do you think we have to make so much of it? Honestly, there are that many hungry mouths around this place, I'll be lucky to freeze half of it."

"It's great that there are so many people around, though, isn't it?" Rihanna replied. "I remember when I was growing up that we always had a full house. We lived in the country and my grandparents owned a large house just down the lane, and three of my aunties lived in the little village, just a ten-minute walk away. There was always someone popping in for something. And my mum and I always baked on weekends." She smiled at the memory, which had eluded her for years. It was as though her childhood had been relegated to the back of her mind for some reason, while she'd gotten on with her life in the city.

"Did you prefer it in the country, then?" Carla licked her fingers before putting a couple of bowls into the sink.

Rihanna thought for a moment. "Do you know what? I did. When we moved to the city, I sort of *had* to fit in with everyone, and I stopped baking and gardening and all that stuff I'd grown up doing. My education became really important, as everyone in my class seemed to think I was stupid because I'd moved from the country, and I felt the need to prove them all wrong. I guess I forgot how nice it is to be away from all the hustle and bustle."

Just then the door opened, and Ace removed his hat as he came in. "Something smells good."

"Come on in and get warmed up." Carla immediately poured him a hot drink and he sat at the table, which was awash with baked goodies. "What can I get you to eat?"

"It all looks delicious," he said with a smile, looking around at the array of cakes. "I heard you had some of that gooey butter cake somewhere. Is it out of the oven yet?"

"Funny you should ask that, Ace. Rihanna's just fetching it out now." Carla grinned.

Rihanna brought it over to the table, while Carla lifted a plate of chocolate chip cookies to make room for it.

"It's hot," Rihanna warned with a smile.

"In that case, maybe I should try one of these sugar cookies while I'm waiting for it to cool down." Ace took one from the plate in front of him with a cheeky smile. "Hmm, delicious," he moaned before anyone could object.

Carla nodded toward Rihanna. "Now you see what I mean about having to bake twice as many as we need for the freezer?"

Rihanna chuckled.

"Hey, I've been working hard all morning. I need a little sustenance," Ace informed them with a grin.

"I think we all do," Carla conceded with a smile. "Come on, Ri. It's time for a sit down."

Rihanna brought over a fresh pot of coffee while Carla made some room on the table. They joined Ace, sighing as they sat.

"I hadn't realized how tired I was getting," Carla remarked.

"It's been fun, though." Rihanna beamed at her.

"I think I'll have an oatmeal and raisin cookie." Carla chose one from the cooling rack, and Rihanna had the same.

"You sure look like you've had a nice time," Ace said, turning to Rihanna, who was sitting next to him.

"It's been ages since I baked anything, let alone in these sorts of quantities," she replied, glad of the opportunity to gaze into his gorgeous face. He seemed much more relaxed today, thank goodness.

"Are you from a big family then?" he asked, in surprise.

Rihanna nodded, munching on her cookie. "Yeah, fairly big. And we always had friends and neighbors dropping by, too. It was like open house all the time when I was growing up."

"In the city?" He raised his eyebrows.

She shook her head. "No, when I was really young, we lived in the country."

Rihanna noticed his face relax even more.

"Oh, right, of course, you mentioned that yesterday. Until then, I kind of assumed you'd always lived in the city." Then he quickly added, "But that's me. I always make assumptions when I shouldn't." He gave a self-deprecating smile and her heart lurched, remembering the conversation they'd had yesterday morning.

"I think it's a natural assumption to make," she assured him with a soft voice. "I probably come off as a bit brash and haughty until you get to know me. It comes from spending too much time trying to compete with my city-slicker peers instead of just being myself."

She surprised herself with her own admission and could see the others hadn't expected it, either.

"I like this side of you," Ace said quietly. "I feel more relaxed around you — not having to keep on my toes in case I say or do the wrong thing."

Rihanna's stomach warmed, and she felt her cheeks flush. He seemed different today — more open and laid-back. She liked seeing him like this. She smiled.

"Have you thought any more about the apartment over the grocery store?" Carla asked, standing up to cut the gooey butter cake.

Rihanna tore her eyes away from Ace and nodded. "Yeah. I think I'll inquire about it later. You're both right about it being the better option. I just hope I can afford it."

"I'm sure you can on a bank manager's wage." Ace smiled, then his face immediately fell. "I'm sorry. That was presumptuous, wasn't it?"

Rihanna felt them both looking at her and bit her lip. Then she smiled. "Yes, it was a bit," she admitted with a giggle. "But I can see why you might think that."

He put his hands up. "I really am sorry."

"Don't be. Most people would assume I'm on a good wage — and I am. It's just that, unfortunately, I've also got a lot of debt to pay off. But that's just between us, right?" She looked warily at them both.

"Of course." Ace nodded.

"It's no one's business but yours," Carla assured her, passing around the gooey cake. "Though I still think you should make the dumbass pay what he owes you."

"Anyone I know?" Ace asked with a frown.

Rihanna shook her head, giving Carla a pointed look. "No, he's not from around here. Just someone from my past."

Carla rolled her eyes, and Rihanna knew she'd expected her to divulge the story to Ace. She wasn't so keen to show him what a complete idiot she was, though, not yet, anyway. For some reason she'd rather impress him if she could. Did that mean he was growing on her? She had to admit she really liked him, but whether anything could come of it was another story. Besides, she hardly knew anything about him.

As though reading her thoughts, Ace smiled. "We've all got a past, Rihanna. Don't worry about it. I'm kinda glad you're a country girl, though. No wonder you look like you belong around here."

She gasped. "Do I?"

He nodded. "You were a natural in the saddle yesterday, and you sure can bake." He took another bite of his cake, as if to make his point. "And you're clearly at home with a house full of people, even when you don't know them all that well."

"I don't know any of you all that well," she replied with a shrug, secretly flattered.

"I've told you all about me," Carla said, pouring out more coffee. "What about you, Ace? Care to tell us your life story?" She grinned.

Ace chuckled. "There's really not much to tell. I'm a country boy through and though. Heck, even Almondine gives me hives. I've worked with horses all my life. Came to Pelican's Heath about a month ago when I got this job, and here I am. My family are over in Reedlake County, so not too far away, and I've got a place in town. What more do you wanna know?"

"And you're single?" Carla was tenacious, and Rihanna gasped.

He grinned. "Oh yeah, I'm single all right. Never cheated on anyone in my life, and never intend to. Had a few girlfriends when I was old enough, but nothing too serious on either part. No skeletons in the closet or regrets to keep me awake at night. Just a boring old open book."

"There's nothing boring about you." Rihanna spoke without thinking, and immediately put her hand to her mouth when she realized she'd actually said the words aloud.

He grinned. "Why, thank you, ma'am. That's very kind of you to say." He bowed his head, graciously, making them both giggle.

"I meant there's nothing boring about being a good person — not cheating and all that." Rihanna blushed as she quickly tried to clarify her statement.

He grinned before finishing his coffee. "Well, thank you, ladies, for the cake and the scintillating conversation — including the compliments." He nodded at Rihanna. "But I guess this cowboy had better get back to work before the boss realizes how long of a break I've taken." He grimaced and stood up.

"You're most welcome, kind sir." Carla stood and curtseyed, while Rihanna just watched him put on his hat.

He turned and winked at her before he left, and her heart just about melted.

Chapter Eleven

Monday morning brought with it a hint of positivity and a whole lot of hope for Rihanna, who, for some reason, couldn't wait to get to work.

Instead of her suit, she pulled on a warm, woolen dress, which looked great with her boots, and a pretty cream scarf. She put on her makeup as usual, but left her hair in a half-up, half-down style. Maybe if she appeared a little more approachable, people might give her half a chance.

She arrived before the staff and put on a fresh pot of coffee, ready for their arrival. Not that she felt the need to soften them up a little, but she was going to make some changes today that she figured they might not be all that happy about. But she was the boss, and, despite her slightly relaxed appearance today, they needed to understand that.

Paul and Sarah arrived together, as usual, chatting quite happily until they saw her. Paul's eyes widened, but Sarah frowned.

"Good morning." Rihanna let them in with a cheerful smile.

"Morning," they mumbled back in their usual fashion.

"Did you both have a nice weekend?" Rihanna chirped on, ignoring the odd looks they were giving her.

"Yes, thanks."

Making conversation was like pulling teeth from both of them.

She followed them through to the back room and poured their coffees as they removed their coats.

"Just so you know, there's a bit of a change to the lunchtime arrangements." She was handing Paul his drink as she spoke and sensed his whole body tense.

"What do you mean?"

She smiled. "Well, as you know, we've been working for a week now with the original schedule, and it's not working. I've decided the best thing is for both of you to man the desk at the busiest time of day and take your breaks before or after the rush, That means one of you can go from eleven until twelve and the other from two until three."

"And what about you?" Paul sounded quite accusatory, and she tried to ignore his audacity.

"I'm happy to take two half-hour breaks during the day instead of a whole hour," she replied, forcing a smile. "I usually only have a sandwich in the office, anyway."

He huffed, looking over at Sarah.

"But it's in our contracts," Sarah pointed out.

"Your contracts state that you have an hour's break," Rihanna reminded her. "It doesn't state at what time."

"But Mr. Williamson agreed to the times." Paul wasn't giving in easily.

"When we spoke last week, he agreed with me that whoever had made up the roster hadn't thought it through. We need to have at least two members of staff on the premises at all times, and by changing the schedule, we can now have three of us available at the busiest times and still not compromise that rule."

"But what if I don't *want* to take my break at eleven?" Sarah piped up, obstinately. "It's too early for lunch."

"Then take the later time." Rihanna smiled, but her face was firm enough to show them that it was a fait accompli. She turned and went over to unlock the front door, aware of their disgruntled mumbles as soon as she left them.

"Eleven isn't lunchtime," Paul protested, taking his seat behind the counter.

"Your contract doesn't stipulate that you have to have a meal during your break, though it is expected in order for you to remain in peak condition to work. Nowhere does it mention that it has to be during lunchtime. Obviously, the bank's busiest time is when our customers break for lunch, so we have to accommodate that."

"I don't see why it had to change. We did all right last week," Sarah moaned.

"If I hadn't helped behind the counter for two hours straight, you both would have had a very stressful hour working on your own. Not only that, but the service would have suffered, and we aim to offer our customers the best we can, don't we? Isn't that the reason we're here?"

They both mumbled, which was almost an agreement.

"You can decide between yourselves what time you'd like to take your break, but we need to stick to the new schedule." She was firm but not overpowering and left them grumbling as she went back to her office.

Luckily, she'd taken the time to thoroughly check their contracts and was certain she was right. She wondered how long it would take for Paul to ring Mr. Williamson to complain, but at least she knew he could do nothing about it.

The first thing she did was to contact HR at the head office to ask for the complete résumés for her staff. She had been given a highlighted version but was curious about their experience. Speaking to Dyson on Saturday had also piqued her interest. As the sheriff, he was obviously interested in people, and she realized that, as a boss, she should be, too. Unfortunately, her staff members weren't as forthcoming as they might have been, so she'd have to take the official route.

Over the phone, the woman at head office sounded very surprised that she hadn't been given the information in the first place and happily agreed to send it over as soon as she could.

It sounded like it was getting busy in the bank, so she popped her head out of the door to see if everything was all right. There was quite a queue, so she went through, smiling at the customers.

"Fucking cheek, if you ask me," she heard Paul say.

"Can she do that?" His customer was clearly annoyed at something.

"We shall see," Paul replied with a chuckle. "Just you wait till I've had a word with Dwayne."

They both laughed, and the man walked away, giving her a surprised look then a grimace as he left the branch. She watched him go down the street shaking his head and was desperate to ask him what the conversation was about.

Paul must have realized she was there, as his voice was a little quieter when she returned. A rather scruffy-looking guy whom she recognized had been sitting outside the café and she half-wished she could go over there, too, just to escape the tense atmosphere.

"Can I help anybody?" she asked, looking around at the customers.

"I just need to open a new account," a pretty girl with bright pink hair told her.

"Come on through. I can get the paperwork for you." Rihanna smiled at the girl, who was probably about the same age as her, and led her into her office. It was so refreshing to see a smiling face, and the girl looked so cute with her spiky haircut and big green eyes.

"Can I get you a coffee?" Rihanna offered.

"That would be great, thank you."

Rihanna popped to the kitchen and quickly made the drinks, aware of Paul and Sarah grumbling on the front desk nearby. She seethed. Although she knew they weren't happy with the new arrangements, she had hoped that they were professional enough to keep it to themselves in front of the customers.

"Here you go." She went back to her office and put the drinks on the desk before closing the door.

"This is really kind of you. I've had such a rough morning, and I really need it," the girl enthused, picking up her cup. "I'm Trinity Parker-Bray, by the way."

"Hey, Trinity. I'm Rihanna Richards."

Trinity beamed. "Are you from around here?"

"Not originally. I only came to South Dakota for the job. I was living in the city before."

"I was in Nebraska before I came here," Trinity offered with a nod. "Bit of a culture shock, isn't it?"

Rihanna smiled, glad that someone understood how she felt. "It takes a bit of getting used to, but the place is growing on me."

"It does. Cavern County's got a way of seeping into your bones and not letting you go. I love it here, now. Wasn't so sure when I first came, though. I wasn't planning to stick around, to be honest. But then the people and the place and the whole atmosphere sucked me in somehow, and now I wouldn't be anywhere else."

Rihanna nodded. She was starting to experience the same, she realized with a smile. "I was afraid I wouldn't fit in," she admitted with a grimace.

Trinity gestured toward the door with her cup. "You've got your work cut out with those two, haven't you?"

Rihanna felt hot. "What do you mean?"

Trinity gasped. "I'm sorry. I shouldn't have said that. Ignore me." She shook her head.

"You can't unsay it," Rihanna told her. "Do you know Paul and Sarah?"

Trinity narrowed her eyes. "I'm sure my Cordell's had trouble with him," she said quietly, "when he was working for CC Carpentry. Cordell and Jarrod were building our house at the time, and they'd ordered some wood. Paul turned up late with it and they were in the middle of a storm. He hadn't got it covered and it was soaked through. When the guys asked why, he got quite antsy with them, saying he wasn't accountable for the weather. But he'd only had a twenty-minute drive, so it had to have been raining when he'd set off. Anyway, they had a few choice words, I believe, and used a different supplier after that. It put them back weeks on the build. I tend to avoid him now."

Rihanna frowned. "So, he hasn't always been a bank teller? I thought he'd had years of experience." She glanced over at her computer, wondering whether HR had sent his details through yet.

Trinity raised her eyebrows. "No, he's had all sorts of jobs — handyman-type stuff. I don't think he's had a regular job for some time." She shrugged. "That's why I was surprised to see him in here, to be honest."

Rihanna nodded. "Can you tell me roughly when he worked for the carpentry firm?"

Trinity thought for a moment. "It must have been just over a year ago," she said, reaching for her phone. She pressed a few buttons before saying, "Oh yes, I remember. It was in the spring. We had some really bad storms in April of that year, I recall, so it must have been around then."

Rihanna scribbled a quick note, her eyes narrowed slightly.

Trinity put her cup on the desk and bit her lip. "Do you mind if I say something?"

Rihanna swallowed her drink. "Of course."

"Well, I don't know if you realize it, but he was being quite derogatory about you to the customers out there." She'd lowered her voice again. "I don't mean to cause trouble, but I just thought you should know."

"I know he's not too happy in his work," Rihanna conceded, her stomach churning with embarrassment.

"It's not just that." Trinity leaned forward, her eyes wide. "He said that you'd get your comeuppance. I think he's got something up his sleeve, which wouldn't surprise me, knowing him. I always thought he was a bit slimy. I mean, I know he doesn't get along with my husbands after that incident, but that's no reason to take it out on me, is it?"

Rihanna shook her head. "Well, thanks for tipping me off," she said, in an equally quiet voice. "I've certainly got my eye on those two—between you and me, of course." She suddenly realized how odd it was that she was confiding in a complete stranger—and a customer, at that. But Trinity had an openness about her that seemed to encourage her to be the same. She was similar to Carla in that respect, and Rihanna assumed it must be something to do with having two husbands.

"Of course." Trinity frowned, picking up her cup again. "I just hope I haven't upset you. I honestly don't mean to. I just thought it was only fair you should know."

"I really appreciate it," Rihanna assured her with a smile. "I don't have many friends around here yet, and it's good to know someone's got my back."

Trinity beamed. "I think we're gonna be *great* friends."

"Me, too." A warm feeling enveloped Rihanna as they chinked their coffee cups together and giggled.

* * * *

Rihanna sighed after seeing Trinity out. It was always hard to hear that someone was being mean behind your back, but she'd grown quite a thick skin in this job and could cope with it.

One thing she didn't like coping with, though, was angry customers, and when one raised his voice to Paul, she was shocked to hear her teller shout back.

"You know full well I put that money in on Thursday," the man pointed out. "So why isn't it in my account?"

"If you show me the receipt, I can look into it for you," Paul replied belligerently.

"You never gave me one!"

"We always give receipts."

"Well, you didn't on Thursday!"

"If you can't prove that you paid it in, then how do you expect me to look into it for you?" Paul's voice got even louder, and everyone was looking over at them.

"What seems to be the trouble?" Rihanna swooped over to the customer, smiling politely.

"I want my dang money!" the man demanded.

She looked over to Paul. "Do we have this gentleman's money?" She kept her voice at a respectful level, hoping to defuse the situation. This sort of thing wasn't doing the bank's reputation any favors at all.

Paul shrugged. "Nope. It's not in his account, so I can't give it to him, can I?"

"I paid it in on Thursday," the man insisted. "To you, personally. I remember."

"Well, *I* don't, and there's no evidence of it," Paul replied, matter-of-factly, his eyebrows raised.

Rihanna's heart pounded as she was aware that the other customers had started whispering now, and she could only guess what they were telling each other.

"Could you come into my office, sir? I'll look into this myself," she offered, still forcing a smile.

The man huffed but followed her.

"I might have known I couldn't trust him," the man groaned, slumping into the seat opposite her. "Once a liar, always a liar, if you ask me. I don't know how he managed to get a job here in the first place."

Rihanna was beginning to wonder the exact same thing.

Chapter Twelve

Sarah did nothing but moan about having to take her break an hour earlier than usual, but reluctantly gathered her things, frowning at Rihanna on her way out of the door. It wasn't very busy in the bank, which was a relief to Rihanna, who was desperate to open the email that had just arrived from HR.

"I'll leave my door open so I'll hear if it gets busy," she told Paul, as cheerfully as she could manage. "You can always phone me if you need me."

Paul grunted as she returned to her office.

It would appear that Paul Michael Rogers had had many jobs in his fifty-two years, only one of them being in a bank, apart from his current position. He had all the necessary qualifications, however, which surprised Rihanna, given that he hadn't gone straight into banking. She desperately wanted to call his last bank to ask about the glowing reference they had given him, but with the office door wide open, she decided this wasn't the right time. She made a note of the details, though, as well as the college where he had taken his exams.

Luckily, Sarah Maureen Lake's résumé seemed to ring true. There had been a short break in her employment after she'd left her last job, which Rihanna knew coincided with her getting divorced, which was what had tempted her to leave her job in a nearby town and look for a new location. Her qualifications and references looked to be in order, and Rihanna had been given no reason to doubt them. Sarah, it seemed, had always been a quiet worker, who efficiently got on with her job without any fuss or bother. She had always been competent and trustworthy, and her last manager had been very impressed with her, according to her reference. It seemed a great pity that Sarah seemed quite content to voice her discontent now, though, and Rihanna wondered if it was part of Paul's attitude rubbing off on her or whether she had been told to make her feelings so clear. It would be just like Mr. Williamson to tell her to shout up about anything she wasn't happy with, just to make Rhianna's job a little harder.

It turned out to be a good thing that all three of them were available to help out at lunchtime, as the bank was a hub of activity. Unfortunately, there was only room for two tellers behind the counter or Rihanna would have been tempted to jump on and help out, but as it was, she was probably more use sticking to her job and keeping an eye on things, while intercepting some of the customers before they got as far as the long queue for the cashiers.

She had placed a large pile of application forms on the shelf near the door, which saved many people from venturing too far into the building before getting what they needed and going on their way.

"How long does it take for cash to reach my account, dear?" An old lady's inquiry sent shivers down Rihanna's spine, and she quickly ushered the woman into her office and closed the door. This was too much to be a coincidence.

"On Friday, I paid my money into my bank account, and I went to use my card today but the shop declined it," the lady told her, close to tears.

Rihanna frowned, offering her a box of tissues. "I'm so sorry to hear that," she said, sympathetically.

"It was all right," the lady assured her. "That pretty girl was working at the time — the one with the lovely dark hair — and she let me have my groceries anyway, but she wasn't able to take the money for them. She said I could pay next time I was passing. She's so good, that girl." The lady sniffed before smiling.

Rihanna could imagine Carla being kind about the situation, but it must have been harrowing for the poor lady.

"Did you definitely pay it into *this* bank?" Rihanna asked, softly.

"Oh, yes, dear. My daughter had my account switched over from Almondine as soon as we were allowed to, and I had all my details sent over last Monday. I came in on Thursday and paid in my money. I hate to carry too much around with me, you see. I know I probably sound a little paranoid, but you can never tell who's around, especially with those strangers hanging around the place all the time."

Rihanna narrowed her eyes. "Strangers?"

The lady nodded. "Yes, dear. That vagrant-type and the young man he's usually with — always outside here, or just over the road when I come down." She lowered her voice, conspiratorially. "They give me the creeps, I don't mind telling you." She shivered.

Rihanna was aware that the guy in the red shirt seemed to be around most times she ventured outside the door but hadn't realized he was making such a habit of it. Perhaps the sheriff was right to be suspicious, after all.

"How much money did you deposit on Thursday, Mrs. Hills?" Rihanna asked, bringing up the lady's bank account on her computer. There was no sign of a deposit in the past week, and the previous one had been made in Almondine about a month ago.

"I paid in a hundred dollars," she said, her trembling hand reaching into her leather handbag. "My son sent it for my birthday. Here." She passed over a pink envelope with a beautiful birthday card inside. "Read the message," she urged.

Rihanna read it aloud. "To Mom, I hope you have a wonderful day. Sorry I can't be there, but I'll come home soon. Take this hundred dollars and buy yourself something nice. I wasn't sure what you'd prefer. Lots of love." She couldn't read the signature but it didn't matter. The fact was that this lady had definitely been given one hundred dollars. She replaced the card in the envelope and handed it back to her with a smile. "You have a very generous son."

"I do." Mrs. Hills nodded, her short, white curls bouncing softly. "But you're going to tell me this isn't proof that I paid it into the bank last Thursday, aren't you, dear?"

Rihanna's heart sank. She wished she was rich enough to give the lady the cash herself from her own purse, but she just didn't have it. "I'm afraid this doesn't prove it, Mrs. Hills, but I might know of a way I can check."

The old lady's eyes lit up.

"Can you give me until tomorrow to look through the security tape?" Rihanna asked. "If I can see you make the transaction on there, it will prove that something has gone awry, and I can give you back your money without any problem. I'll ring you first thing to confirm whether I have the proof or not."

The old lady smiled. "That would be wonderful. I know I'm old, dear, but I'm not too doddery to know when I pay money into my bank account. I'm not sure what's happened here, but I trust you'll sort it out for me."

"I'm not sure, either, Mrs. Hills," Rihanna replied, standing slowly. "But I intend to find out. Are you all right to get home? Do you need money for the bus or anything?"

Mrs. Hills stood, too. "No, thank you, dear. I'm meeting my friend. Thank you for your time."

"Not at all, Mrs. Hills. I'm sure we can sort this out. It's just…" She bit her lip, causing the old lady to frown at her, curiously. "Could I ask you a favor? Would you mind not telling anyone about this? Not until I've had a chance to sort it out? If it's an innocent misunderstanding…"

"You have my word, dear. I'm not the sort of person who spreads malicious rumors, believe me. And, besides, my friend and I have better things to talk about." She beamed. "My daughter's having a baby. I'm going to be a grandmother again." Her whole face lit up and she suddenly looked ten years younger.

Rihanna smiled back. "That's wonderful news. Have a lovely time with your friend, and I'll speak to you again tomorrow." Rihanna gave Mrs. Hills her arm and helped her to the front door, where they said goodbye.

On her way back into the branch, Rihanna glanced up at the security cameras. There were two, which seemed to be angled more at the foyer than the counter, which irked her. A lot of good they'd do like that. It would be too obvious to move them now, so she left things as they were and returned to her office to make some phone calls.

After arranging for a couple of extra cameras to be installed behind the counter early the following morning, she called Trinity to ask if either of her husbands might be available to do a job at short notice. To her delight, Cordell was there at the time and promised to call in that afternoon to discuss her requirements. It seemed things were looking up, after all.

* * * *

Rihanna was tired when she got up the following morning, but figured it was worth the lack of sleep to get things sorted at the bank.

She drove up to her place of work just after seven-thirty a.m., minutes before a van arrived with a couple of workmen.

"I'll get the coffee on," she promised, after they'd introduced themselves, and they brought their ladders and equipment into the building.

The guys, Jeff and Trevor, were really friendly, as well as efficient.

"I can't see those being of much use," Trevor said, gesturing to the original cameras as she handed him his drink.

Rihanna rolled her eyes. "You can say that again. At least they show the customers, but not what they do once they reach the counter." She'd discovered that to her cost last night when she'd run through last Thursday's tape.

"Who moved them?" Jeff asked, from his position up the ladder.

"What do you mean? They've always been there." Rihanna frowned, putting his coffee on the counter for him.

Jeff shook his head. "Nope, sorry. The one nearest the door was focused on the customers, the other on the counter."

"Are you sure?" Rihanna's heart beat a little faster.

"Yes, ma'am. I installed them myself," Jeff assured her.

"He's right. We've got the copy of the job sheet right here," Trevor told her, handing her the paperwork. It clearly stated the positioning of the cameras, with figures to back up Jeff's claim.

"Look," Trevor said, pointing to the numbers on the sheet. "These are the measurements to show the exact position that they were installed in." He took another ladder and a tape measure and climbed up to the camera nearest her office. Then he read the distance between the camera and the ceiling, and the angle of it. "Is that what it states on that sheet?" he asked, climbing back down.

She shook her head, suddenly feeling hot. Turning the page, she recognized the signature of the person who had signed for the job. *Dwayne Williamson.* They had only been installed the day before the bank had opened, so there hadn't been much time for anyone else to come in and alter their positions.

"Can you write down the position they're at now, please?" she asked Trevor, her mind whirling.

"Sure." He took the pen from his pocket and wrote down the new positions with today's date.

"I wasn't too keen on the guy who had the job done, to be honest, ma'am," Jeff called over. "I told him you'd need cameras behind here as well as over there, but he wouldn't hear of it. Practically accused me of just trying to make more money." He shook his head. "I kinda had an inkling we'd be back to finish the job, sooner or later."

"You advised him to have these put in?" Rihanna frowned, watching him attach one of the cameras.

"Of course. It's part of the job. I'm glad to see you listened about the window there, too. Real clever making it a two-way mirror, I like that." He nodded toward Cordell and Jarrod's handiwork, which had kept her there past nine o'clock last night.

"That was my idea, too," she admitted.

"Looks real nice. I like a good, neat job." Jeff looked impressed.

Trevor had already moved the ladder back to the position of the other camera and was drilling a few holes to mount it.

"Would you mind sitting behind the counter for me?" Jeff asked her. "I just want to position this one."

"Of course." Rihanna sat where Paul usually did.

"Is the teller about the same height as you, ma'am?" Jeff asked.

"A little taller," she told him.

"No problem. Right, that's about it." He checked the position again. "This should show right over his shoulder, and it's high enough to see over his head. It's pointed at the counter, showing the till and all the drawers, too. You'll be able to check everything this person does."

"Thanks." Rihanna sighed with relief before positioning herself in Sarah's chair. Trevor aligned the second camera with the same views over the other side of the counter.

"I really appreciate this," she told them, looking anxiously at the clock.

"No problem. Let me just adjust those other two," Trevor said, setting up his ladder again. "I'll put them back to their original positions, shall I? One showing everyone who comes in or out of that door, the other recording everything that goes on at the counter from the customer's point of view." He was already doing the job as he asked.

"Could I take a quick copy of the last job sheet as well, please?" she asked.

"Of course." Jeff sorted out the paperwork while Trevor returned all the equipment to their van.

She thanked them profusely before seeing them out. They'd done a great job and had been very neat and tidy about it, too. She looked around the room, feeling much more secure than usual.

After making another coffee, she went back into her office. She and Trinity had been chatting away happily here last night, while the guys had worked on the two-way mirror. She really liked all three of them and was glad to have made more friends already.

Sitting down, she pulled her notebook from her bag and opened it. It wasn't hard to tell why those two customers had been so upset yesterday. Both had definitely visited the branch last Thursday and approached Paul at the counter. She had seen Mrs. Hills reach into her purse and pull out the same pink envelope she had seen yesterday. Even without seeing the actual transaction being made, it was clear that the old lady had been telling the truth. It was the same with the man. Paul had definitely served him, and she had even seen a wad of notes being passed from the man's large hand. She quickly rang the bank's head office for advice, praying she would finish the call before the staff arrived.

Bypassing her area manager, she asked specifically to speak to the regional manager. She hadn't met the guy before and could only hope that he was on the level, unlike Dwayne Williamson, it seemed. He sounded surprised to hear from her, but when she explained the reason for her call, he was glad she'd spoken to him personally.

"Say nothing for now," he told her. "I'll get there as soon as I can. With the rush-hour traffic, it might be a couple of hours, but keep your cool. I'm on my way."

His name was Josh Treadwell, and he seemed a little older than her, with a very reassuring voice. She sighed with relief when she replaced the receiver.

Glancing up at the camera in her own office, she wondered if it had been tampered with as well. It seemed to be facing right at her, so she could only assume it had been left untouched, and she wished that she'd checked with the security guys before they'd left. It hadn't really occurred to her before.

A few minutes later her thoughts were interrupted by impatient banging on the front door. Paul and Sarah must have arrived, she thought, checking the time. This was going to get interesting…

Chapter Thirteen

"What the hell...?" Paul ignored her greeting and immediately fixated on the cameras behind the counter.

"Morning, Sarah," Rihanna kept up her sing-song attitude as they both snarled and stared at the new additions to the room.

"What's that?" Sarah demanded, pointing to the mirror.

"It's a window that will allow me to see when it gets busy in the bank so I can come and help out if I'm free," Rihanna replied, matter-of-factly. "Much more efficient and private than leaving my door wide open, don't you think?"

"It's a fucking two-way mirror," Paul snapped, "so you can spy on us."

Rihanna ignored the sickly feeling in her stomach. She'd guessed that he'd recognize it straight away. He was a handyman, after all.

"Why would I need to do that?" she countered. "I'm sure you must be trustworthy to be in the job in the first place. Mr. Williamson wouldn't have hired you if you hadn't been security checked, now would he?"

Looking straight at him, she wasn't surprised when Paul couldn't meet her eye. The truth was, there was no evidence that Paul had had a security check, according to his résumé, something she'd had HR investigating yesterday afternoon.

She waited by the door, watching as Paul glared at the cameras on his way to the back room. A few minutes later, they both re-emerged, having put their coats and belongings away, and took their seats, as usual.

"I don't see what we need those for," Paul said with a huff, gesturing with his head to the new cameras.

"They're a prerequisite of the bank," Rihanna informed him. "They should have been installed before we opened last week, but there must have been some delay."

"Well, we managed all right without them," he said, sulkily.

"Did we?" She narrowed her eyes at him and he gaped at her. Suddenly realizing she might have given the game away, she quickly shook her head. "They're as much to protect you as anything else. As you know, we had two customers in here yesterday claiming that they'd deposited money into their accounts when they had no proof either way. Don't you see that this will give you the proof you need to dispute it when it gets to court? Security camera footage is admissible as evidence. This is what will clear your name if the need arises. You're entitled to that much, surely?"

Paul frowned even harder, his jaw dropping. "Court? What do you mean?"

"If these people honestly think they've got a case, what's to stop them taking it further?" She wasn't surprised at how shocked he was, just at how blatantly he was showing it. For all his bluster, he wasn't very good at hiding his feelings. "We have to be prepared for any eventuality, and this way we've covered our backs, haven't we?" She smiled. "Literally, you might say."

Neither of the others saw the funny side, so she ignored their grumpiness and opened the door to the first of the day's customers.

Back in her office, she could hear the grumblings of her staff and see the sideways looks they kept giving the two-way mirror. Judging by the customers' reactions, they must have been surprised at the new additions, too, though she couldn't help thinking, yet again, how unprofessional it was of her tellers to moan to them about their grievances. Actually, she noticed, Sarah hadn't said much about any of it, seemingly taking it all in without passing an opinion, for a change.

Another new addition was a coffeepot in her office. It was a nuisance having to leave clients on their own when Sarah or Paul were too busy to make them a drink, and she felt it put her at a disadvantage. She was also certain her tellers weren't as busy as they claimed, but she could do nothing about that right now. They seemed determined to undermine her.

She'd set up a little coffee station in the corner by the door and was looking forward to the delivery of a tiny refrigerator where she could keep her milk. It was due later today and she only hoped it didn't arrive while the regional manager was making his visit. The room smelled of coffee, which she hoped would make the clients feel welcome when they came to see her. After all, a meeting with the bank manager could sometimes be quite unnerving.

She was surprised by a personal call from Carla regarding the flat above the grocery store.

"Good news." She could almost hear the smile on Carla's face as she spoke, and Rihanna reciprocated. "I know you're busy, but I just wanted to let you know that the flat upstairs can be yours for the same price as the one down the road. What do you think?"

Rihanna didn't really have time to think. With everything that had gone on here the past couple of days, she'd hardly considered her living arrangements since Sunday. "Oh, my gosh!"

"I know. It's a once-only offer, I believe," Carla told her.

"I don't know what to say." Rihanna's mind was reeling.

"Say you'll take it." Carla urged. "It's a great opportunity."

"It is." Rihanna swallowed hard, wondering how Carla had managed to persuade her boss to reduce the price so much. She only hoped it wasn't the karate-thing that had swung it. "Yes," she blurted out. "Yes, I'll take it."

"Great. I'll get all the details and call you tonight," Carla promised.

"Thank you."

Putting down the receiver, Rihanna grinned to herself. It was a start. More than that, it was *progress*. She was ironing out the problems here at the bank, she was making friends and it looked like she might just be about to put down some roots. She'd even had a call from Ace last night, apologizing for not being in touch all day, though she hadn't really expected to see him.

As it was, she was in the middle of watching the security tapes, so wasn't very chatty, but it was thoughtful of him to phone.

As the morning wore on, she became more and more nervous about speaking to the regional manager. Josh Treadwell had sounded very nice over the phone, but that didn't mean he'd agree with her assertions about Paul. However, she had heard back from HR, who informed her that they had still not found any security checks on him, and that they were still investigating. That must have *some* impact on proceedings, surely?

It was half past ten before she received a call from Sarah to say that her visitor had arrived. She looked through to take a peek at him before going out to meet him. He looked a little younger than she'd expected, but just as self-assured as she'd imagined him to be.

"Mr. Treadwell, do come in." She flashed him a smile, which he returned graciously.

"Thank you. It's nice to meet you, Miss Richards." Once inside her office, he turned and shook her hand politely.

"And you, sir. Would you like some coffee?"

"It does smell lovely." He nodded, removing his coat, which she immediately took from him and hung on one of the hooks behind the door with her own. "This is nice," he said, looking around the room. "I haven't been here before." He pointed to the two-way mirror. "And I like that."

"I had it installed last night, sir," she explained, taking the drinks over to the desk. "As well as additional security cameras, as we had none behind the counter at all."

He frowned, taking his seat after she had sat down. "Really? They're supposed to be in all the branches."

"The security guys who came today said that they'd suggested them, but whoever had had the job done said it wouldn't be necessary." She neglected to tell him who was responsible for their lack of installation.

Mr. Treadwell frowned.

"And there's something else," she said, pulling the job sheet from her drawer. "Someone had changed the position of the cameras after they'd been installed. One of the security guys noticed it this morning when they did their routine check."

"Routine check?" He raised his eyebrows.

"Well, they said whenever they did a job, they always double-checked on their previous work, to make sure there were no problems. Just part of the service, I believe." She was thinking on her feet.

"I see."

"They wrote down the measurements here." She pointed to the note on the papers she had copied earlier.

He picked them up and studied them. Then he turned the page before returning them to the table.

"You think someone had purposely tampered with them?" He narrowed his eyes.

"It looks that way, sir. Anyhow, what I needed to speak to you about was these two allegations that customers had deposited money last week that hadn't been recorded." She was a little unnerved by the way he was looking at her.

"Ah yes. There's no record on their accounts of the money ever being there, and your figures tallied at the end of the day, so there's no surplus to account for."

Rihanna raised her eyebrows, guessing he'd had his staff look into it all while he was driving over here. At least he was efficient.

"I checked the security tapes, sir, and both customers definitely came into the branch on Thursday and were served by Paul."

"And what exactly did he do for them?"

"He said he doesn't remember either of them, so he doesn't know what they were here for." She refrained from rolling her eyes but was perturbed by his lack of reaction to the news.

"Do you have the tape?"

"Yes, sir." She'd loaded it ready in her computer, which she spun around to show him. "This is the first one, Mr. Bettinger. You can see him come in and go up to the counter," she pointed out.

Mr. Treadwell frowned as he studied the screen. "We can't see exactly what the teller is doing, can we?"

"Well, no, not exactly. But the customer definitely has the money in his hand. Look." She pointed to the screen with her pen. "Then he doesn't have it." She pointed again to a very grainy picture as the guy moved his hand.

"But we can't see it in the teller's hand," Mr. Treadwell replied, pursing his lips.

"Well...no...but it's obvious, isn't it?" She looked as incredulous as she felt.

"It's still not proof, though, Miss Richards."

"But if the camera had been installed like it should have been, we would have the proof, wouldn't we?" she countered.

"Proof, yes. But proof of what? Either the man deposited the money or he didn't. Without the proof, we can't say for certain which he did. Even if the money was over at the end of the day, we could only *surmise* that it was his."

"But surely the customer's always right?" She gaped at him in disbelief.

Mr. Treadwell raised his eyebrows. "Maybe in retail, Miss Richards, but this is a bank. We can't assume everyone who comes through our doors is honest, much as we'd like to." He shook his head in a condescending manner that rankled her.

Rihanna bit her lip to stop herself saying something she might later regret.

"What about the other one? Have you any proof there?" He sounded like he was cajoling her now, which did nothing to abate her anger.

Without a word, she loaded the tape to the place where she had seen Mrs. Hills come in and pressed play.

She knew exactly what he was going to say before he opened his mouth. It was obvious.

"Again, we have no proof, Miss Richards." And there it was.

"Two customers claim to have deposited funds into their accounts on the same day with the same teller, and yet there are no receipts for the transactions, nor is the money over at the end of the day, and you think that means that the *customers* are dishonest?" she fired at him.

He narrowed his eyes. "Are you suggesting something different?"

She swallowed hard.

"Think carefully before you speak, Miss Richards. Remember that any accusations would need to be substantiated or you could be held liable for slander."

She took a deep breath, suddenly wishing she hadn't bothered to call him in the first place. What good had it done? He seemed to regard her as an inexperienced manager who didn't know what she was talking about.

"I'm not suggesting anything, Mr. Treadwell. I'm simply offering you the facts. It is my duty to report any anomalies to a member of senior management, so that is what I'm doing."

"And you didn't wish to report it to your area manager? Why is that, Miss Richards?" He seemed more curious than annoyed.

"I wanted to speak to someone completely impartial, sir."

"And you don't feel that Mr. Williamson would be?"

She pursed her lips in thought before replying. "As you can see from the records, sir," she began, pointing to the security guys' job sheet, "Mr. Williamson is already involved in this...matter." She chose her words carefully.

He tilted his head to one side. He really was quite handsome. "Are you suggesting some kind of involvement in — "

"I'm not *suggesting* anything, sir. I'm merely showing you the facts. Mr. Williamson had the security cameras put in, though they were tampered with afterward. And Mr. Williamson was advised to have extra cameras put behind the counter to record the tellers' transactions, but he declined to have them installed. I am certainly not casting any aspersions. What I *am* saying is that had the existing cameras been left in their original positions and if the advice of the security guys had been followed and the extra cameras installed, we would have all the proof we need. I think you can see that from the current footage."

He nodded. "I see." He licked his lips slowly while clearly contemplating his next move. He went to get up but stopped when she spoke.

"Oh, and another fact which you may or may not deem important is that HR are currently trying to locate a security check that should have been carried out on Paul before he took up his position." She put her hands up in submission. "Just in case you weren't aware of the situation."

"Right." He looked pensive as he elegantly rose from his seat. "Well, thank you for your concerns, Miss Richards. I'll certainly be looking into the matter."

"I hope so, sir." She wasn't really convinced. "And, in the meantime, I have two customers who are expecting a call back from me today with regard to the incidents we've just discussed. What will you have me tell them?"

His shoulders sagged slightly. "Well, without proof, there's not much we can do."

"Do you really want me to say that?" She frowned, hardly believing her own ears. "I mean, it's your decision, of course, but I'm just thinking about the reputation of the bank. When word gets into the papers that we've washed our hands of the situation, we're bound to lose all the accounts we've just accrued, including most of the businesses of Pelican's Heath. The branch will be forced to close before we've really got going. Is that fair, do you think, on the customers *or* the staff?"

He frowned back. "The papers? What do you mean?"

She raised her eyebrows, standing slowly. "Well, of *course* it'll get into the papers — and not just the local ones, I'd expect. All the financial supplements will hear

about it, and the whole bank will be held in disrepute —
whether we have proof or not."

"It's their word against ours," he pointed out,
irritably.

"Yes, sir. And, as individuals, the customers have
nothing to lose, whereas the bank — "

"I see what you mean," he snapped.

"And once it gets to court..."

"Who mentioned court?" His voice raised an octave
or two as he stared at her.

"If we tell the customers we have no proof and as
such won't be investigating the matter any further, they
will take it that we don't believe them. No one likes to
be called a liar, Mr. Treadwell, either directly or
indirectly. Defamation of character is a serious charge,
and I doubt the bank could — "

"You're suggesting we take their word for it?" he cut
in. "Despite the lack of evidence, and the fact that the
money wasn't even over that day?"

"I'm suggesting that we give the customers the
benefit of the doubt, and, as a gesture of goodwill,
refund their money. At the same time, we launch an
investigation into what happened. After all, if they *are*
telling the truth, then the money has gone *somewhere* —
clearly not into the bank. *If* anything untoward should
be uncovered, wouldn't it be better that the bank finds
out before the court or the newspapers? It has got to be
better to clean up our own mess than have it on show
for the whole world to see, surely?"

"And if they're trying it on? Customers are only
people, after all, Miss Richards."

"Then we might have lost a few hundred dollars, but
that's still got to be better than having to shut down the
branch because we've lost a few hundred accounts,

don't you think?" She was struggling to keep the tremble from her voice, and she wasn't sure whether it was due to nerves or anger.

His jaw tightened. "We will *not* lose money, Miss Richards," he announced resolutely. "All right, you can refund their money, but make sure they know this is a gesture of goodwill and *not* an admission of guilt."

"Thank you, sir."

He shook his head. "No, don't thank me. I intend to get back every penny. I will personally make it my mission to investigate this matter, and I *will* get to the bottom of it. I will find out exactly what happened here and where that money is. You can count on that." He stalked over to the door.

"I appreciate it, Mr. Treadwell," she told him. "And if I can help in any way, please let me know. I'm very interested to find out what happened, too."

"I should think so, Miss Richards." He turned to face her again before opening the door. "Because your job may very well be riding on the outcome."

Chapter Fourteen

The next few days went quickly for Rihanna and, despite the atmosphere between her and the staff, she enjoyed her job much more. Being able to keep an eye on how busy it became on the floor meant that she was able to pop through when she wasn't tied up with paperwork and alleviate some of the pressure on the counter. Most of the people she dealt with wanted to open new accounts, so it was a simple matter of pointing them in the direction of the pile of forms by the door, anyway.

She was planning to move into her new apartment on the weekend and had arranged for her things to be removed from storage and delivered to the premises first thing on Saturday morning. It would be nice to have some of her belongings back, especially her books. Something she wasn't looking forward to seeing again, however, was the myriad of wedding paraphernalia she still needed to sell. Her plan was to put it on the Internet and just get whatever she could for it, even though it meant taking a big hit on what she'd paid. The sooner it was out of her life, the better.

Mercifully, she didn't get a visit from Mr. Williamson all week, which, she surmised, meant that neither of her tellers had recognized Mr. Treadwell when he'd come for his meeting. She was sure that if they had, they would have been straight on the phone to the area manager, and Mr. Williamson would want to know why she'd gone over his head with her concerns. She still hadn't figured out what she would say to him.

Friday afternoon was quite quiet, and she was surprised to get a visit from Ace. She knew he'd been working hard all week, so they'd only had the odd phone conversation in the evenings, which suited her fine as she was busy checking through the security tapes after work each day, as well as making arrangements for her move from the hotel.

He wore his work jeans and a checked shirt, and his face wasn't as clean-shaven as usual, but he looked every bit as handsome.

"Hey, are you busy?"

"Not too busy for you. Come on in." She smiled as he strutted toward her.

"How's it going?" He took the seat opposite her in his usual, casual manner, smiling brightly, despite the tiredness that showed around his eyes.

"Great."

"I like what you've done with the place." He nodded at the two-way mirror. "Great idea."

"It's so I can see how busy it is out there in case they need a hand," she told him, with a smile. "Although the staff think it's so I can spy on them."

"Seriously?" He frowned incredulously.

She nodded, leaning toward him. "As if I had time to watch them all day."

He raised one eyebrow. "That just sounds like a guilty conscience to me."

"You think?"

"Why else would they assume that?"

"Maybe they're just suspicious of me being their new boss and all."

He shook his head. "There's a reason for everything," he told her. "If that was their first thought, there's something behind it, believe me."

"You seem very knowledgeable on the subject."

"I like studying people. It's what helped me get the foreman's job over at the ranch. I can read between the lines, get the nuance of what they're saying, even when they haven't actually used the words. Those two always seem on the defensive to me—especially that guy, Paul. I wouldn't trust him as far as I could throw him."

"He's a hefty guy," Rihanna commented with a giggle.

"My point exactly."

"Is there anyone else you've been watching?" She flashed her eyes at him suggestively.

To her disappointment, he sat back in his chair with a sigh. "Yeah. Those guys who keep hanging around outside. Dyson's right to be suspicious of them. They're up to something."

Rihanna huffed, crushed that he hadn't answered in the way she'd hoped and irritated that the strangers were still causing speculation around the place. "I think the old guy might be homeless," she said, a little curtly. "Maybe he hangs around the café because it's warm there and he can get a hot drink."

Ace shook his head. "I don't think so. Look... I know you like to see the best in people, and that's real generous of you, but you have to admit that there's something odd about a couple of strangers in town who spend most of their time hanging around by the bank."

She bit her lip in annoyance. "I wouldn't say I'm generous. I'm just a decent human being who doesn't automatically suspect strangers of wrongdoing when I don't even know the first thing about them."

"That's kind of why they're strangers." He gave a lopsided grin that did nothing but exasperate her even more.

"You don't know what it's like being a newbie in town—everyone making up their own minds about you without knowing the first thing about you." She raised her voice a little in her annoyance. "Not everyone you meet is up to no good just because you don't know them. It seems to me this town's full of negative thinking and paranoia, which just puts strangers off settling here."

"I'm still a newbie around here myself," he pointed out, calmly. "I told you that I only came here a short while ago. Compared to most folks around here, that still makes me a stranger."

"Then you of all people should know how it feels to have people raise suspicions about you without any cause."

He grimaced. "I guess. But I, like you, just get on and do my job. I don't hang around the local bank."

She raised her eyebrows. "*Don't* you?"

He swallowed hard, clearly taken aback. "Would you rather I didn't come in here?"

"I don't have a problem with anyone coming in here, but I also don't automatically feel paranoid about it."

He straightened his back. "I only came to ask what time you needed me to come and help out tomorrow — with your move, I mean."

Her jaw tensed. "Don't worry. I can manage just fine on my own, thanks."

He frowned. "Aw, come on. You must have loads of stuff that'll need carting up them stairs. It'll be much quicker and easier with two of us."

"Carla's helping me."

"It'll be even easier with three."

"Ace, the place is already furnished. I only have a few boxes of personal items to move in. I'm sure we can manage that without you. Thanks all the same."

"Are you mad at me?" He ran a hand through his dark hair.

She wasn't really sure how to answer that. "You look tired. You should get some rest if you're not working."

"It's been a long week, I ain't gonna lie, but I'd be happy to help you get settled in your new place." He looked slightly anxious.

She shook her head. "Honestly, we can manage."

He stood, clearly affronted. "Okay, if that's what you want."

"It is."

"Maybe I could stop by in the evening? Pick up a takeout or something? Join you for your first meal in your new place?"

She narrowed her eyes. "I'm not sure if Carla will want to do that, actually."

"I see. Well, in that case, I'll let you get on. Good luck with the move. Call if you want me." He picked up his hat and headed for the door, not half as confidently as when he'd walked in.

Rihanna felt glued to her seat. She didn't really want him to leave like this, but right now she was too aggravated to stop him.

"Thanks, Ace."

As soon as the door had closed behind him, she felt like crying. He'd only wanted to help, but she felt so annoyed at his attitude that she couldn't bring herself to accept his offer. She forced herself to concentrate on her work for the rest of the afternoon, wiping tears from her eyes when they became too blurry to read.

* * * *

It felt strange checking out of the hotel the following morning. Although it wasn't exactly homey, she'd got used to staying there and was surprised at how much stuff she'd accumulated in the past couple of weeks.

Bundling the last of her things into her car, she skipped breakfast and made her way straight over to Pelican's Heath in order to meet the van from the storage unit.

Carla was already waiting for her when she pulled up, as well as Dyson, who wasn't in uniform for a change.

"Happy moving day!" Carla was clearly excited for her as she went over and gave her a big hug as soon as she got out of her car.

Rihanna smiled. "Thank you. I can't believe this is actually happening."

"I brought along some muscle as well, just in case." Carla gestured to Dyson, who grinned at them.

"That's real kind of you." Rihanna felt a lurch in her stomach. Carla must have heard about her conversation with Ace yesterday.

"Have you got much in your car?" Carla asked, looking over.

Rihanna grimaced. "More than I thought."

"Let's get that up there first, in that case," Carla suggested. "Give us a chance to get the coffee on, too, before the van gets here.

"I'll need to get some, actually." Rihanna had planned to shop for food later and hadn't given a thought to the coffee they'd need to keep them going while they worked.

"Don't you worry about that." Carla went over to Dyson's truck and took out a basket full of groceries and what looked like home-baked goods. "I came prepared."

Rihanna beamed. "You're such a good friend! Thank you."

"Hey, I wouldn't have offered if I hadn't known I'd be kept in caffeine and chocolate cake," Dyson said, smiling as he put an arm around his girl and gave her a squeeze.

Carla rolled her eyes playfully.

"We'll start with your trunk." Dyson went over to Rihanna's car, and she opened it.

It didn't take long to get all her things from the hotel transferred into the bedroom of the new apartment, and the smell of fresh coffee made it feel instantly homey.

"The van's here," Carla said, peering out of the window as they sat taking a well-earned break with their coffee and cake.

They went down to meet the driver.

"Wow... I can see why you wanted the bigger apartment," Carla teased as they looked at all the boxes piled high in the back of the van.

"Most of this is getting sold," Rihanna told her, with a sigh.

"Well, let's get it all upstairs so you can sort through it at your leisure," Dyson cut in, cheerfully. "Where do you want these?" He'd already reached in and picked up a pile of boxes.

"The bedroom, I think." Rihanna was aware that the bedroom was going to be full of most of her stuff, but it seemed the best option. At least any guests she might have wouldn't have to look at her wedding things.

The delivery guy helped them, too, and they soon had everything stored in various rooms of the apartment. The driver even stayed for a coffee and some of Carla's delicious cake before leaving them to sort it all out.

"I hope the place won't look cluttered once I've unpacked everything." Rihanna looked around anxiously. The apartment suddenly seemed much smaller now.

"It always looks like more when it's still in boxes," Dyson said, kindly.

"And once we've got all that stuff in the bedroom sold, you'll be able to move around in there a lot easier," Carla added, gathering up the cups and plates and taking them to the little kitchen.

Rihanna smiled, grateful for their encouragement.

"Well, I think my work here is done. I'll let you ladies unpack or gossip or whatever it is you've got planned for the rest of the day." Dyson stood with a smile.

"Thank you so much for all your help," Rihanna said, standing up, too.

"My pleasure, ma'am." He grinned, before putting an arm around Carla, who'd just returned to the sitting area. "You just holler when you need a ride back, okay?" He took her in his arms and gave her a sensual kiss that made Rihanna look away and go stare out of the window. She couldn't help thinking how nice it would be to have someone love her as much as Dyson clearly loved his girl.

"Where shall we start?" Carla had just seen Dyson to the door and was looking around the apartment.

"The kitchen, I think. At least I'll be able to fix myself something to eat once these boxes are out of the way," Rihanna said, decidedly. "Are you sure you wanna stick around, though?"

Carla frowned. "Of course. I told you I'd help out."

"I know, but…"

"What is it?"

Rihanna smiled. "I just can't help thinking if I had a guy like that, I don't think I'd want to be apart from him for too long — especially if I didn't have to be."

Carla laughed. "I'll see him later. Besides, he's got errands to run. I think I got let off easy today."

Rihanna grinned. "As long as you're sure?"

"Positive. Now, pick a box."

* * * *

It only took a couple of hours to get everything unpacked except the bedroom boxes.

"These are all wedding things," Rihanna explained, pointing to a large pile of boxes stacked by the window.

Carla nodded. "You sure were organized for it."

"I was such a fool. I spent all that money without an inkling of what was really going on." She felt tears sting her eyes as she gazed at the labels on the sides of the boxes.

"He was very cruel," Carla said, softly.

Rihanna nodded. "Sometimes I wish I could go tell him exactly what I think of him," she admitted. "He can't have loved me, not really. He played me.

"Where is he now?" Carla asked.

Rihanna shrugged. "Last I heard he was still in New Moldington, going out with a girl called Vanessa Trent-Balister. Her family's rich, and she likes to throw money around like confetti."

"Ouch." Carla winced.

"Yeah. See a pattern emerging here?"Rihanna grimaced.

"Rich women who can pay for all the things he can't. Yeah, I get it."

"I wasn't exactly rich, but I would have been real well off if I hadn't wasted it all on the damn wedding." Rihanna kicked one of the boxes in frustration.

"We need to find him and make him pay his share. This just isn't fair." Carla shook her head.

"I don't think I could face him," Rihanna admitted. "At the time all I wanted to do was get away from all the sympathetic faces that surrounded me. I didn't bother to argue with him about the money or anything else. I guess I just felt numb."

"And now?" Carla asked, gently.

Rihanna thought for a moment. "Now I feel angry. How dare he put me in this position? He's lied to me, made false promises and practically stolen my money. I never would have paid out all this if he hadn't assured me he was going to pay his share into my bank. Now he's just made a damn fool of me, and I let him. Why should he be allowed to get away with this?" Her voice became a little louder, and her whole body tensed.

"What would you *like* to do about it?" Carla asked.

"I'd like to make him pay me back. That'd really hit him where it hurts. Right now, it looks like he's just gotten away with it. And he's moved on without even a second thought as to what he's done. At least Vanessa's not likely to be taken in by him. From what I've heard, she's not the type to want to settle down. Too busy having fun."

"Well, I suppose that's something," Carla mused.

"Yeah, I wish I'd been more like that." Rihanna gave a self-deprecating laugh. "I suppose I'm just too much of a romantic."

"That's not such a bad thing," Carla assured her. "You're just you. We can't all be the same."

"It's a good thing." Rihanna nodded. "I just wish I hadn't let him walk all over me like that, though. I'd love to see him get his comeuppance."

"Perhaps he will." Carla had a thoughtful look on her pretty face.

Rihanna hoped she was right.

Chapter Fifteen

After a busy start at the bank the following day, Rihanna was grateful to be able to pop over to the café for her break. It was quieter over there and she'd taken the opportunity to check out a few websites on her phone.

Three boxes' worth of her wedding items were now listed on the Internet, too, thanks to Carla insisting they start right away, and Rihanna was pleased to notice that there had already been a lot of interest.

Walking back into the bank, she was surprised at how busy it had suddenly become. A man was yelling at Paul over the counter with several customers watching. Rihanna was too late to hear what the argument was over, as the man finished by shouting something rather insulting about the bank before flouncing out of the door. She was about to follow him outside when another customer approached her, looking worried.

"Are you the manager?" the elderly man asked.

"Yes. Rihanna Richards. Would you like to come into my office?" She unlocked the door and gestured for him to take a seat while she quickly poured them each a coffee. "Is everything all right?"

His face was pale, and anguish spilled from every pore. "I need to ask about my money," he began, his voice a little wheezy. "It's just that I heard what that man was shouting about, and I wondered if it would be the same with me."

"What was he shouting about?" Rihanna took a sip of her drink, suddenly wishing she had something much stronger. This wasn't looking good.

"He'd paid his money in on Friday, and it still hadn't reached his bank account. I've come to take some money from my account that I paid in last Wednesday and I'm worried that it might not be there, either."

This was too familiar to be a coincidence. Rihanna fired up her computer and brought up the man's bank account, holding her breath. "Mr. Carding, I can see that you deposited fifty-six dollars on Wednesday, which went straight into your account." She wasn't sure which of them was more relieved.

The old man closed his eyes as though sending up a silent prayer. "Thank you so much."

"You're welcome." She smiled at him, before taking another sip of her drink.

"Well, I mustn't delay you any longer," he said, going to get up.

"Not at all. At least finish your coffee, unless you're in a hurry?"

He looked surprised as he shook his head. "No, not at all. If you're sure, though? It is rather good coffee."

"Of course. Is there anything else I can help you with?" She still had his account details on the screen in front of her.

"No, I don't think so, dear, thank you. It was just that I heard all that shouting, and I suddenly thought, what if my money is missing, too? Whatever would I do?" Tears came to his eyes at the mere thought, and Rihanna's heart went out to him.

"I'm sure it's just some misunderstanding, Mr. Carding," she assured him. "When you deposit cash into your account, it goes in straight away. If there was a problem with the other man's account, I'm sure we can fix it for him. He just needs to speak to us about it."

He nodded. "I can see that flying off the handle and walking out hasn't solved anything."

"Exactly, sir." She smiled. "Don't worry. I'll find out who he is and look into it this afternoon. It's probably just a computer glitch or something—or maybe he didn't pay it in when he thought he did. Whatever it is, I'm sure it can be easily rectified." She was trying to convince herself as much as him.

She accompanied him to the counter when he'd finished his drink, thankful that the color had returned to his cheeks. There was only one customer in the bank now, and she was at Sarah's counter.

"Paul, could you serve Mr. Carding for me?" she asked politely.

He looked a little taken aback, but took the man's card from him and brought up his details on the screen in front of him.

"I need to take out thirty dollars, please," Mr. Carding said.

"Of course, sir."

Rihanna watched the transaction then accompanied the elderly man to the door.

"Thank you so much, dear," he said, yet again. "I'm sorry for taking up your time like this."

"It's what I'm here for, Mr. Carding," she assured him with a bright smile. "If you have any other concerns, please don't hesitate to knock on my door."

"You're very kind."

She watched him walk unsteadily up the road.

"A satisfied customer? That's a change."

Rihanna spun around to see who was speaking and recognized the man in the red checked shirt. Despite his comment, she forced herself to smile at him.

"I don't think we've met. I'm Rihanna Richards." She reached out a hand and he had the grace to wipe his on his shirt before shaking it.

"You can call me Frankie."

"Do you live around here, Frankie? I think I've seen you before, haven't I?" She played it cool.

"Yeah, not far."

She was desperate to ask him why he was always hanging around the bank, but felt that would be a little too confrontational.

"Do you have an account with the bank?" She smiled, knowing full well what the answer would be.

"No."

"Would you like to open one? I have the form right here, and I could fill it in for you now if you'd like?" It was worth a try, she thought. A great way to get his personal details, which could allay Dyson's concerns about him.

"Nothing to put on it." He gave a gravelly laugh before walking away.

Rihanna went back into the bank, which was still quiet.

"Who was that man I saw shouting when I arrived?" she asked Paul.

He shrugged. "Dunno. Just came in to complain, I think. But the manager wasn't here, so he took it out on me." He gave her a pointed look.

"I was on my break, as you well know," she reminded him, curtly. "It's not just you and Sarah who are entitled to take them, don't forget."

He sniffed, showing his disdain as well as his bad manners.

She seethed, having had just about enough of this attitude from her staff.

"I think it's about time you started showing me some respect," she told him, her stomach getting all jittery as she spoke. "Whether you like it or not, I'm your boss, and I deserve to be treated as such."

He raised his eyebrows, clearly shocked.

"From now on, I expect to be treated as your manager, not something you trod on. And I will not tolerate you bad-mouthing me or the bank to the customers. It's unfair and totally unprofessional. If you want to keep your job here, I suggest you remember that. Do I make myself clear?" Anger kept the tremor from her voice, and she found it hard to contain herself. There was much more she wanted to add, but this wasn't the time.

"Yes, ma'am."

"Good. And if you could try that again without the gritted teeth, I'd be much obliged." She knew she was asking a lot, but she was at the end of her tether. She stared at him, expectantly. For a moment she thought he wasn't going to reply, but eventually he sighed and replied, "Yes, ma'am."

"That's better." She knew he'd hate being patronized, but then, so did she.

"Now, I understand the customer was concerned that his money hadn't been deposited into his bank account when he thought it had," she went on.

Paul nodded. "Yeah. They often try it."

"So, you checked his account, and it wasn't there?" she clarified.

He rolled his eyes. "Yeah."

"Then he must have given you his name. Can you give me his details, please? I think I need to check what's happened, as it has given a really bad impression to the other customers."

Paul tutted before pressing a few keys on his computer. With a sigh he jotted down a name and account number and passed it over to her.

"Thank you." She was about to let it lie, but she just couldn't. She turned back to him and leaned over the counter. "And do remember what I said. Tutting, huffing and eye-rolling are all considered very disrespectful, especially in a business such as banking. But then, I'm sure you'll already know that, having had so much experience in banks."

Rihanna was pleased to return to her office. She checked the man's account and, sure enough, there was no deposit made the last week at all. She recalled that he'd said it had been Friday that he'd come into the branch. She'd already checked the security tape for that day but had found nothing untoward, so she made a note for herself to look through it again tonight. She must have missed something.

She was already cross with herself for her parting comment to Paul. The fact that she doubted he had ever worked in a bank before was supposed to be kept under her hat until she'd found any evidence. There was no time like the present, she reasoned.

Paul's résumé showed that he had worked at TNOT Bank for four years. She rang their manager.

"Hello, my name is Rihanna Richards. I'd like to speak to the manager regarding a reference he has supplied, please."

The lady was very friendly and put her straight through.

"Hello, am I speaking to Mr. Leahy?" she asked, politely.

"I'm sorry, ma'am, but there's no one by that name here. Are you sure you've got the right bank?" a young man replied.

"The TNOT Bank on Upper Vale Street?"

"Yes, ma'am, but no one by that name works here."

"I'm sorry. I wonder if it's a previous manager?"

"No, ma'am. Mr. Suffrocote was the last manager here, and that was for fifty-two years. I've only just taken over last fall, so I'd know if anyone else had managed the place."

"I'm sorry to trouble you," she went on. "I had a reference from your bank for a candidate at my bank here in Cavern County. Are you able to confirm that this person actually worked at your bank, in that case?"

"Of course, ma'am. What name is it?"

"Paul Michael Rogers."

As she surmised, the poor man had never heard of him. She gave him the dates that Paul supposedly worked at the branch, but it still yielded no results.

"I'm real sorry, ma'am, but no one by that name has ever worked at this bank. I've got the HR records up in front of me, and there's no result for him at all."

"Thank you so much for your help, sir. I'm sorry to have taken up your time." She put the phone down with a sigh. Just as she'd suspected, the guy was a fraud.

Out of interest, she called CC Carpentry.

"Hello there, I'm calling for a reference for one of your previous staff. Could I speak to your manager or head of HR, please?" She was put through to a very gruff-sounding man.

"Stan Porter here, manager of Cavern County Carpentry. How can I help you, ma'am?"

"Hello, Mr. Porter. I'm looking for a verbal reference for one of your previous staff. I'm sorry. I know he worked for you some time ago, but I need the dates of his employment and any details you can provide with regard to his work ethic. The name is Paul Michael Rogers."

"Are you kidding me?"

She was rather taken aback by his response. "No, is there something wrong? He *did* work for you, didn't he?"

"Yeah, right up until I fired him for thieving our stock. He was also doing dirty deals, and I'm not certain but I reckon it was him who was lifting cash from the till, too. If I were you, I'd steer well clear of that one, ma'am."

"Thank you, Mr. Porter. You've been most helpful."

Glancing through the two-way mirror, she noticed Paul scowling as he spoke to Sarah, who must have just returned from her break. Judging by his expression, he was probably telling her about the dressing-down he'd just received. *Good*. Hopefully Sarah would get the message loud and clear, too.

* * * *

She was surprised when Ace knocked on her door just after lunchtime. They hadn't been in contact all weekend, and she hated how they'd left things on Friday.

"Are you sure you don't mind if I come in?" he asked, a little sheepishly after she'd opened the door.

"Of course." She frowned slightly, concerned that they were going to have a similar conversation to the last.

"Coffee?" she offered.

He waved a hand, shaking his head. "No, thanks. It's just a flying visit."

"Won't you sit down?"

"No, honestly, I can't stay. I just wanted to see you. I heard you got moved in okay at the weekend."

She nodded. "Yeah. There are still boxes of wedding stuff to unpack, but most of it's sorted."

"D'you mind if I come over tonight? I'd love to see the place." He took a step toward her, and she was treated to a waft of his gorgeous aftershave.

She'd missed him over the last few days and would have given anything not to have argued the last time they had been together.

"Ace, I'd love to spend some time with you, but I've got something I need to do tonight."

His face fell and he immediately took a step backward. "I see. Never mind."

"No, you don't understand." She took a step toward him this time. She lowered her voice. "I need to check the security tapes from this place."

He frowned. "Seriously?"

She nodded. "I can't talk about it now."

"Can I help?"

She raised her eyebrows. "Would you want to? It's not all that exciting, believe me."

He nodded. "I don't mind what we do. I just want to see you. I need to explain a few things."

She smiled. "Okay. I'll be home around six. Come any time after that."

He grinned, making her stomach burn. He really was a handsome cowboy. "I'll see you tonight." He winked before heading out of the door.

Rihanna found it hard not to smile all afternoon.

Chapter Sixteen

After the staff had left, she took the security tapes and locked up the bank. Then she had to go to the recycling center several miles out of town where she deposited the cardboard boxes she'd used for packing. Having emptied a lot of the items she had earmarked for selling into her cupboards and drawers, she was pleased at how much space was freed up in her bedroom.

She was pleased not to have to make the trek over to Almondine and arrived back in Pelican's Heath just before six. Walking up the stairs and into her own apartment felt really special, and she smiled as she put down her bags then waved her arms in the air as she swooshed around the large, open space that was hers to do with as she liked. She felt very much like Maria from *The Sound of Music*, taking in the fresh air and freedom of the Austrian mountains.

"If you start singing, I'm outta here," Ace teased her from the open doorway, and she realized she'd forgotten to close the door.

"Just enjoying all this space," she told him with a smile. "You've no idea what it's like being cooped in one small room for weeks on end. I'm making the most of this."

He chuckled, closing the door behind him. "I don't blame you, darlin'. It must have been hell being holed up in that hotel with staff to clean your room, wash your bedding and even cook your meals. I don't know how you suffered through it for all that time."

Ace placed a bag on the floor next to hers before she reached him and swatted him playfully on his ass. "Cheeky!" she accused.

"Yeah, and that's just what you love about me. Admit it." He was still laughing as he turned around and caught her arm just as she was about to swat him again. He gently kissed her fingers, making her insides burn.

When he put his arms around her and took her in his strong arms, she sighed at his closeness, then his lips crashed over hers. His kiss was determined but also soft. It made her feel wanted in a way she'd never felt before.

Surrounded by his scent and his warmth, she allowed herself to melt into his body and lost herself in his affection.

Opening her eyes as he finally freed her lips, she saw how dark his pupils had become as he gazed into her face, and she studied every inch of his, as though seeing it for the first time. She'd always known he was handsome, but this close up, he looked beautiful. His eyes shone, no longer tired or wary. His stubble was close to his skin, and his teeth were perfect and pure white as he smiled back at her.

"I think I'm falling in love with you," he whispered gently.

Her whole body sagged. She'd been thinking a similar thing herself, having missed him so much this past weekend, but she was aware that they hardly knew anything about each other.

"I know it might not be what you want to hear right now, and I get it, but I wanted to be honest and upfront with you." He grinned. "That's it. No expectations, just pure honesty, because that's what I want with you, Rihanna. Is that okay?"

She continued to stare into his gorgeous face, his words ringing in her ears.

"Say something," he urged. "Even if it's just 'go away'."

Shaking her head, she replied in a whisper, "I don't want you to go."

His face relaxed at her words, and he leaned in and gave her a chaste kiss on the lips. "Well, that's all right then."

She smiled, feeling deliriously happy for the first time in forever. "I'm falling for you too, Ace," she admitted. "I know it's too soon, but I'm willing to wait if you are?"

"We've got all the time in the world, darlin'," he assured her with another sexy smile. "I only told you because I think it's so important to be honest, don't you?"

She nodded. "I agree."

"Good. Well, now we've got that sorted out, is there any coffee in this place?" He looked over toward the kitchenette.

"Follow me." She took his hand and led him over to where the coffee machine was waiting to be switched on. After setting it going, she opened a couple of cupboards. "This is where the coffee and tea are kept," she said. "And this here's for the crockery." She showed him the stack of two dinner plates, two side plates and two small bowls neatly piled on the bottom shelf, with mugs and glasses on the upper shelf.

"You don't expect much company, I see," he said, incredulously.

She smiled with a sigh. Truth was, she'd had a lovely bone china dinner set given to her and Phil as an engagement gift from her parents, but Phil had somehow managed to commandeer it in the split. She wasn't about to ruin the mood by talking about it now, though.

"This is the dining area," she said, pointing to the small table with four chairs just by the window. "And this is the sitting area." She waved a hand toward the sofa and armchair at the other end of the room.

"It all looks so different with your pictures and photos up," he said with an approving nod. "Much more homey." He went over to a shelf and picked up a photograph. "Is this your folks?"

She smiled. "Yeah, that's them."

"They look real nice." He replaced it with a grin.

Rihanna went over to pour the coffees, which she placed on the table. "Were you serious about helping me with the security tapes?" she asked.

He raised his eyebrows as he turned to face her. "I sure am. Look... I've even brought my laptop and everything. I figured we might get it done quicker with both of us." He strolled over to where he'd left his bag by the door and picked it up, along with hers, and took them over to her.

Her heart lurched. "You didn't have to do that."

"I do have an ulterior motive," he admitted, a little sheepishly. "I thought the quicker we get this done, the quicker we could make use of that comfy-looking sofa over there."

"You've got a good point," she agreed with a giggle. "Take a seat."

"Okay, what exactly are we looking for?" he asked as the laptops fired up.

Rihanna took a deep breath. "This is only between us, okay? I mean, it's strictly confidential. Bank business. You can't tell a soul what's going on. Promise?"

"Cross my heart," he said, doing just that.

"Right." She went on to explain about the customers who'd claimed their deposits hadn't reached their bank accounts and how she'd called in the regional manager, who had objected that she had no proof that anything untoward was happening.

"You think that proof might be on these disks?"

She nodded. "These two are from behind the counter, whereas these are from the foyer area and the front door." She picked them up to show him.

"You take the counter, and I'll do the door." He took one of the disks and quickly loaded it into his computer.

Rihanna skimmed through the other disk until she spotted the man who had been shouting in the bank today. "Okay, this is him," she said, pointing to her screen. He had been served by Paul at eleven-seventeen, which was while Sarah had been on her break.

"Let me just pull that up on here," Ace said, skimming through his copy until he saw the man entering the bank. He went straight up to the counter and pulled his wallet from his back pocket. "Okay, he has a wad of notes in his hand, but I can't see the teller." He leaned over to where Rihanna sat next to him, his aftershave wafting over her. "Let's see what you've got."

"He has handed them over, and Paul has taken them from him." Rihanna had studied this the last time she'd checked the footage. "Paul placed the money in the drawer, put the card into the slot and completed the transaction." She frowned. "It doesn't make sense."

"That's what he's supposed to do, right?" Ace clarified.

"Yes. But when I checked the account, that transaction hadn't been entered. But the money was right at the end of the day. If it hadn't been entered correctly, the money would be over." She shook her head, sitting back in her chair.

Ace flipped back to look at his own screen. "The guy leaves and puts his card in his wallet." He enlarged the picture. "Definitely just the card. And his wallet's thinner, so the cash has gone."

Rihanna's heart pounded. Whether it was the nearness of the gorgeous hunk or the enormity of what they were doing, she wasn't sure. Probably both.

"Let's look again at that transaction." He leaned toward her again. "Can you slow it down a little?"

Rihanna did as he'd asked. The man put his card in the reader. Then Paul took it out and put it in again.

"Let's break it down," Ace suggested. "Why would he do that? Doesn't the customer normally handle their own card?"

Rihanna nodded. "Yeah. We're not supposed to touch them so we can't be accused if it gets dropped or lost or whatever. It's just to cover our backs. The customer handles it at all times."

"Well, this one didn't."

The disk kept rolling.

"There, look." Ace stopped the footage and pointed to the screen again. "This Paul guy's taken the card out and handed it back to the customer."

"Okay. Perhaps he's just being polite." Rihanna shrugged.

"Is he usually polite?"

"Not especially," she admitted.

"So, why does he need to handle it?" Ace was tenacious.

"When you insert the card, you have to press it right in," she suggested. "Maybe the customer hadn't pushed it in hard enough. That would be why Paul had to take it out and do it again."

"Wouldn't you usually ask the customer to do that?"

"*I* would."

"Okay. So just how hard does Paul need to push it in?" Ace leaned over and rolled that part of the footage again. "Doesn't look all that hard to me. More like he's just placed it in the top."

Rihanna frowned. "It wouldn't bring up the account if it wasn't in properly," she pointed out. "Can we check his screen?" She focused on Paul's computer and enlarged the place she needed.

"Is it usually blank?" Ace frowned.

"No. It might just be taking its time to upload."

"Do we get sound on this thing?" Ace asked.

Rihanna unmuted it and turned up the volume.

They heard the sound of tapping keys and studied the screen on Paul's computer. It was just a bunch of random numbers and letters.

"Is that some kind of code or something?" Ace asked, frowning again.

"That's all done for you. Thank you, sir," Paul's voice said as he took the card from the reader and handed it back.

"I'm much obliged to you, son," the customer replied, putting the card back into his wallet as he turned to leave.

Rihanna stared at the screen. "He didn't put it through."

"Okay, so where's the cash?" Ace narrowed his eyes as he slowly played the footage again. "Keep your eyes on the money," he told her.

Paul could plainly be seen putting the cash into the drawer, but he'd folded it with a flick of his finger and tucked it in front of some other notes. While he made the pretend transaction, he didn't close the drawer, but kept it open just a little way. After the customer left, Paul slipped his right hand back into the drawer. By slowing the footage down frame by frame, they could see how he'd tucked the money into the palm of his hand, closed the drawer, then it looked like he'd straightened the hem of his sweater. When his hand came back into view, however, it was empty.

"It's in his sweater." Rihanna's voice came out as a horrified whisper.

Ace played it again. "There." He stopped the film and pointed. As Paul straightened his jumper, his forefinger and middle finger were missing. "That's how he's slipped the cash into his pocket or whatever he's got hidden up there to put it into."

"So, I was right." Rihanna didn't feel as elated as she'd expected. It was horrid to think that someone was stealing from right under her nose.

"No wonder he was so sore about those dang cameras." Ace's jaw was tight. "Should we call Dyson?"

Rihanna shook her head. "No. I need to contact Mr. Treadwell first. They'll want to sort this in-house, though I'm sure we'll have to call the sheriff tomorrow."

"Why waste time? There's a thief out there on the loose. The sooner he's put behind bars, the better. I say we call it in now."

"No." She stared at him. "You promised you'd keep this between us. It has to be handled through the bank."

"Okay, if you're sure." He shook his head, a dubious expression on his face.

"Ace, I told Mr. Treadwell the facts. I was real careful not to tell him what I thought was going on, but I know he got the message. I want to be able to show him that I was right."

His body sagged beside her and he smiled. "You've got it, darlin'. It's your call."

"Thanks, Ace."

"What's the thing with the fingers, though?" he asked, chuckling.

She frowned. "What?"

"Why does the teller have to hold up his fingers every now and then? Is it some kind of signal to you or something?"

"Show me."

He went back to his own computer and rewound some of the footage. "There."

Rihanna looked to where he was pointing, and, sure enough, Paul was holding up two fingers.

"Earlier it was three," he told her.

Rihanna's mind whirled. "Hang on." She widened the picture, trying to see more, but it only showed the empty bank.

She reached over the table and picked up another disk. "This one shows the doorway," she said, handing it to Ace. "Let's see who he's signaling to."

They played the tape, matching up the times. There were no customers in the foyer, but a red shirt could be seen just by the door.

"It's that guy that's been hanging around the place." Ace stared at the screen.

"Frankie," Rihanna said, slowly.

"You got his name?" He turned to give her an incredulous look.

She shrugged, still watching the screen. "I introduced myself, so he did the same."

Ace raised his eyebrows. "Yeah, I can see how that might work," he conceded. "So, what does two mean?"

Rihanna shook her head. "Did you say he did it for three as well?"

Ace nodded. "Just those two numbers as far as I've seen. Does it mean anything to you?" He frowned.

Rihanna searched her brain before it dawned on her. Her whole body went hot, and she grabbed his hand. "Oh my God, Ace," she whispered, staring right at him. She turned back to the screen, her heart hammering. "That was eleven-twenty-seven a.m. There would have been two of us in the bank. I'm guessing the three was either before eleven a.m. or after two p.m., when we were all there."

"It's a fucking tip-off. They're planning to rob the damn bank." Ace shot to his feet. "Now we've *got* to call the sheriff." He reached over the table for his phone.

"No...we don't." She stood up, too. "You promised. We let the bank deal with this."

"But the dang place could be robbed at any time. You're not safe in there, Ri, and I, for one, am not prepared to stand by and let anything happen to you." His face was red.

"You *promised*," she pointed out. "What was all that stuff about honesty when you first walked in here? Doesn't that count for *anything*? You made me a promise. Now, are you about to break it already?"

"I need you to be safe." The urgency in his voice surprised her.

"I will be." She nodded. "I'll call Mr. Treadwell first thing. I'll show him what we've found out. He's sure to call the sheriff."

"And what if Treadwell isn't available? Or he gets delayed? Or just doesn't show up? What then?"

"Then I'll think about calling the sheriff. But it will be *my* decision, okay?"

"I still think we should tell him now. We could just forewarn him. Then he'll be ready for the call from your boss tomorrow." Ace seemed to have made his mind up.

"Are you working tomorrow?" she asked him, thinking on her feet. She couldn't allow him to run roughshod over her. There were procedures that had to be followed, and she was almost sure Dyson wouldn't sit on the information until Treadwell called him in.

He nodded. "I'm working late. Starting at eleven."

"Then you can hang around the bank if it makes you feel any better...keep an eye on things. My guess is they're not going to rob the place while there are customers in there, are they? Paul's giving them the heads-up about how many staff are in the place when the place is free of customers — the actual number of people in the building. If you're there — or anyone else for that matter — they're not going to try anything, are they?"

He closed his eyes for a second, clearly thinking it through. "All right. But if that Treadwell guy isn't there by eleven, we call the sheriff. Deal?"

"Ace," she whined.

"Come on, baby. You need to meet me halfway."

She looked into his pleading eyes. He was worried for her. He cared that much. And she cared for him and wouldn't want him to be in a similar position.

She nodded slowly. "Okay." She owed him that much.

Chapter Seventeen

Rihanna was early for work the following day, after a sleepless night. Although Paul's betrayal had really irked her, she'd spent most of the night remembering the sensual kiss Ace had given her when he'd eventually left. It would be great to see him again this morning.

She had everything ready to show Mr. Treadwell, though his secretary advised that he wasn't in the office yet.

"I need to see him urgently," Rihanna explained. "Can you ask him to come to the Pelican's Heath branch right away? I'm expecting trouble here today, and I need to speak to him immediately."

The secretary agreed to have him call her as soon as he arrived for work, and Rihanna just prayed he wasn't going to be late.

"Could I have his email address, please?" Rihanna asked. "I may not be able to speak too freely when he calls, so I'd like to send over an outline of the problem, if that's possible."

She could just imagine trying to explain everything and being overheard by Paul or Sarah. The secretary obliged, and Rihanna emailed the information over.

After her fourth cup of coffee of the day, she heard the knock at the door that signaled the staff had arrived. With a deep breath, she went through to let them in. Paul sounded his usual sour self as he grumbled something incoherent, and Rihanna found it hard to look at him. Her heart hammered. Sarah didn't look much happier.

"Good morning." Rihanna forced a smile and a cheery tone as she welcomed them inside. They didn't reciprocate, but then, she'd learned not to expect them to. Sarah wasn't quite as bad as Paul, and she *did* manage the occasional smile, but Rihanna somehow got the impression that Paul was influencing her in some way. Hopefully, not for much longer.

The private phone rang in the office, and Rihanna went straight through to answer it.

"Miss Richards?" She recognized the regional manager's voice.

"Yes, sir. Did you get my email?"

"I did. I'm already on my way to you now. Don't say a word to anyone until I arrive. I want to talk to you before we inform the sheriff."

"Of course, sir."

There was a knock at her door a few minutes later and she opened it to see Ace smiling at her.

"Come in."

He looked around the room as he removed his hat. "Is he here yet?"

"He's coming," she assured him. "Would you like some coffee?"

As she poured, she was aware of his arms around her waist. "Are you okay?" he whispered.

"I am now."

"I'll just have this then I'll make myself scarce," he promised, taking the cup from her and following her over to the desk. "I don't want your boss getting the wrong idea. Besides, we don't want to arouse any suspicion out there, do we?" He kept his voice low as he gestured toward the two-way mirror.

Rihanna nodded. "True. Mr. Treadwell's told me not to tell anyone."

"My lips are sealed," he said. Then he grinned. "Though I'd rather they were sealed around yours again."

She felt her cheeks go hot as she giggled, a memory of last night returning to her mind.

"Fancy another ride up the mountain at the weekend?" he asked, raising one eyebrow suggestively.

Her stomach burned as much as her face now. "I'd love that."

He nodded before taking another large sip of his drink. "Great."

She sighed. "I don't think I'll get much work done this morning," she told him. "I'm so on edge."

"Is there a back door to this place?" he asked with a thoughtful frown.

"Yeah. It's down past the staff room. It's only to be used in emergencies—I'm not even allowed to use it as the staff door—and it only opens from the inside, for security reasons."

Ace nodded. "I guess that makes sense."

"What're your plans for this morning?" Rihanna asked, not wishing to part company with him but knowing it would raise suspicions if he didn't leave soon.

"I thought I'd go over to the café," Ace replied. "I can keep a good eye on things from there. It'd also be good to watch out for those two guys who've been hanging around the place and see if they've got any friends who might be involved."

Rihanna's stomach jolted. She hadn't thought of that, though it made perfect sense. Frankie was a little long in the tooth to be holding up banks all on his own, and the guy in the gray shirt hadn't been around for the past few days.

"Don't worry." Ace must have noticed her alarmed expression as she stood to say goodbye. "We've got this, remember? With any luck, they'll give up on the idea once Paul's out of the equation. He is their inside man, after all. Or he might just spill the beans and the sheriff can pick them all up."

She stood and went straight into his open arms. "I hope you're right."

"I won't let anything happen to you, I promise." He took her lips in a searing kiss that she felt right through to her core. She held him tighter, grabbing at his short hair, not wanting to let him go.

"Just try to act normal," he whispered, when he finally freed her mouth.

Rihanna watched him go, thinking that she'd never be 'normal' again after that kiss. Ace Blenheim sure was a gorgeous cowboy, and she couldn't believe that she hadn't even liked him when they'd first met. Not that she'd been actually looking at his face at the time, truth be told, as she'd been too busy screaming at the horse rearing up in front of her car to notice its rider. It was hard to believe that had only been a short while ago. She felt like she'd known him forever, somehow.

Despite her earlier reservations, she managed to bury herself in paperwork for the next hour or so until her private line rang again.

"I thought it best if you met us in the foyer, Miss Richards. I don't want to arouse suspicion among the staff if they recognize me or my name, if I need to be announced."

"Of course, sir. I'll be right out."

He was just walking through the door with two other men when she went through to greet him. There were several customers in the bank, so she was fairly sure they wouldn't be noticed as she greeted her boss and led them all into her office where proper introductions were made.

"This is Dave Tranter, our head of security, and James Hatton is from HR," Mr. Treadwell told her, as she shook hands with his colleagues.

Both men had dark hair. Dave Tranter's was almost black. Tranter also had a bushy mustache that made him appear older than both his colleagues. James Hatton was very tall and handsome, with warm, brown eyes and a kind smile.

Although very nervous, she was glad that the regional manager had taken her concerns seriously.

Mr. Tranter eyed the security camera in the corner of the office and the two-way mirror with a satisfied nod.

"I believe you've got some proof to show us," Mr. Treadwell prompted, when they all sat down with cups of hot coffee.

"Yes, sir." She'd already loaded up the disks, so she turned the screen so they could all watch and set it running.

"Certainly looks like he's signaling to the guy by the door," Mr. Tranter agreed, as Paul could be seen raising three fingers. You think that's how many staff were in the branch at the time?"

"Yes, sir." Rihanna pointed to the timestamp. "I've changed the staff's breaks to eleven and two o'clock so we're all on site at the busiest time, between twelve and two."

"You mean they weren't doing that to start with?" Mr. Hatton asked, incredulously.

"No, sir. They told me Mr. Williamson had given them permission to have their lunch breaks at noon and one. I spoke to him about it, though, as it made it very difficult with me having to cover the front desk for two hours each day." She bit her lip.

The men exchanged a look she couldn't decipher.

"What's this, then?" Mr. Tranter asked, pointing at the screen.

"What?" Mr. Treadwell frowned as he studied the tape.

"Hang on." Mr. Tranter rewound the film then pointed again. Paul was holding up four fingers this time.

"Do you have four members of staff?" Mr. Hatton asked.

"No, sir." Rihanna blushed, her heart hammering. Had they been wrong about the hand-signals after all? Mr. Treadwell would be angry if she'd got them all here on a wild goose chase.

"There's no one else in the foyer," Mr. Tranter pointed out, shaking his head.

"Maybe there's someone in here with me," Rihanna suggested, reaching for her diary. She checked the time on the recording and a wave of relief washed over her. "Yes, I had a customer with me at that time. A Mr. Jackson came to discuss a loan," she told them.

"That makes sense," Mr. Treadwell said, with a nod. "So it looks like he's definitely giving the guy at the door the heads-up about how many people are in the branch."

Rihanna let out a long breath. It had occurred to her last night that it was odd that Paul didn't just tell Frankie their new times so he could work out how many staff were in the branch at a given time, but, of course, he would have to account for customers, too.

"So it looks like the guy's been keeping an eye on the comings and goings in here." Mr. Hatton huffed.

Rihanna nodded. "Yes. Not everyone who comes to see me has an appointment, and often I'll just go through when it's busy to see if I can help any of the customers to save them waiting in line. Otherwise, he'd just be able to check the diary at the front desk."

Mr. Treadwell finished his coffee and put his cup back down, pursing his lips. "Is the back door always kept locked?"

"Yes, sir. We never use it. I leave the alarm connected, too."

"So, if they were planning anything, they'd have to use the main entrance," Mr. Tranter affirmed, glancing at the bars on the windows.

Rihanna felt a jolt in her stomach. Hearing them talk about the possibility of a robbery made it all sound much more real, and she'd hate to think what could have happened if she and Ace hadn't uncovered this when they had.

"Hang on. What's going on there?" Mr. Hatton squinted at the screen. "Rewind that bit and slow it right down," he instructed Mr. Tranter.

"Look at that." Wide-eyed, Mr. Hatton pointed to where Paul was taking money from a customer before his hand slipped under his sweater.

Rihanna immediately checked her notes. "That's one of the days we had a complaint about," she told them. "The man wanted to know why the money wasn't deposited in his account."

"Well, we can see why," Mr. Treadwell seethed. "And you did give them their money, right?"

Rihanna nodded. "Yes, sir."

"Good. At least this won't have to get out." He raised his eyebrows to her. "You were right to be concerned, Rihanna. The press would have had a field day if this had been leaked."

She felt a warm glow inside her. It was good to be proven right. She just nodded in response.

"I looked into Paul's résumé, too," she said, quietly. "He claims to have worked at a bank, but when I rang them, they'd never heard of him. I also heard that when he claims to have been working there, he was actually working at a carpentry company in town. They fired him for suspected theft."

Mr. Hatton's eyebrows furrowed, making him appear quite thunderous. "Who hired him? Williamson?"

"I think so, sir." She swallowed hard.

"I'll leave that one with you," Mr. Treadwell said, shaking his head to his colleague.

"I'll be more than happy to look into it." Mr. Hatton tapped a note into his phone. Rihanna wouldn't like to be in the room when *that* conversation took place.

She'd been keeping half an eye on the two-way mirror during proceedings, as was her usual routine. It was good to know what was going on out on the floor, even if she wasn't required out there.

"Sir, Sarah will be due her break at eleven," she told Mr. Treadwell, glancing at the clock.

He squeezed his lips together. "Can you ask her to hang on, please? She'll have to take it later. We need to get the sheriff in here, and he'll want to speak to Paul, so we're going to need her to mind the desk."

"Is she usually quite amenable?" Mr. Hatton asked, as Rihanna rose to her feet.

She swallowed hard. "Not really, to be honest." She shook her head slowly.

He stood up with a smile, his anger seemingly forgotten. "Don't worry. I'll have a word with her," he offered.

Mr. Treadwell grinned, making him suddenly look much younger. "He could charm the birds from the trees," he said to Rihanna, with a roll of his eyes. "If anyone can sweet-talk her, *he* can."

"In that case, be my guest." Rihanna smiled, relieved not to have to have that conversation with Sarah, especially in front of Paul, who was bound to have something to say on the subject, should he get the chance.

While Mr. Hatton left the room, Mr. Treadwell reached for the phone and called the sheriff.

Rihanna watched with interest as the head of HR approached Sarah, his smile already in place. It was odd to see her twirl her hair as she smiled back at him, nodding to whatever he was asking her. Her body physically relaxed in his presence, and she practically melted in front of him. Rihanna giggled to herself before turning her attention back to Mr. Treadwell, as he replaced the receiver.

"He'll be here in a few minutes," he said, sounding quite impressed.

Rihanna nodded, wondering if maybe she should have given Dyson the heads-up last night, as Ace had suggested. It would have been quite embarrassing if he'd been out of town and her boss would be kept waiting for a visit from him, but she was glad it seemed to have worked out well. Besides, Mr. Treadwell had specifically asked her not to breathe a word of this to anyone.

Mr. Hatton still hadn't returned to the office when the sheriff knocked on the door, and Rihanna let him in with a smile. After introducing him to Mr. Treadwell and Mr. Tranter, she made them all some more coffee before taking her seat behind her desk again.

She watched the proceedings in the bank while the two men filled in the sheriff about the events and showed him the footage that backed up their allegations. Paul seemed quite unnerved at the arrival of the sheriff, and she guessed Mr. Hatton was keeping an eye on him to make sure he didn't disappear. *Clever.*

Chapter Eighteen

Ace was relieved to see the sheriff's truck pull up outside the bank. He'd sure had his fill of coffee for one day and was desperate to know what was going on in that bank.

The guy in the red shirt had stuck his head around the door earlier but looked really annoyed as he turned away. Ace had watched him stroll back down the street but hadn't seen anything of him after that.

"Hey, boss." He caught up with Dyson before he got to the bank's door.

"Hey, yourself. Aren't you late for work?" Dyson frowned.

"Yeah, I was just on my way. I saw you coming, though, and just wondered if everything was okay." Ace tried to look innocent but wasn't sure he was actually pulling it off.

Dyson's narrowed eyes suggested he suspected something was amiss. He looked into the bank then back at Ace. "I'm not sure, to be honest. Could you stick around for a while without looking too obvious?"

"Sure." Ace grinned, happy to be included at last.

"Thanks. I don't want either of the staff to leave the premises until I get to the bottom of this."

"You've got it, Sheriff."

Ace watched him walk straight into the bank and knock on Rihanna's door. Immediately, Paul's face tensed. A man in a smart suit, whom Ace had seen arrive earlier with a couple of other men, stood by the counter and the woman, Sarah, was serving a customer.

"I'm just going to the bathroom," Paul announced, standing up.

The guy in the suit frowned at him as he locked his drawer and disappeared down what Ace remembered was a short corridor. Suit-guy looked quite perturbed but stayed where he was.

Ace went around to the back of the building and waited by the door. Sure enough, about a minute later the door opened, followed by a deafening alarm. He caught Paul as he hurled himself outside and pulled his arms back up behind his back.

"What the...?"

"You planning on going someplace?" Ace asked, calmly.

"Let me go, you fucker!"

"Not a chance."

"Who the hell are you? You've got no right — "

Ace ignored his protestations and grinned as the sheriff came around the corner.

"Well, now, if that ain't an admission of guilt, I don't know what is." He pulled the cuffs from his back pocket and swiftly clipped them onto Paul's wrists.

"He's broken my fucking arm," Paul yelled. "I want him arrested for assault."

"I don't know what you're talking about," Dyson replied, shaking his head. "I didn't see anything."

"Shall I accompany you in the car, Sheriff?" Ace offered, as the alarm stopped and someone slammed the door shut from the inside.

"That'd be a real help." Dyson grinned as he led the prisoner to his truck and helped him into the back seat.

Ace took great delight in climbing in next to him.

"Just give me a minute, will ya?" Dyson went over to the two men standing with Rihanna in the bank's doorway. "Well, I was gonna do this in your office, ma'am, but it looks like this guy's got other ideas. Mind if we continue our conversation down at the station? I'm afraid you'll need to close the bank for an hour or two."

"That's not a problem, Sheriff," one of the guys in suits said, graciously. "We'll follow you down."

"Much obliged to you, sir." Dyson nodded before climbing back into his truck and firing up the engine.

Ace winked at Rihanna, who looked gorgeous standing there with the suited men, especially when she smiled back at him.

Down at the station, Dyson helped Paul into a chair.

"I want my lawyer," Paul snapped right away.

"By all means. If you just give me the number, I'll call him for you right away." Dyson couldn't have been more helpful.

Ace waited around in the doorway, relieved when a couple of expensive-looking cars pulled up outside. He was surprised to see Sarah with them, looking quite scared. Rihanna was muttering something to her, probably trying to reassure her, but Sarah didn't seem to be listening.

Catching a waft of Rihanna's flowery perfume as she passed him in the doorway, he smiled to himself. He hoped his presence had lifted her confidence, as she looked so professional walking into the sheriff's office with her boss. Ace just wanted to grab her and give her a long, lingering kiss, but kind of got the impression that wouldn't be considered too appropriate right now. He'd just have to wait.

* * * *

Rihanna loved that Ace was waiting for her when she arrived at the sheriff's office, especially as Mr. Hatton had informed them that it had been Ace who had caught Paul as he'd tried to make his escape through the back exit.

Any guilt she might have felt for getting Paul into trouble vanished at the thought of him trying to run — a clear indication that he definitely *was* guilty of something.

The sheriff obviously wanted to ensure that Sarah had no involvement in Paul's antics, but Rihanna was concerned that they had had to close the bank at the busiest time of the day. She'd said as much to Mr. Treadwell, who had told her not to worry, but she didn't want to let the locals down.

Luckily, Mr. Treadwell took the lead in explaining everything to the sheriff, while Paul scowled at everyone, huffing and snorting at each allegation. His lawyer was present, as he'd requested, though the guy looked as shocked as everyone else when he heard what had been going on.

Sarah shivered when she was asked about her connection with Paul's theft and his alleged plans to help with a bank robbery.

"I had no idea." Her face was pale as she shook her head, clearly in shock. Tears streamed down her cheeks. "He just told me to make life hard for Rihanna. I thought it was just because she was young and had come from the city to take a job that should have been given to someone more local. I had no idea he had planned anything like this, and I certainly knew nothing of him stealing from the bank." She turned to Rihanna. "I'm sorry."

Taking a deep breath, Rihanna nodded. Poor Sarah looked so appalled and upset that she couldn't help feeling sorry for her. She stood and put her jacket around Sarah's shoulders.

"Did you bring a coat?" the sheriff asked Sarah.

"I left it at the bank, sir." Sarah's voice was croaky, and she sounded like she was holding back a large sob.

Just then Rihanna's phone rang, and she pulled it from her purse with a frown. She knew she should have switched it off but hadn't thought about it earlier.

"It's Mr. Williamson," she told them. "The area manager."

"Put him on speakerphone," Mr. Hatton told her.

Mr. Treadwell nodded, so Rihanna quickly obliged.

"Hello, Mr. Williamson."

"What the hell is going on? I'm at the bank and you've damn well closed it! How dare you close during business hours—especially at lunchtime? Do you realize how much money you're losing the bank? Money that will be taken from your wages, young lady. Make no mistake about that!"

Mr. Hatton took the phone from Rihanna. "Hello, Dwayne. James Hatton here. We're all down at the sheriff's office. Come and join us, won't you? You can apologize to Miss Richards while you're here, too."

There was a momentary silence at the other end of the phone before Williamson blustered, "What? I don't understand. Where is the sheriff's office anyway?"

Mr. Treadwell rolled his eyes. "Looks like one of us will need to go fetch him."

"I can go if you like?" Rihanna offered, hopeful of some reprieve from the tense atmosphere. "I can grab Sarah's jacket while I'm there."

"Take my car." Mr. Treadwell offered her the keys.

"Oh gosh." Rihanna had forgotten she hadn't driven herself there.

Ace got up. "I'll go with you."

"Actually, Ace, I was going to ask you about when you caught Paul trying to escape," Dyson said.

"I'll be fine," Rihanna assured him with a smile.

Leaving them talking, she went outside and took large gulps of fresh air on her way to the large, shiny car. Sitting behind the wheel, she was surprised by how quietly it burst into action, and she enjoyed the short journey over to the bank. She could never afford a vehicle like this, and it was way too big for her needs, but it was a joy to drive.

Mr. Williamson was standing outside the branch, surrounded by a crowd of locals, all waving their arms around and talking at once. He turned to frown at Rihanna when she emerged from the car. "I hope you've got a good explanation for all this, young lady. The things I've been hearing — "

"I do, sir."

"Just what's been going on around here?" he demanded. "And why's James Hatton here? He doesn't make branch visits."

"He came with Mr. Treadwell and Mr. Tranter," Rihanna replied. "They're all at the sheriff's office now. I'll show you the way in a minute. I just need to collect something from the bank." She pulled out the keys to the bank as she walked over to the door.

"I'm not hanging around while you run your errands!" Mr. Williamson was most indignant at the thought.

"I won't be a minute, honestly," she told him. "I just need —"

"I don't care what you need. *I* need to get to the sheriff's office right now and sort this mess out. And mark my words, young lady, your days around here are well and truly numbered."

"But I just have to —"

"You just have to take me to the sheriff's office. That's what you have to do...*now*."

"I can do that," a man from the crowd offered. "It's not that far."

All of a sudden everyone started pointing out the directions for him, and again, talking over one another.

"Show me," Mr. Williamson ordered the man who had first offered. Then he turned back to Rihanna. "I'll expect you there in five minutes."

She said nothing. It would take longer than that for him to get there, anyhow.

The crowd dissipated as Mr. Williamson and the other guy went to their cars, and Rihanna let herself into the branch and locked the door behind her. It seemed really strange to be empty at this time of day, and the eerie silence caused her to shudder as she made her way to the staff room behind the counter. Sarah's red coat had been hung on the hook on the outside of her locker door, and Rihanna quickly took it down.

She went straight back to the main door and unlocked it again. As she did so, it was swung open, hitting her on the forehead with the immense force. For a few seconds she was dazed, but then she saw a familiar face snarling at her as he pushed his way inside and slammed the door shut behind him. He grabbed the key from her hand and quickly locked the door again. That was when she noticed his gun.

* * * *

Ace watched Dwayne Williamson saunter into the sheriff's office, a sour look on his ugly face. His gray hair seemed quite disheveled, and his beard needed a good trim.

"Ah, there you are." Mr. Treadwell stood and shook his hand politely, as did the other two men. "This is the sheriff, Dyson Shearer," the regional manager offered, before turning to introduce Ace.

"Ace Blenheim." He shook the guy's clammy hand.

Mr. Williamson gave him a look of disdain before taking the seat Dyson had just pulled over for him.

"What the hell's going on?" Mr. Williamson stared at Paul, who was sitting by the sheriff, still cuffed.

"We were hoping you might be able to fill in some blanks for us, actually," Mr. Hatton replied, matter-of-factly.

"Me?" Mr. Williamson looked most indignant as he raised his eyebrows.

Ace glanced over to the door before interrupting them. "Actually, where's Rihanna?" An ominous thud hit the pit of his stomach.

"She'll be here in a minute." Mr. Williamson shrugged. "Said she needed to fetch something from inside the branch."

Ace leaped to his feet, his heart hammering. "And you *left* her there? *Alone?*"

"One of the locals showed me the way." Mr. Williamson looked over to the sheriff. "Is there any coffee?"

"I'm taking your unmarked truck." Ace quickly took the keys from the hook where Dyson kept them, not waiting for a reply, and rushed out of the office.

He couldn't reach the bank fast enough.

Rihanna's truck was still in its usual place and the huge Lincoln Navigator she had borrowed was parked neatly at the side of the road.

Right in front of the bank stood a rusty old pickup, the engine running, and at the wheel was a man he recognized in a red plaid shirt.

Ace surveyed the scene before getting out of his truck and sent a message to the sheriff.

Something's up.

His heart hammered at the thought of Rihanna being in danger, and he felt sick to his stomach. He couldn't show it, though, or arouse any suspicion.

He casually got out and went over to try the door of the bank. *Locked.* He put his ear to the door. Nothing. It was hardly surprising, given the thickness of the door, but it had been worth a try. He peered through the barred window at the front of the branch, but the blind had been pulled down. At the side of the building he looked into Rihanna's office, but there was no one inside, and the door had been closed. The blinds on the other side of the building had also been pulled down, and the back door was still locked. *Damn!*

He sent a text to Rihanna, on the off chance that she might get it.

Where are you? Xx

"It's shut!" the guy from the truck called over to him as he went back to the front of the building.

"Is that right?" Ace strolled over to the guy's open window. "Bit strange to be closed at this time of day. What's going on?"

The guy shrugged.

"It's Frankie, isn't it?" Ace asked, as casually as he could.

The man frowned. "How d'you know that? Do I know you?"

"I've seen you around."

"Is that a fact?"

Ace nodded.

"So what you doin' hangin' around the bank?" Frankie asked.

"I could ask you the same thing."

"I'm just waiting for someone."

"Yeah, who?"

"You're mighty nosey, ain't ya, son?"

Ace grinned. "I just haven't seen you in a truck before. Is it yours?" Ace had already clocked the registration.

Frankie scowled. "Now that really is none of your dang business."

Ace put his hands up in a submissive fashion. "Only asking."

"Well, don't."

"Okay, okay." Ace backed away from the guy, resigned to the fact that he wasn't going to get any information from him. He had to be waiting for someone who was inside the bank, though, that much was obvious. What concerned Ace was whether that 'someone' had hurt his girl or not.

He checked his phone but there was no reply from Rihanna. He wasn't really surprised, though he couldn't help feeling disappointed.

He was itching to bang on that door and demand entry but knew full well that was unlikely to happen and would only warn whoever was inside that he was onto them. Goodness knows what a riled bank robber—if that's what this was—could do to an innocent girl who might already know who he was. The best thing had to be to wait for Dyson, but where the heck was he?

His question was answered a few minutes later when a huge black ICON Bronco pulled up and the sheriff, along with the other guys from the bank, piled out.

"It's all locked and I think he's the getaway," Ace mumbled as soon as Dyson got near enough to hear. "I'll take the back door."

Dyson nodded, and Tranter immediately ran to the side of the bank.

As Ace passed the pickup, he heard Frankie on the phone, warning someone that the sheriff was here. He quickly pulled out his gun and shot holes in the front tires.

"Hey, what the—?" Frankie's look of shocked betrayal did nothing to extinguish the anger Ace was feeling.

"You're with me, Grandad." James Hatton suddenly jumped into the seat next to the old man, a gun in his hand.

"Open up. It's the sheriff." Dyson hammered on the front door.

Chapter Nineteen

Ace held his breath. The guy only had two ways out, and one of them would take him straight into the hands of the sheriff. However, that route was also where his getaway was, and he might not realize the old pickup wasn't going anywhere.

On the other hand, he could easily misjudge the sheriff's support and try the back door. Either way, Ace couldn't wait to get his hands on the fucker.

It was only then that it occurred to him that there might be more than one thief in there. What if there was a whole gang of them? He shook his head. No, that pickup only had a single cab, and he doubted bank robbers would be comfortable in the bed of a pickup with the possibility of the sheriff shooting at them.

He heard movement, and suddenly Dave Tranter appeared, coming toward him. "No way will he try to get out of the window," the guy whispered, shaking his head. "My money's on this door."

Ace nodded. It seemed the obvious choice.

"Sheriff's got a spare key," Tranter went on. "He and Treadwell are going in the front."

Ace raised his eyebrows. They'd clearly got this all figured out on the way over here.

He held his breath. Tranter stood behind the door, while Ace took the front, careful to position himself far enough away to be able to duck any bullets that were sure to come firing his way.

He sure was right about those bullets. As soon as the back door opened just a smidge, the guy started shooting. The noise mingled with that of that damn alarm, and the whole place seemed to be in utter chaos. Ace could just about hear shouting, but if someone was barking orders, he had no idea what they were.

His gun was poised, focused on the tiny slit in the door. The first thing he saw was a slither of fabric. It wasn't gray, as he'd expected, but blue. A feminine, cobalt blue, that he recognized as being the color of Rihanna's suit. His heart thumped painfully in his chest as he realized she was being used as a human shield.

Shaking his head at Tranter, he prayed the guy would understand what he was telling him.

Movement up front told him the sheriff and Treadwell had had no luck inside and were coming to join them around the back. *The more the merrier.*

Slowly, Rihanna emerged, walking warily out of the door. With a hand across her mouth and a gun pointed at her head, she stared at the scene in front of her. From where she was, she wouldn't have seen him, hunched by a bush, his gun pointed at the door. The sheriff and Treadwell were also hiding behind a low wall that ran partially along the side of the building.

Her eyes darted everywhere, as though she was straining to see some kind of help. Her hands were tied behind her back, and she clearly found it hard to balance with that fucker pulling her head back while she tried to focus on where she was going.

"Don't you dare try anything." The coward in the gray shirt was threatening her through gritted teeth. He had a large bag hanging from his shoulder, presumably stuffed with money from the bank's vault. With the time he'd had available to him, Ace guessed he could have taken a lot more, if only he'd had more people to help and a reliable getaway strategy in place.

"What a fuckup!" he muttered under his breath. This guy was a chancer. Sure, he might have had some foolproof plan in place when Paul had been their inside man, but since his arrest, he must have just seen his opportunity and taken it. Once he realized that Frankie was in no position to help him, he'd become desperate, and where would that leave Rihanna? He dreaded to think.

"We've got you surrounded," Dyson shouted over the incessant alarm. "Let the girl go."

"Fuck off!" the guy scorned. "Any move on me and she gets it."

"You can't get away," Dyson replied, calmly but firmly. "Your only hope is to give up the girl. Taking a hostage won't help your case. Believe me."

"She's my insurance," the guy spat out, slowly edging nearer the sheriff, though he didn't know it.

Ace's heart pounded painfully against his ribs. As soon as the guy realized he had nothing to lose, Rihanna would no longer be of any value to him. The fear in her eyes suggested she knew it.

Rihanna stumbled slightly as she tried to walk in her heels across the grass, the weight of the guy's arm lying heavily across her shoulder as his hand was clenched tight against her mouth. Her wrists hurt as the rope cut into her skin, and she'd long since given up on trying to untie herself. He'd noticed her moving her hands and had made lewd comments about her trying to touch his groin, which had made her stomach churn. He was dirty and smelled of stale sweat and cheap beer. At least Frankie had been friendly, but this guy was just horrid. He clearly rated himself much higher than anyone else would and had some ill-founded notions about being God's gift to women. He was clearly deluded, especially as he actually thought he was going to get away with robbing the bank and using her to facilitate it.

It was hard to look around with him holding her head firmly in place, but she knew that Ace had to be somewhere nearby. She just wished he'd been allowed to come with her, then none of this might have happened, though she understood the sheriff's need to get his side of the story. He'd played a major part, after all, having actually stopped Paul from escaping. A proud warmth spread through her.

Ace hadn't been far from her thoughts for the past hour or so. She was pleased he'd been at the sheriff's office, even though she could hardly hold his hand — something she'd been desperate to do at the time. She'd do more than just hold his hand when they got out of this mess, though — much more. And she was sure they *would* get through this. They just had to.

"Throw the bag on the ground," Dyson ordered.

"Fuck off," came the reply.

"Do as he says," came a shout from the main road.

Rihanna felt his body stiffen next to hers.

"What?" Horror was evident in his voice.

There was then a muffled sound, as though someone were stopping the old man from speaking, but it didn't matter. The guy who held the gun to her head had got the message loud and clear. *Damn!*

"Frankie! Are you all right?" The guy sounded frantic, and Rihanna caught the tremble in his voice.

"He's fine," Dyson yelled back. "No one's going to hurt him — just like you're not going to hurt that girl in your arms there, are you?"

"Only if you don't let us go — me and Frankie." He just sounded obstinate now.

Rihanna could see they'd reached a stalemate. The sheriff was hardly going to swap the old man for her and let them go free after all this, was he? As a feeling of resignation started to smother her, she noticed a flicker from the bushes beside her. Someone was there. It had to be Ace!

Her logical mind took over and she made a swift mental inventory of the man who held her captive. He had one hand on her mouth and the other held his gun. The heavy bag was perched on the shoulder of the arm that was around her shoulder, gagging her mouth. He was no longer walking forward but had stopped halfway up the side of the bank.

She leaned back against him, taking a deep breath in through her nose. His hand covering her mouth shifted slightly with the movement. Trying to roll her shoulders seemed to loosen the hand on her mouth a little more. Then she leaned right back, as though missing her footing, and made a noise against his palm. He jerked and the bag slid from his shoulder. At the same time, she grabbed his groin and squeezed his balls hard. He let out a loud yelp and fired a shot aimlessly into the air.

Rihanna spun around and pushed him over as he grabbed his painful crotch, dropping the gun at the same time. She reached for the gun but he was too fast, and quickly snatched it from the grass. Ace suddenly sprang from a nearby bush and grabbed the fucker's wrist, his own gun now pointing at the guy's head.

"Drop it!" Ace commanded.

The guy lay on the ground, clutching the piece of metal in one hand, the soft flesh of his genitals in the other. His face was a harsh stare, tense with fear and pain, determination and anger.

"You heard the man." Mr. Tranter suddenly appeared from behind the bank's back door, a gun pointed at the guy on the ground, too.

Then the sheriff and Mr. Treadwell came forward from their positions up ahead, both also with guns poised.

Rihanna's mind whirled with relief and confusion, just before everything went black.

* * * *

Ace was relieved when Rihanna regained consciousness a short while later. He had caught her before she'd slunk to the grass and lifted her into his arms. Her bosses from the bank had offered their jackets, which they'd placed on the soft grass, and Ace had laid her down gently, her feet elevated on his own rolled-up Carhartt, her face cradled with his arm.

Dyson had already bundled the prisoners into the back of his truck and he and Mr. Treadwell had gone back to the sheriff's office. The other two men had gone over the road to fetch some hot drinks. They returned just as Rihanna started to sit up, aided by Ace.

"Hey, baby." He smiled at her.

She looked around her in bemusement.

"Ah, you're with us again. Here."

Mr. Tranter handed her a cup of cold water. "I've got you coffee for afterward," he promised.

She smiled with gratitude and slowly sipped the water, which seemed to help bring some color back to her cheeks. "Thank you," she said.

"Thank *you*," Mr. Tranter replied, his eyebrows raised. "Looks like you've saved the bank from being robbed."

"Did they get much?" Ace asked.

"Sheriff's taken the haul with him as evidence," Mr. Tranter explained. "We'll know more when they've counted it up. Sure was a heavy bag, though."

"He made me open the vault," Rihanna said, with a shiver. Her voice sounded very small and weak.

"You did the right thing," Mr. Hatton told her.

"You sure did," Mr. Tranter agreed, nodding.

"Let's get you into the warmth," Ace suggested. "It's freezing out here."

The two men put on their suit jackets while Ace wrapped his girl in his thick Carhartt and they quickly went over the road to the café. On the way, Rihanna gasped at the sight of the old truck with two flat front tires.

"I don't suppose you know anything about this?" she asked Ace with a frown.

He put on his most innocent expression. "Me? Why would I know anything?"

She narrowed her eyes.

"Well, we couldn't just let them escape now, could we?"

She raised her eyebrows. "That was the getaway vehicle?"

The other men were chuckling now.

"You should have seen the guy who was supposed to whizz them out of town at a moment's notice," Mr. Hatton remarked with a grin.

"Frankie," Ace explained.

Her jaw dropped. "Oh no."

They all sat around one of the tables that had a bench seat on one side, where Ace and Rihanna sat, while the men took the chairs opposite them.

"Could we get more coffee over here, please?" Mr. Hatton called over to the waitress, offering her one of his winning smiles.

Ace was surprised at how laid-back Dave and James — as they insisted on being called — were, despite their designer suits and flashy cars.

"I thought I'd never get a look-in," James said, as they went over and over the incident. "Honestly, I was just getting cold waiting behind that door, waiting for the nod from Ace."

"I didn't dare make a move," Ace admitted. "Especially once Frankie started yelling to let him know it was all over."

"Yeah, that was pretty frightening." Rihanna shivered again, despite the warmth of the café and the guy who held her close.

"You were real brave," Dave told her, and the other guys agreed.

"I had to do something," she said, a little self-deprecatingly. "I could see how tense he was getting once he knew they had no chance of getting away. Once desperation really sank in, he'd have no reason not to hurt any of us. I couldn't let that happen."

"You took a risk," Ace said, with a sigh.

"But it paid off," she reminded him.

"Yeah, but—"

"We all had guns pointed at the guy," Dave was quick to point out.

"Except me. Hey, maybe I should hire out my babysitting services," James chirped. "Cantankerous old guys a specialty."

"You didn't do a very good job of keeping him quiet," Dave jibed.

"Hey, that wasn't my fault. I thought he was cooperating nicely. I didn't wanna go gagging the old timer. He might have had a heart attack or something." James rolled his eyes at his colleague.

"But he gave the whole game away. Up till then that mad fucker thought he was home and dry. Er...sorry, Rihanna." Dave quickly put his hand to his mouth, clearly realizing the colorful language he'd used.

She smiled. One thing the guy had never given her was his name, which was probably just as well, really. She felt a sort of affinity with Frankie, despite what he did—or nearly did, just because she'd spoken to him and knew who he was. It was best the same hadn't happened with his accomplice.

"D'you reckon Dwayne's involved in all this?" Dave asked, frowning.

Rihanna shook her head. "Mr. Williamson? Why would he be?"

"He hired Paul without checking his references," Dave replied.

"He was very friendly with both Paul and Sarah," Rihanna admitted. "They used to have whole conversations while I was unaware he'd even arrived in the branch. That was before I had the two-way mirror installed, of course."

Ace grinned, proudly. "That was a good move, baby."

He held her a little tighter, unable to hide how proud he was of her.

Dave frowned. "Yeah, that's something that should have been done before you'd even taken over the position. Every other bank has something similar in place. I can't believe Dwayne overlooked it."

"I'd be surprised if he had anything to do with it," James said calmly, putting a hand out to placate his colleague. "Honestly, why would he risk his job like that? He makes enough money in his position. He'd be a fool to throw all that away."

"You think?" Dave shot him a dubious look before taking another sip of his coffee.

James nodded. "Yeah. That's not to say I think he deserves the dang job after all this. He's clearly slacking in his duties. I wouldn't put it past Josh to demote him now. Serve him right, too."

Ace was surprised how freely the guys spoke in front of him and Rihanna, but then, after what they'd all gone through, they were more like friends than anything else. He sure would like to see these two again in more relaxed circumstances. They seemed like good guys.

"I thought I'd find you in here." Josh Treadwell's voice from the doorway made them all look up. "You want more coffee?"

"Need you ask?" James replied with a grin.

Josh ordered the drinks and came over to join them, pulling up a chair from a nearby table.

"So, how are Butch and Sundance?" Dave asked. "Behind bars?"

"Hey, I had to spend time with Frankie. More like Bonnie and Clyde, by my reckoning," James piped up.

Ace grinned, glad to feel Rihanna relax a little more beside him. The fresh coffees arrived just then and they handed them around, delighted that Josh had even treated them to cookies to go with them.

"They're in a couple of cells for now," Josh replied, shaking his head.

"And where's Dwayne?" Dave frowned, looking over toward the door.

"He's gone home. I've told him we want to see him first thing in the morning," Josh replied, a little more seriously.

"All of us?" Dave checked.

"Of course. I'm sure you've both got questions for him, the same as me. Better that we all sleep on it and go at it with a clear head in the morning, I thought." Josh nodded before turning to Rihanna. "I'll arrange for someone from Almondine to replace Paul temporarily, just until we find a replacement."

"Sarah will be there, though, won't she?" Rihanna asked.

"Yeah. Sheriff seems to think she had nothing to do with all this. I sent her home. Though it was disgraceful for her to treat you the way she did. She said she's real sorry about that. She wanted to talk to you about it."

"She has already apologized," Rihanna pointed out with a frown.

"I guess she wants to explain herself," Josh said with a kind smile.

"So, the sheriff doesn't suspect Dwayne of knowing anything about all this?" Dave looked a little dubious.

"Not from what he can tell. We'll give him a good grilling, don't you worry about that. Oh, and, James, you'd better look into recruiting a new area manager. Even if he's not involved in any of this, he hasn't exactly done a good job in that role, has he?"

James nodded. "I'm on it."

Rihanna sighed, and Ace guessed how relieved she must feel not having to put up with Williamson anymore. It seemed the guys were right on the money about him being demoted. It was completely justified, too.

"Oh, and another thing," Josh added, looking at Rihanna. "Could you use another teller over there? I'm thinking that with all those new accounts you're setting up for us, you don't really have time to help out on the floor at lunchtimes — and I doubt you're getting all the breaks you're entitled to."

She blushed. "Well...um...yes, that would be a massive help," she replied.

Josh nodded to James, who quickly replied, "Duly noted."

"And I want Rihanna to get a pay raise," Josh added. "After all, she's brought us in all this new revenue, and saved us from a bank robbery. I reckon it's the least she deserves."

The other two men nodded. "I'm on that, too," James promised.

"And you let me know if you need any more security measures," Dave told her. "I've actually got a few ideas to run by you...when the dust has settled a little."

"Thank you." She smiled shyly.

"Well, on that note, I reckon you should take the rest of the day off, young lady. And we'd best be making tracks." Josh finished the last of his coffee before they all started standing up.

"Let's get you home," Ace told his girl after they'd all said goodbye.

"Don't you have to work?" she frowned.

"Nah. Dyson must have told Matt what was going on earlier," he said, with a grin. "Matt told me to take the day off. Said I'd earned it."

"You have. You managed to catch Paul then that gray-shirt guy. I'd say you've more than earned it." She reached up and kissed him on the lips.

Ace felt a warmth inside him and put both arms around her. She was bundled up in his jacket, as hers had been left with Sarah. "And what about you? You managed to take that guy down all on your own. I'd say you've earned more than the rest of the day off." He winked at her.

"Have you got something in mind, cowboy?" She gave a cheeky smile.

"I sure have. Let's get a takeout on the way home. After we've eaten, I'll show you *exactly* what's on my mind."

Chapter Twenty

They were both more than ready for a meal that evening, having missed lunch altogether with everything that had been going on. Afterward, Rihanna washed their dishes.

"You still unpacking boxes?" Ace asked after a visit to the bathroom.

She guessed he must have taken a peek in her bedroom on his way past. It was a pity, that she'd put everything in there to keep the rest of the apartment tidy, and yet now she really wanted the bedroom to feel appealing.

"Yeah, just some stuff I need to sort out, that's all." She didn't like to admit that it was mostly things left over from the wedding that had never happened — things she was trying desperately to sell on the Internet.

"Maybe I can help?" he offered.

"No, honestly." She shrugged, wiping her hands in a dish cloth. "I'll get around to it eventually."

He came over and took her in his arms. "How are you feeling?" he asked.

"I'm fine," she assured him. "I can't believe I fainted like that." She shook her head. "It's never happened to me before."

"He was probably cutting off your oxygen supply with that dang hand over your mouth," Ace replied. "Perhaps we should add attempted murder to his list of charges."

"It wasn't that bad," she said with a giggle. "I think I just got a bit overwhelmed by it all. I've never been in a position like that before. At one point I actually thought he might kill me."

He held her even tighter. "Now you know there's no way I'd ever let that happen."

"I felt much better when I saw you were nearby," she admitted.

"You *saw* me?" He feigned a shocked expression. "Well, there goes my application for the Special Forces." He rolled his eyes.

Rihanna laughed. "No way. I couldn't stand to think of you doing anything like that every day."

"Aw, does that mean you really care about me?" he asked with a wink.

"You know I do." Her voice was soft.

"Well, that's good." He pressed his soft lips against hers as their bodies squeezed together.

Their kisses became more fervent, their breaths more rapid, as they stroked and caressed each other. He brushed a finger down her cheek while also running a hand up and down her spine, making her tingle. She ran her fingers through his short hair before feeling the hard muscles of his arms and shoulders through his shirt.

"Wanna take this somewhere cozier?" he whispered.

She nodded, unable to speak as her heart hammered with desire and hope. He was so gorgeous, and she couldn't help wanting him right then.

He led her to the bedroom, hardly breaking their kiss for more than a second, then heeled off his boots after laying her on the bed. Watching as he stripped his shirt over his head, not bothering to unfasten the buttons, she felt her whole body heat up even more.

"Can I help you?" he asked with a sensual grin, leaning forward.

"Be my guest."

He wasted no time in unzipping her skirt and pulling it down her bare legs, before slowly unbuttoning her blouse. His fingers were warm and gentle, as well as admirably competent, as the cotton fell open and was then swiftly whisked from her body.

She shivered, although it wasn't really cold in the room. Lying in just her white frilled underwear with matching bra, she reached up for him and caught hold of his belt.

"My turn," she murmured.

His eyes glinted with mischief and pleasure, and he placed his hands behind his head to allow her full access.

Rihanna subconsciously licked her lips as she unfastened his belt, then his jeans, running a hand down his hard cock as she unzipped the denim. She pulled them down his legs, and he then moved his hands to remove them while she stroked his huge erection through his shorts.

She watched him raise one eyebrow in question, and her heart beat even faster. He couldn't know what that expression did to her — but he was about to find out.

After he'd pulled down his shorts, he gasped and his body tensed slightly. His eyes had turned almost black with desire as he looked down at her, and she couldn't resist licking at his massive cock while he hissed in response.

"Oh, baby," he whispered.

She wrapped her lips around his girth and sucked, while he ran his hands through her hair, panting heavily as she laved her tongue over his velvety length before tugging very gently with her lips.

"Oh, my God, Ri," he gasped.

"Hmm-m," she hummed against his skin, driving him wild.

She'd never enjoyed this before, but with Ace it seemed different — perhaps because it was her choice to do it, and maybe because she didn't have to ask if she was doing it right or not. He made that much perfectly clear!

One of his hands found her left breast, and she was aware of the fabric of her bra being pulled to one side while he circled her nipple, making her hard and tingly. She felt the thrill in her core and was sure her panties must be soaked by now.

Her eyes closed as she sucked and pulled at his throbbing cock, his yelps of delight spurring her on.

"Oh, yes, baby. Yes, go on. Please, baby."

She found the hole at the tip of his cock and she dipped her tongue in and out, before circling the bulbous head then returning to long sucks up his whole length.

"I'm gonna come!" His voice had risen a few octaves, signaling his pleasure, and Rihanna just quickened the pace, losing herself in his desire.

Instead of pulling her mouth away, as she had always done in the past, she continued sucking until she felt his cream slide easily down the back of her throat. She drank it down greedily before slowing slightly as she felt his weight on her when his arms came around her shoulders.

"Oh my God, Ri," he whispered breathlessly. "Oh wow. I've never... You're just so..."

She moved over on the bed, allowing him to lie next to her as he gulped for air, his arms still holding her close.

"You're unbelievable," he managed after a minute or two.

"I could say the same about you," she whispered, running her hands over his taut chest.

"You ain't seen nothing yet," he replied with a flash of mischief in his eyes and a big grin on his lips.

He rolled her onto her back and tucked his fingers into the top of her panties. Watching her face all the time, he slowly pulled the wet lace down her legs before discarding it on the floor.

"Beautiful." He gazed at her pussy.

Instead of feeling embarrassed, as she usually did, she loved his admiring look, and smiled back at him. He leaned down and laid a reverent kiss on her mound, making her yelp as a jolt of electricity shot right through her.

He grinned before reaching up for her bra. Quickly unfastening it, he pulled it off her body, again throwing it onto the carpet while he gazed adoringly at her pert breasts.

The look on his face as he studied her body made her feel beautiful, wanted. She'd never felt quite like it before. Usually, she'd be frantically trying to get under the covers so Phil couldn't look at her nakedness for too long. For some reason, she'd always felt self-conscious with him, embarrassed even.

"You are so gorgeous." Ace's voice was soft and sincere.

Leaning over her, he took her right breast in his mouth, nibbling at first, then licking and kissing it hungrily. He did the same with the left, while his hand continued to massage the right. Again he wound his finger around her nipple, making it hard and pointed. His tongue did the same with her left nipple, before he nipped at it, making her squeal. Another delicious shock went through her, ending at her core.

He trailed his right hand between her legs and found her clit, which he circled mercilessly with his thumb, making her gasp and moan with delight.

"Ace," she whispered.

"Is that good, baby?"

"Oh God, yes."

She could hardly breathe as pleasure swamped her whole body while he touched and caressed her in all the right places.

He lavished her breasts with attention, moving his mouth from one to the other, sucking and nipping at them in equal measure.

Slowly he ran his tongue down, over her stomach, while one hand still played with her nipple, the other exploring her wet pussy.

Her back arched with anticipation as he neared her mound and he covered it with his hot breath, then his lips, as he kissed and licked all around her aching clit.

She knew it wouldn't take much more to make her come, but she wanted to prolong her orgasm as much as possible, enjoying his ministrations too much to let him stop.

He circled her clit with his tongue and she yelped, grabbing at his short hair, almost pushing his mouth closer. He moaned as he kissed and licked at her hot pussy, sending shivers and electric shocks through her body. She jerked with the most wonderful spasms as his tongue became more inquisitive, poking in and out of her, the way she longed for his massive cock to do. He invaded her hole with his fingers, getting deeper with each thrust.

Rihanna felt herself nearing the edge and her breaths became shorter and more rapid. Suddenly he swiped his tongue over her clit and she screamed, still clutching his hair as a wave of ecstasy washed over her. It felt like it lasted for ages but was probably only a few seconds, before her whole body started shaking as she came slowly back to earth.

She didn't remember releasing his hair or Ace crawling back up the bed, but she found herself in his warm, strong arms as tears rolled down her cheeks.

"Hey, it's okay," he murmured. "It's fine."

She clung to his ripped chest, her eyes closed, breathing him in as though her life depended on it. She had no idea why she was sobbing so hard, but he didn't seem to mind as he shushed and whispered reassuringly to her, still holding her tight.

Slowly she started to compose herself, feeling a little silly for her reaction.

"I'm sorry. I don't know what happened," she told him, sheepishly.

He lifted her chin with his thumb, forcing her to look at him. "Don't apologize, baby. As long as you're all right? I didn't hurt you or upset you, did I?"

The concern in his eyes almost made her cry all over again. She shook her head. "No, it was beautiful. I've never..." She sniffed back a large sob. "I've never felt like that before," she admitted.

"You made me feel things I'd never felt before, too," he told her, coming down to kiss her lips with his. "Thank you."

She sniffed again, then wiped a hand over her wet face. "I'll just use the bathroom," she muttered before sliding out of his embrace and heading for the door.

Her reflection took her by surprise. She looked...different. Her eyes were much darker, and her face was flushed. Her lips were bright red. She washed plenty of cold water over her skin, at first glad of the coolness, but afterward feeling quite cold. Still her face looked pink, and there was a slight sheen across it.

Her heart was slowing down now, but she couldn't forget the way he'd made her feel just a few short moments ago. She'd never experienced an orgasm like it in her life. Everything seemed different with Ace—more intense, more loving. Her heart jolted. Yeah, that was it. She *loved* him. She knew that now.

She smiled at herself in the mirror. She was in love. And the way she felt right now proved to her that she couldn't have been in love with Phil Cartwright at all, though she thought she'd been at the time. But this was so much more.

Should she tell Ace? She wasn't sure. He hadn't said it, so she didn't want to look a fool if he didn't feel the same way. Although she'd only just realized it herself, so maybe he was just catching her up—or had he already felt it and was just picking the right moment to tell her? She'd bide her time and play it by ear. It was exciting, though.

After freshening up, she took the robe from the back of the door and wrapped it around her. She didn't want to spoil the mood, but now that she'd well and truly recovered, she was feeling a little chilly. Grinning, she went back into the bedroom. And that's when the smile fell from her face.

Ace sat on the edge of the bed, still half-covered in the sheet. The drawer of the nightstand was open, as was the ring box in his trembling hand. In his other hand was the band of gold. Her wedding ring.

He turned to face her, shaking his head. "Why didn't you tell me?"

She frowned, suddenly glad she was no longer naked. His face was a mixture of hurt and betrayal.

Suddenly, he was putting the ring back in the box. He slammed the drawer shut and pulled on his clothes.

"What are you doing?" she gasped.

"What I should have done before any of...this." He waved a hand over the bed.

"Ace, I don't understand." She took a step toward him, then, on seeing his expression turn to anger, she stopped.

"*Don't* you?" He was pulling on his boots now.

His tone and the loudness of his voice irked her. He had no right to act like this. "No, I don't. And I could ask you what you were doing snooping around in my things." She folded her arms across her chest in defiance.

He shot her an incredulous look, before standing up straight. "I'm sorry. I wasn't snooping around. I was looking for a condom, if you must know. I hadn't expected things to go the way they did tonight, and I just thought..."

"Oh." She suddenly felt mean for being annoyed with him. It was heartening to think he hadn't assumed they'd do anything tonight, especially after the day they'd just had. And she felt it was a mark of respect that he wasn't the kind of guy to carry condoms around just in case he got lucky.

"Yeah."

She frowned as a thought occurred to her. "Why would you think that *I'd* have one?"

He shrugged. "I didn't. I just thought that *if* you should happen to have one, that was the logical place to keep it."

"Well, I don't have any. I'm not that kind of girl," she pointed out.

"No. I didn't think you *were* that kind of girl," he said, his jaw tight as he crossed the room to the door. "But then, I didn't think you were the *married* kind, either."

Chapter Twenty-One

"Come on in. I've some pancakes cooking," Carla called over from where she stood at the large stove. "And there's coffee in the pot there." She smiled at Ace brightly. "I heard you were quite the hero yesterday."

"I ain't hungry. I'll take some coffee, though." His stomach churned at the memory of yesterday. It was one hell of a rollercoaster, for sure.

"Help yourself." She gestured to the pot on the kitchen table. "I've just made it."

"Thanks." He slumped heavily onto one of the wooden chairs, which creaked under his abuse.

Dyson came into the room, looking as fresh as a daisy. He gave a big smile when he saw Ace. "Well, if it ain't the hero of the hour." He nodded to him before going over to give Carla a big hug from behind.

"Pancakes are ready," she told him with a giggle.

"Music to my ears," Dyson replied, watching her place them on a hot plate. "Here... Let me carry that for you, darlin'."

He took a cloth and she followed as he took the plate over to the table.

"Hey, you okay, buddy?" Dyson frowned, catching Ace's expression.

"I'm fine," he lied. Watching them interact made him feel worse, somehow. He wasn't into sharing, but he could see the love that emanated from Carla and her husbands every time she was with one or both of them — or even when they just talked about each other. He'd hoped for that sort of joy in his life, but now it looked like he'd never get it. Having thought that Rihanna was 'the one', he felt like his world had just come crashing around him.

"Was Rihanna okay when you got her home last night?" Dyson asked, offering him the pancakes.

Ace put a hand up to decline them.

"He's not hungry," Carla offered, in answer to Dyson's look of surprise.

"All the more for me." Dyson grinned, placing the plate back on the table and taking a couple for himself.

"Hey, man, don't you even think about missing me out here." Matt suddenly appeared in the doorway, heeling off his muddy boots. He hung his coat and hat behind the door before joining them at the table where Carla was already pouring his coffee. "Some of us have been working already."

"Get out the violin. St. Matthew has arrived," Dyson joked, shaking his head.

"Well, we can't all have a desk job now, can we? Some of us actually have to *work* for a living. Ain't that right, Ace?" Matt shot him a cheeky grin.

"I think Ace'll be the first to testify that Dyson's job's a lot more than that after yesterday, ain't that right?" Carla giggled as she looked over at him.

Ace put his hands up in submission. "Hey, now, just you leave me out of this. No way am I coming between married folk." He quickly finished his coffee and shot up from his chair, the ache in his heart becoming too much. "I've got work to do."

He couldn't get out of the house quick enough. Pulling on his coat as he embraced the bitter cold air, he gave a loud sniff before forcing his feet to take him over toward the stables. It was still early, and the hands were just starting to tend to the horses. Titan, his own horse, was housed at the end of the stable block, with some of the other privately owned beasts, and he went straight over to him. For a moment he just buried his face in the horse's flank, glad of the softness. As he felt tears begin to roll down his cheek, he quickly wiped his face and set about saddling up and was soon riding the monstrous animal out of the ranch and up toward the mountain.

There was plenty of work he could be doing, instead of heading off into the foothills, but nothing that couldn't wait. No way could he let the hands see how upset he was today, and he sure couldn't stand to see the pity on Dyson's and Matt's faces if they realized how he felt.

He took the same route he'd taken with Rihanna and remembered the look of sheer bliss on her face at the time. It had been a magical day, and one that he'd never forget. But he *needed* to forget her. He'd come to think of her as his, although they'd never actually made anything official. Now he could see why. She'd told him she'd come out of a relationship in the city that had left her feeling vulnerable and distraught. She hadn't mentioned that it was a marriage.

Thinking about her now, he felt a huge lump hit the pit of his stomach. Was the reason she'd chosen the larger apartment so that her husband could come back and live there? Was he already living there, and he'd been too dumb to notice? Her bedroom had been filled with boxes and filled suit-covers hung on the outside of the wardrobe. Was that all his stuff? It sure made sense. She'd got that place looking real nice as soon as she'd moved in. Was that all for her husband?

He dismounted Titan at a clearing partway up the mountain, and looked over the edge. They sure had come a long way already. He guessed the old boy had been glad of the exercise, and he sure was grateful for the time alone in the fresh air. Taking large breaths of the coldness into his lungs, he tried to calm the niggling feelings that engulfed him.

"I really thought I'd fallen in love, boy," he told the horse, who munched contentedly at some frost-covered grass. "It just felt so right with her."

His thoughts drifted back to their antics in her bedroom the previous night. It had been perfect. Holding her while she cried afterward had made him feel like a king. She wasn't upset or hurt, she was just emotional. That's how he'd made her feel — or so he'd thought. Was she really upset that she was with him when she was, in fact, married to someone else?

When she'd gone to the bathroom, he'd felt sure they would make love on her return and had cursed himself for not thinking to bring protection. He'd never been the type of guy who carried condoms in his wallet, knowing that he was never likely to need them. Sex with someone he didn't care about had never been his thing, and he'd imagined making love with Rihanna would be something they'd have talked about and planned. But life didn't always turn out that way.

When he'd checked her nightstand, he'd known it was unlikely that she'd have any condoms in there but felt that it was the obvious place if she *did* happen to keep any. He'd been half-hoping to find some so they could continue their night of passion, and half-hoping she wouldn't have any. After all, she really wasn't that kind of girl, was she?

Tears blurred his vision as he recalled finding the ring box. Out of interest he'd opened it. Although the box was clearly new, he'd thought it might contain an antique ring, a family heirloom of some sort, or a really modern-looking shiny piece of glittering silver that she might wear on a night out or something. Never in a million years had he imagined finding a wedding band. He'd taken it from the box, hoping to find it was either huge, or too tiny for Rihanna's finger, but he'd known as soon as he saw it that it was exactly her size.

He hadn't given her the chance to deny it. What was the point? He'd never known her to lie to him but couldn't bear for her to start right then. How could he have been so stupid as to not suspect something like this? It was too perfect. *She* was too perfect. Of course something had to be wrong. Had he been too blind to notice the signs?

* * * *

Rihanna was trying her hardest to bury herself in her work. Having stayed up bawling her eyes out all night, she felt tired and irritable, as well as angry.

Sarah had tried to apologize to her first thing, but she hadn't been in the right frame of mind to accept it. Normally she would have accepted it graciously, but she felt anything *but* gracious today.

"That doesn't explain why you thought it was okay to come in here and treat me the way you did," Rihanna had told her, ignoring the tears that welled in her

colleague's eyes. *"I was new to the area as well as new to the job. I thought you, of all people, would have understood that and offered me some kind of respect, if not friendship."*

"I'm sorry," Sarah had wailed again, her face turning red. *"Paul said that Mr. Williamson felt that you weren't up to the job. He'd had someone much more experienced in mind but had been overruled by Mr. Treadwell and the guys at head office. I didn't realize at first that the person he'd favored was the woman he was dating. When I did, I tried to be a bit nicer to you, but Paul told me I was a traitor and that I couldn't just change my mind like that. He said we had to stick together."*

"And you believed him? You're a grown woman, for goodness' sake," Rihanna had snapped. *"Surely you can make up your own mind about someone?"*

"I know. I should have." Sarah had given a loud sniff, wiping her eyes with a tissue. *"I'm so sorry I didn't."*

"And you knew nothing about Paul's plans to have his friends rob this place?" Rihanna fired at her, though she knew the answer already. Dyson had been very thorough in establishing that Sarah had no involvement in Paul's plan whatsoever.

Sarah had shaken her head. *"I swear. I had no idea."* More tears had gushed down her face.

Rihanna had sat back with a sigh. *"All I ask is some respect and loyalty,"* she'd said, a little more softly.

"And you'll get it, I promise." Sarah had looked back at her with sincerity and remorse, making Rihanna feel bad for being so hard on her.

"Okay. Then let's make a fresh start," Rihanna had relented.

Sarah had nodded. *"Thank you. You won't regret this."*

Rihanna had watched her leave the office thinking of all the other things she *did* regret right then. And right at the top of the list was letting Ace Blenheim into her heart.

Mr. Treadwell had been as good as his word, sending over a really competent cashier, Betsy, from Almondine to replace Paul, temporarily. Betsy was real friendly and polite, and couldn't be more helpful. Her southern drawl seemed to ingratiate her with the locals, too.

Of course, the customers all wanted to know the details of yesterday's sudden closure, and Rhianna had informed her staff to only tell them that it was a matter in the hands of the sheriff. She knew the gossip-mongers would make their own assumptions – and probably be quite right – but she didn't want to fuel the fire, and certainly didn't want the staff giving them information that could jeopardize the case against anyone. She shuddered at the realization that Paul had sat out there planning to rob the bank and wondered what else he might have been capable of. After all, that guy who'd tried to take her hostage had had a gun!

Her phone rang, yanking her from her sobering thoughts.

"Sheriff's here to see you, Miss Richards," Betsy told her, cheerfully.

"Thanks, Betsy. And you can call me Rihanna," she told her. "Send him through, would you?"

"Of course, ma'am. Thank you."

Rihanna smiled, wondering if Betsy didn't quite feel ready to use her first name. She guessed the management over at Almondine were probably a little more aloof than over here.

"How are you, today?" Dyson smiled as he came in, removing his hat as he neared the desk.

"Morning, Sheriff. I'm fine, thank you. Do you have any news?"

"There's a court date for early next week," he said, with a nod. "You might be called to testify, but you'll just have to tell the judge exactly what happened. Nothing to worry about."

Her stomach clenched. "Really?" She'd been worried about that all night. It made sense, given her position as well as her involvement, that she'd have to speak out in court, and the thought just about terrified her.

"Those three have a lot to answer for," he replied, gravely.

"D'you think Frankie'll go to jail?"

"He's an accessory," Dyson replied.

Rihanna frowned as another thought crossed her mind. "Will Ace Blenheim be called to testify, too?"

The sheriff narrowed his eyes, slightly. "I should think so. After all, he caught Paul trying to escape. And he was involved later when I arrested Michael Gittings."

She raised her eyebrows. "Is that the guy in the gray shirt? I never knew his name."

"That's him."

She nodded.

"Can I ask you something?" he asked, a little cagily, studying her face.

"Of course." She held her breath.

"Is everything okay with you and Ace?"

She frowned. "Why do you ask?"

"He didn't look too happy this morning, that's all. I know yesterday was pretty darn tough for both of you. I was just wondering if he'd taken it bad, you know?"

"You'd have to ask him."

She felt her jaw tense as she spoke. No way was she prepared to discuss her private life with anyone, let alone the sheriff. It was interesting to hear that Ace wasn't his usual cheerful self, though that was on him. If he hadn't jumped to conclusions like that, neither of them would feel so bad right now. But that was Ace all over—jumping to conclusions before he knew the facts.

"I will." Dyson picked up his hat and stood up. "Well, I can see you're busy, so I won't keep you. You just give me a holler if you need anything, won't you?"

"Of course." She stood up and followed him to the door.

"Thanks, Sheriff."

Her phone rang again, and she quickly went to answer it. It was Mr. Treadwell, who sounded quite friendly.

"I was just wondering how you're feeling today?"

"That's real nice of you, sir. I'm okay, thank you. Better when I'm busy."

"Well, that's good. I just wanted to let you know I'm sending a couple of workmen over this afternoon. They should get to you just after closing time, if that's okay?"

"Of course." She frowned, puzzled.

"Their names are Tom Pikeman and Ronald Tighe," he went on. "They're going to install another counter so you can fit in another teller, like we spoke about yesterday."

She gasped. "Thank you, sir. That's great news."

"How's Betsy working out for you?"

"She's great. Everyone seems to love her, and she's real good at her job."

"That's nice to hear. I'm considering making her permanent over there if that's agreeable with you? She lives nearer to your branch than Almondine, anyhow."

She smiled, probably for the first time all day. "I'd love that, sir. She seems to fit in real well here."

"I thought she would. Don't say anything just yet. We'll discuss it further in a day or two, when we interview for the third cashier. I've got James Hatton setting up some candidates as we speak. I thought maybe early next week we could all get together and do it at your branch? Makes sense for them to see where they'd be working." He seemed to have it all worked out.

"That sounds good, sir. Only, I think the sheriff said the court hearing might be early next week. I'll have to attend. Apparently I have to answer some questions or something." She sighed at the thought.

"Great. We'll all be there for that, anyhow. I'm not sure if we're needed, but we wouldn't miss it. We can schedule the interviews later on, in that case. I'll be in touch with some dates and times when Hatton's got it all figured out. In the meantime, have a think on Betsy. You don't have to take her on if you'd rather not. Let me know next week."

"Thank you, sir." Rihanna put the phone down with a smile. It was good to know that *someone* was listening to her without making assumptions.

Chapter Twenty-Two

For the first time since she'd started working at the bank, Rihanna was able to take a whole hour for her lunch break. It was something Mr. Hatton had insisted on when they'd spoken yesterday. Although she felt slightly nervous leaving the bank with just the two tellers in place, both women had assured her that they were more than capable of holding the fort, and, besides, with Gittings in jail, there was no longer any threat.

"Hey, how's it going?" Carla was working in the grocery store when Rihanna went back to her apartment.

"Yeah, it's great. Thought I'd make the most of my lunch hour and get some more unpacking done while I have the chance." Rihanna forced a smile.

Carla didn't look convinced as she took a step toward her, her forehead slightly furrowed. "Are you sure you're okay?"

"Of course." Rihanna tried to sound bright.

Carla sighed. "I saw Ace this morning."

"Oh."

"Now, I know it's none of my business, but he did *not* look happy."

Rihanna glanced around the shop, glad to see it was empty. Closing her eyes momentarily, she felt tears sting at the edges, so she quickly opened them again, blinking hard.

"You don't have to tell me if you don't want to, but I really thought you two looked great together yesterday." Carla's voice was gentle.

"I thought we were great—better than great, actually. I thought I was falling in love with him." She couldn't hold back the tears this time, and Carla swiftly reached behind her, turned the shop sign to 'Closed' and put an arm around Rihanna, ushering her into the back room where they sat at the little table.

"He thinks I'm married," Rihanna blurted out. "He found the ring and just assumed..."

"Oh no." Carla enveloped her in a warm hug. "Did you tell him he had it all wrong?"

Rihanna shook her head. "I didn't get the chance. He left right away."

Carla grimaced. "Well, that explains why he looked so pissed this morning," she said, with a tut. "Honestly, I thought that face of his was gonna turn the milk sour at the breakfast table."

"Sheriff said he wasn't too happy," Rihanna recalled. "But, honestly, Carla, he wouldn't even stay to discuss it. He just flew right off the handle, jumped to his own conclusions and walked right on out."

"You two need to talk."

Rihanna bit her lip. "I wanted to last night. Then I got to realizing that it probably wouldn't do any good. I mean, yeah, I could tell him he's got it all wrong. I could explain all about Phil and what happened, but I'm not sure it would be enough."

Carla frowned. "What are you saying?"

"I let my guard down." Rihanna gave a self-deprecating laugh. "We did stuff last night I've never done before, and it was magical. I really started to think that it was going to be okay, you know? Phil was in the past, and now I'd gotten Ace and he was everything Phil wasn't. But I was kidding myself. Ace didn't want to listen to me. He just made up his mind what was going on and ran with it—literally. Phil never listened, either. It was either his way or no way. I don't think I could go there again, Carla, no matter how much I love Ace. It just won't work."

"It *will* work if you both want it enough," Carla said softly. "Even a blind man could see how much you two love each other. Sure, he ain't perfect. He *is* a guy, after all." She chuckled, and Rihanna rolled her eyes in agreement. "But, let's face it. Your relationship's been like driving on a dirt track since you met. Isn't this just one more little bump in that road? One you can overcome with a little more communication and a little less assumption?"

"I don't know." Rihanna sniffed hard. "The way he looked at me last night? It was like I'd just betrayed him. He thought I'd been lying all along. If he can't trust me, give me the benefit of the doubt, hear me out, then what chance do we have? I can't keep fighting like this, Carla. I had all that with Phil, and it just didn't work."

"Well, I'm not giving up the fight." A familiar voice in the doorway made them both jump. Ace stood with his hat in his hand, a contrite expression on his face.

Another tear trickled down her cheek.

"I'm an idiot," he went on. "I was taken for a fool in the past and I guess I'm just so determined not to let it happen again that I go around looking for problems that ain't even there. You're right, Ri. I jump to conclusions, make my own mind up on the spot and run with it. I need to take a step back and listen. I'm sorry."

Rihanna stared at his handsome face. She'd never seen him look so tense, so anxious. She had to look away. It was too much. *He* was too much. All she wanted to do was run into his arms and tell him it was all okay and that they would figure it out. But what good would it do? Patch it over until the next time.

"I think you two should go upstairs and talk properly," Carla suggested.

"And I think Ace should learn to read. The shop's closed. That means you shouldn't have come in here and listened to our private conversation," Rihanna snapped as embarrassment and anger raged inside her. How much had he heard?

Ace looked taken aback. "I'm sorry. The door wasn't locked."

"It didn't need to be. The sign said it was closed." Rihanna took a deep breath.

"Ri," Carla interjected firmly, "you guys need to talk."

"No. We needed to talk last night. Ace didn't want to. Now *I* don't want to. We'll just leave things as they are, shall we?"

"No." Ace took a step forward, his face tense. "We can't leave it like this. Carla's right. We need to discuss it."

Rihanna sniffed again, trying to swallow beyond the hard lump in her throat. "I need to get back to work shortly." She stood.

"Then we'll talk quickly." Ace was tenacious.

Rihanna huffed. It was clear she was outnumbered here, and she knew she was just being stubborn.

"You might wanna wash your face before you go back," Carla suggested, softly.

With a nod, Rihanna led the way upstairs and unlocked the door to her apartment.

"What was his name?" Ace asked, breaking the awkward silence once they were inside.

"Phil Cartwright."

"Is he from around here?"

"No. New Moldington."

"He asked you to marry him?"

"What do *you* think?" Rihanna led him into the bedroom where she opened the door to the nightstand again. Behind the ring box there were jars of crystal table decorations.

She went over to the pile of boxes and pulled out a handful of beautiful artificial flowers. Another was full of the finest tulle and satin ribbons, and yet another had cut-glass vases.

Ace gaped. "You'd bought everything already?"

She nodded slowly. "I believed it was happening. I was preparing for it, planning, making arrangements." She stood back and shook her head at the pile of boxes. "There's a small fortune tied up in all this. Money I won't get back, but I'm getting what I can."

Ace frowned. "Isn't he contributing to the cost?"

She raised her eyebrows incredulously. "Nope. He insisted we — or, rather, I — pay for everything outright, to save running up credit before we got married. Being on the higher wage, he decided I should pay for the wedding while he paid for the household bills and stuff. It wasn't until after he'd left me for someone else that I discovered that he hadn't paid anything, and we were massively behind with the rent and all the expenses. I ended up having to pay for it all when he disappeared. He'd insisted that I paid non-refundable deposits on the venue and everything to save money, so I lost thousands there, too."

"Oh my God, Ri." He took a step toward her, his arms outstretched. "You should have told me."

Despite longing to sink into his embrace, she took a step back. "Why? So you could see what a dang fool I am? So you'd know how gullible I am so *you* could take advantage, too? You weren't exactly forthcoming about your own love-life, Ace. Why would I tell you about mine?"

His whole body sagged. "You're right. I was with someone...Alice. She dumped me. I suspect she was probably cheating on me, but I had no proof. Suddenly, the whole town heard about it—her family was very influential—only the way it was put was totally the other way around. She made out that *I* was the one who hurt *her*. My life became unbearable, so I moved away. Came out here, somewhere where no one knew me or her. I needed to start afresh, be myself again."

She swallowed hard, grateful that the lump in her throat had dissipated somewhat. It was hard to think that he had been duped, too. It had hurt, too, judging by his expression.

"I'm sorry that happened to you." Her voice was a little softer now.

He shook his head. "It was nothing compared to all this." He waved a hand over the boxes.

"There's more stuff in the wardrobes and those drawers." She gestured to a large chest of drawers that stood under the window. "I've managed to sell some of it over the Internet, but I don't get that much time right now."

He nodded. "I can imagine. He should be paying his fair share, though, especially as he's the reason you broke up."

She shrugged. "Even if I could find him, he'd never pay."

Ace seethed at the injustice. "I'm so sorry," he said. "I guess I've made it ten times worse for you, just running off half-cocked like that. I'm gonna make it up to you, Ri. I can promise you that."

She shook her head. "Don't make me any promises, Ace." She just couldn't take any more disappointment.

"I'm not him." He spoke softly, taking another step nearer to her. "And I get that you're angry with me, and you're protecting your heart, but just don't give up on me just yet. I *will* make this up to you, Ri, and I'll show you what sort of man I really am. But right now, I guess you need some time, and I respect that. I can wait." He placed a warm hand on her arm. "Now, we both need to get back to work, but can I come over tonight and talk about this properly?"

"I don't know." She shook her head, not trusting herself to look him in the eye.

"Then I'll call you later, to see how you feel then."

She nodded.

"I'm sorry, darlin'. And I do love you. That's how I know this'll work out for us." He placed a gentle kiss on her head before heading out of the door.

Rihanna allowed the tears to stream down her face once more before she went to wash her face and get ready for work again.

* * * *

"How good are you at finding missing assholes?" Ace breezed into the sheriff's office, throwing his hat onto a chair.

"Well, now, assholes, I don't have a problem with — they're everywhere — but *missing* ones? Well that's a different matter."

"This one has a name. Phil Cartwright," Ace offered, sitting down opposite the sheriff.

Dyson frowned. "Now that name rings a bell."

"He's Rihanna's ex," Ace explained. "Broke off their engagement owing her a ton of money."

"New Moldington," Dyson said, pointing a finger at him.

Ace frowned while the sheriff tapped at his computer. "How did you know that?"

"Carla told me about him a while back. I thought I'd take a little snoop around, see what I could find."

"And?"

"He'd moved to a place nearby." He frowned at the screen. "Yeah, here it is. Someplace called Hepworth."

"Never heard of it," Ace admitted. "Did you speak to him?"

Dyson shook his head. "Nope. Carla was real worried about Rihanna a while back and she asked me if he could be found. I just made a few preliminary inquiries, and it turned out he hadn't gone far from when Rihanna knew him. I was only able to find him so easily as he'd been caught speeding on the freeway." He rolled his eyes.

"Now why doesn't that surprise me?" Ace shook his head.

"Hey, I wondered where you'd got to." Matt strolled into the office and handed a brown bag to Dyson.

"Sorry, boss. I got caught up in something. I'll make up the time." Ace went to get up but Matt put a hand out to stop him.

"Sounds important," Matt said. He looked back to his brother. "Carla said you left your lunch in the kitchen this morning. She meant to bring it with her but must have forgotten it."

"Thanks, bro." Dyson put his hand in the bag and pulled out a slice of apple cake wrapped in tinfoil. "I'm starving."

Ace eyed the cake enviously. He looked forward to Rihanna baking stuff like that for him and hoped it wouldn't be too long before they got to that stage.

"So, what's going on?" Matt nodded to the screen.

Dyson's mouth was already full of the delicious-looking cake, so Ace explained. "This guy was engaged to Rihanna."

Matt rolled his eyes. "Oh yeah, that shit who left her footing the tab for her own wedding?"

"You knew?" Ace guessed as soon as he'd spoken that he shouldn't be surprised. Carla and her husbands were so open that it made sense she had told them all about it if she'd been worried.

"That poor girl. We need to get this guy to pay up." Matt seethed.

"I told you, bro. It'd need to go through the court." Dyson shook his head. "Rihanna would have to provide all the receipts and prove that every decision they made to spend the money was a joint one. From what we've heard about the douchebag, he'd only lie his way out of it, leaving Rihanna to cover court costs on top of everything else."

"There's more than one way to skin a rabbit," Ace mumbled.

Matt's face split into a shit-eating grin. "I like the way you think there, buddy."

"And I've already told you, violence isn't the answer," Dyson warned them, sternly.

"No, but it'd sure make me feel a whole lot better," Ace admitted.

"I'm not suggesting mindless violence," Matt said, putting his hands up in submission. "Just a little friendly persuasion, nothing more."

Dyson shook his head. "I can't use my position for that. I'm sorry, much as I'd love to."

"Who mentioned *you* getting involved? I'm sure Ace and I could manage quite well on our own."

Ace grinned.

"Well, I'm just gonna go over there and pour myself a coffee to go with my lunch," Dyson said, rolling his eyes.

"Thanks, bro."

As soon as he'd gone over to the other counter, Matt went behind the desk and jotted down the address on the notepad. He grimaced at it. "Where in hell's that?"

"Somewhere in the city. You'd better use your GPS." Dyson returned to his desk. "I'll send out a search party if you're not back by midnight."

Chapter Twenty-Three

It took nearly five hours to reach Hepworth in Matt's truck. Ace dreaded to think how long it would have taken in his own pickup. They both cringed when high-rise office buildings towered over them, as they inched their way through gridlock traffic.

"He lives in an apartment building near a cookie factory," Ace announced, studying the GPS. "Just down here." He pointed.

Matt pulled over in a crowded parking lot.

"How the hell do we get in? It looks like Fort Knox," Matt grumbled, looking over to the skyscraper.

"Maybe we won't have to." Ace slid out of his seat and hurried over to where a group of noisy girls were just emerging from the main door. One wore a veil and her tee-shirt boasted 'Bride-to-Be' in bright pink letters. The others were all laughing in their 'Bachelorette Party' emblazoned T-shirts, and wore deely boppers and short skirts — clearly on their way out for a night on the town.

"Hey, ladies." Ace offered them a bright smile, and they all-but swooned right in front of him.

"Hey, cowboy. You coming with us?" a redhead offered.

He put his hands up in submission. "I wouldn't dare, ladies," he assured them. "I'm just looking for a friend of mine, Phil Cartwright. He lives around here, I believe?"

"Oh, you're with the bachelors," the bride slurred.

"Their party's over in Jerry's Bar," a slightly more sober bachelorette explained. "Phil should be there already."

"Is it far?" Ace asked, still grinning.

"You can walk it from here," the redhead interjected. "Just two blocks down." She pointed down the road.

"Great. Thanks, ladies. Have a great night."

"We will," they chorused back.

Matt emerged from the truck on Ace's signal.

"He's at a bachelor party," Ace murmured. "Come on."

"*His* bachelor party?" Matt frowned, catching up to him.

"Not sure." Ace had an odd feeling about this but was trying not to make assumptions for once.

"He hasn't wasted much time if it is." Matt grimaced.

Jerry's Bar was already heaving with people spilling out into the street.

"Looks like a popular place," Ace commented, trying to ignore the odd looks they were receiving from some of the men in starched suits. He removed his hat before going inside, where the noise assaulted his eardrums. Tuneless rock music blared from behind the bar, and people were crammed around small tables, while the guys had to squeeze their way through to the counter.

Matt ordered a couple of beers, shouting to make himself heard.

"Hey, man, where are the rest of the Village People?" the guy next to him piped up with a grin.

Matt removed his hat, smiling. "You here with the bachelor party?"

The guy nodded. "What else? Sure is a popular guy, ain't he?"

Ace looked around. They had no idea what Phil Cartwright looked like, so the only person they could rule out was the guy they were talking to.

"Sure is. You known him long?" Matt asked, casually leaning on the counter.

"A few months. You?"

"A while." Matt nodded. "But we haven't seen him lately."

"Yeah, I gathered that. Not exactly from around here, are you, boys?"

Ace looked at the guy's suit pants with sharp creases down the front and his white shirt and loosened tie.

"What makes you think that?" he asked, ironically.

Before the guy could reply, they were joined by another suit.

"Hey, no one told me it was a costume party."

Ace frowned. "You mean you didn't get the memo?"

The guy looked puzzled for a minute, then laughed.

Ace took a swig of his beer, already bored at the banter. "So, how well do you know the victim?" he asked the newcomer.

"We all work together, don't we, Isaac?" the guy replied, chuckling as he took his drink from the barman.

"We sure do. Though he's only been with us a short while," the first guy, Isaac, said.

"Where do y'all work?" Matt asked.

"Access Accounting, just over the road there," the other guy replied, pointing his beer-glass in the direction of the door, as though that would explain everything.

Ace nodded. "I'm Ace, by the way. This here's Matt."

They all nodded to each other.

"Trev," the new guy offered, "and I assume you've already met Isaac?"

They nodded again.

"It's real nice to meet you, guys. We were a little worried with not knowing any of the locals and all," Matt said with a grin.

"We'll have to introduce you," Trev offered. "These guys behind us are the technical support guys, like Phil." The three men turned and smiled at them. "This is Paul, Jack and Robert."

"Howdy, guys," Matt offered, clearly playing up to the redneck image they all seemed to take him and Ace to be.

There were mumblings of greeting before Trev pounced on his next victims. "That there's Theo and the one with the mustache is Benny." He pointed to the two men to Matt's right, who turned and nodded to them.

Then Trev frowned, looking over the bar. "Oh my God, look who's here."

Isaac looked over, then he frowned too. "Was he invited, d'you reckon?"

"Must have been. Well, that's one major suck-up, if you ask me."

Ace and Matt craned their necks to see who the guys were talking about and noticed an older man in a smart sports jacket and tie sitting over at the other side of the counter, which surrounded the bar in a sort of U-shape.

"Who's that?" Ace asked.

"Senator Grady," Trev revealed. "Uncle and guardian of the bride-to-be."

Matt and Ace exchanged a look. *This just got interesting.*

"Is he any good?" Matt wanted to know.

"I'd say," Isaac replied with a nod. "He sure has shaken things up over there with his 'honesty is the best policy' motto. Folks are having to watch themselves, and make sure they're squeaky clean now that he's arrived. Any skeletons in closets and they're out. Grady won't stand for any adverse exposure."

Ace tried to hide the grin that spread over his face. This was music to his ears. Judging by Matt's expression, he was thinking the same thing.

"Is the men's room around here?" Ace asked Trev.

The cowboy sauntered over past the senator to find the restroom — not because he desperately needed to pee but it couldn't hurt to get a little closer to their mark, and bathrooms were great places for gossip.

Sure enough, there was a very loud discussion in place about the upcoming wedding when he reached the urinals. It seemed that some of the men weren't as keen on the groom as others, and tempers were already becoming a little frayed.

"He hasn't known her five minutes," the guy beside him was yelling to no one in particular. "How long's he been here? A few months? That's not long enough to fall in love and propose, is it?"

"Of course it is," someone hollered from one of the stalls. "Haven't you ever heard of love at first sight?"

"Doesn't exist," someone from the washbasins shouted up. "It's a myth put about by gold-diggers, if you ask me."

"Which no one did!" someone else from the urinals pointed out.

It seemed Isaac had been wrong about the popularity of the groom, although there were plenty of people who appeared to have just come along for the free food.

"It's no wonder the senator's so against the whole thing," someone grumbled from behind Ace.

"Is that right?" he asked, going over to wash his hands.

"Yeah. He's footing the bill for Sabrina's sake, but he's not convinced it's the right thing," the guy next to him replied.

Ace nodded, then left the room. He went straight over to the bar where the senator stood drinking alone.

"Senator Grady, could I buy you a drink, sir?"

The man turned around, clearly surprised. "Thank you, boy. That's very kind of you."

The bartender obliged.

"Sit down, son," the senator offered, gesturing to the empty stool beside him.

"Thank you, sir. I'm new in town. My name's Ace Blenheim." He offered his hand, which the older man shook with a smile. "I've heard nothing but good things about you, so I thought I'd come over and say hi. I hope that's okay?"

"Sure. That's real nice to hear. You a friend of the groom, I take it?"

"Not personally, sir. I'm with a friend who knows him," Ace replied.

The senator nodded.

"I heard it's your niece that's about to tie the knot?" Ace went on.

"That's the plan," the older guy said with a sigh.

"Do you know the groom well?"

The senator raised his eyebrows. "To be honest, Phil Cartwright hasn't been in town long enough for *any* of us to know him all that well." He pursed his lips. "It was quite a shock when my little Bri announced he'd asked her to marry him, I can tell you."

Ace breathed a silent sigh of relief. At last he could be sure their suspicions were correct, and Phil *was* the groom in question. "I was surprised when my buddy told me, to be honest."

Senator Grady frowned. "I thought you said you didn't know him?"

"I don't, sir." He shook his head. "But most people around New Moldington know *of* him — after the last time, I mean." He hastily put a hand up in submission. "Not that I'm suggesting it's anything like that *this* time. Of course, I don't know anything about the situation, so I'm not casting aspersions or anything."

As hoped, the senator's interest was clearly piqued, and he turned to face Ace head-on. "What do you mean?"

"I was just referring to the last time he got engaged…to Rihanna Richards."

The senator frowned. "He's done this before?"

"He proposed, yes. Dumped her just before the big day, though," he confided in a low voice. "Not that I'm suggesting — "

"What happened?" The senator's voice was quite sharp, his face tense.

"I'm not trying to make trouble or anything," Ace assured him, suddenly feeling sorry for the guy's niece.

"If you know something, son, you'd better spit it out." He spoke through gritted teeth.

Ace took another swig of his beer before replying. "Okay. Well, I happen to know that he hasn't paid for *that* wedding yet. Any of it. He disappeared, leaving Rihanna to pay all the expenses. She's drowning in debt, thanks to him, and he owes her. She left town to escape the shame of it all." He might have been exaggerating a little, not being sure of all the facts, of course, but it all added to the angst in the older man's face.

"Is that right?" The senator was visibly seething.

"Not that I'm suggesting anything here. I mean, I presume he's paid for it all *this* time — especially with you in your position and everything."

"What do you mean?" Grady frowned.

"Well, 'honesty is the best policy' and all that. And with him having such a great job now, I'm sure he wouldn't make anyone else pay for *this* wedding, would he? I mean, it's not like he can't afford it, with all the money he saved last time, letting his girl pay for the wedding *and* all the household stuff. He must have quite a stash put away for this event."

Grady gaped at him.

Ace leaned forward conspiratorially. "I wouldn't have said anything, sir. It's just with you being such a high-profile figure and all, I'd hate for it to come out that your niece's husband is still in so much debt to his former fiancée for the bills he left her with. You've got your reputation to maintain, after all, and I, for one, really admire you for that."

The senator narrowed his eyes. "You're sure of all this, are you?"

Ace nodded. "Rihanna reported it all to the sheriff over in Cavern County, but he can't do anything unless she wants to pursue it through the court, which she can't afford to do right now. She's got plenty receipts and stuff, if you need proof. I don't think she's decided about going to the papers or not yet. It's all so raw for her, being less than a year ago and all."

The senator's eyes widened at the mention of the press and he was glad the message had gotten through loud and clear.

A ruckus from the men's room made them both look over, as a couple of guys came rolling out, fists flying and blood splattering the floor. It sounded like another fight was going on inside, and there was yelling and goading, as though they were in a high school yard.

Grady shot to his feet and strode right over to the guys brawling on the ground.

"When you've finished with him, tell him I'll see him in my office first thing tomorrow," the senator instructed the guy who was on top.

Ace looked at the sniveling bastard on the floor. Even in this light it was clear he wasn't in a great way. The other guy straddled him and gave him another whack across the nose, causing Cartwright to wail loudly. Ace wanted to memorize this scene for a long time.

"Seems like that guy's saved you a lot of trouble," Matt muttered into his ear from behind him.

Ace wasn't entirely sure whether that was a good thing or not.

* * * *

Rihanna was relieved that it was Friday the following day. Ace had sent her a message last night, checking she was okay and telling her he'd been called out of town with Matt, so wasn't able to see her. She was actually quite relieved to be given some space and time to think things through.

Waking up the following morning, she wondered if she hadn't been a little too hard on Ace, telling him it wouldn't work between them. The truth was, she wanted it to work more than anything, but she was scared of being hurt again. She was glad he'd opened up about his past relationship, and she understood better why he acted as impulsively as he did. He must have been scared of being hurt, too.

She smiled when she walked into the bank and saw the third counter ready for a new teller. Life was already easier with Betsy replacing Paul, and Sarah couldn't do enough to try to make up for the way she'd treated her. With another teller, it would be much easier to get her own work done, instead of having to help out at busier times, although even that would be much simpler with the extra cashier point in place.

Her smile widened, however, when she received a call from Mr. Treadwell to ask about the new counter and to update her on Mr. Williamson's position.

"We told him he was going to be demoted back to being a teller for a while," he told her, the smile evident in his voice. "After all, he'd made a really lousy area manager. We planned to send him out to Brandon County, but it didn't seem to appeal to him at all. In fact, he resigned on the spot."

And that wasn't the *only* surprising phone call she took that day...

Chapter Twenty-Four

Ace was surprised when Rihanna smiled as soon as she saw him that evening. He'd been avoiding the bank, for fear of upsetting her again, but had to drop into town to visit the hardware store after work. Rihanna was just on her way back to her apartment.

"How's it goin'?" he asked with a grin.

"Great. Mr. Treadwell arranged for a new counter to be put into the bank, and I've got another cashier here from the Almondine branch until he gets time to get help me interview for another permanent teller." The relief was evident in her pretty face, and he couldn't help feeling happy for her. He hadn't noticed just how tense she'd appeared until recently, but now she really seemed to be enjoying life again. He just wished she was enjoying life with *him*.

"I knew he was a good guy as soon as I met him," Ace replied, nodding.

Rihanna narrowed her eyes. "Oddly enough, someone else said that about *you* today," she said.

He couldn't hide his surprise. That wasn't something he heard very often.

"Really?" He raised his eyebrows.

She nodded. "Have you got a minute?" she asked, a little cagily.

"Sure."

He followed her up the steps to her apartment and went inside. It was as clean and tidy as usual, and he sat on a stool by the breakfast bar.

"Coffee?" She quickly put the pot on and reached into the refrigerator for a milk carton. She emptied it into the drinks, then went over toward the trash can to dispose of it.

"Here...let me." He took it from her, and she went back over to fetch the coffees. Ace couldn't help noticing how many scrunched-up Kleenexes were in her rubbish, and inwardly berated himself for being the cause of her upset, yet again.

"Rihanna, I'm real sorry," he began, as soon as they sat down with their drinks. "I always seem to do or say the wrong thing, and I really regret making you cry."

"It's okay." She shook her head, her voice soft. "I know you mean well."

"I do," he assured her. "I just get it all wrong half the time." He sighed. "I don't know why. I guess I just feel a little nervous around you and I—"

"*Nervous?*" She frowned.

He tentatively stroked her hand across the table. "I meant what I said," he confessed. "I really am in love with you."

She was blushing a little...and smiling. She opened her mouth to speak, but he forged ahead while he kept his nerve.

"When I'm around you, I'm so afraid of upsetting you that I do exactly that," he explained with a self-deprecating smile. "My brain's telling me to go careful and think before I say or do anything, but my heart's pounding so darn fast that I just say whatever's on my mind without thinking. *And* I jump to conclusions way too quick." He shook his head.

"I get it," she told him, gently.

He gaped. "You do?"

She nodded, smiling. "You fear the worst, and so it's the first thing you think of — like with the ring. If you'd thought about it carefully, you'd have realized that it was way too shiny to have been worn at all. And I don't have a mark around my finger. Look." She held up her hand, which was devoid of any rings or marks to ever suggest she wore them.

"I'm sorry." He didn't know what else to say. He could see that she was right.

"I know." She shrugged. "That guy was right. You *are* a good guy."

He frowned as she took a long sip of her drink. "Who said that?"

She narrowed her eyes in thought. "Senator something-or-other."

His eyes widened as she gave him a knowing look.

"He called me today."

Ace swallowed hard. This could easily go either of two ways, and he didn't want to preempt anything, despite the twist in his gut. "Did he now? And what did he want?" He hardly dared ask.

"To ask me how much money Phil Cartwright owed me." She spoke slowly, before taking another sip of her coffee. "Apparently, he knows him. In fact, Phil was all set to marry his niece until last night."

Ace straightened his back, trying to gauge where this was going. "Is that right?"

She nodded. "Yeah. A couple of cowboys rode into town and stirred things up a little, so I hear."

"Uh-huh?"

"He spoke to Phil this morning and asked him all about some allegations one of them had made about him owing money for a wedding that didn't happen."

Ace cleared his throat, trying to calm his breathing. He couldn't read her. She was either real pissed about all this or taking it remarkably well.

"It seems the senator can't have a guy marrying into his family who's so deep in debt, especially to me. It's not good for his reputation. And" — she eyed him carefully — "if the *press* should hear of it, a man in his position would never live it down, especially when they heard that Phil actually left his last bride high and dry with all the wedding debts to take care of by herself while he fled town." She frowned. "Now who on *earth* would go all the way over to Hepworth to tell a senator all about that, do you reckon?" She folded her arms, looking at him expectantly.

He quickly put his hands up in an appeasing manner. "I can explain," he assured her. "Just hear me out, okay?"

"Oh, I intend to," she replied, raising her eyebrows. "Don't you worry about that. After all, I could jump to all manner of conclusions over something like this, but what good would that do? I'd rather hear what actually happened, straight from the horse's mouth — or, in this case, its rider's."

He stood, still holding his coffee cup. "Could we get a little more comfortable? It's rather a long story."

A smile teased her lips. "Sure. I can't wait to hear this."

He still wasn't sure if she was being snarky or if she genuinely meant what she said, so he chose to go with the latter, for once — at least, for now.

"I hate what that guy did to you, darlin'," he admitted when they were sitting comfortably on the sofa. He'd angled his body toward her, keen to watch her expression as she heard what went on. He shook his head. "And I couldn't let that dumbass get away with it."

"Really?" She raised her eyebrows.

"You'd better believe it, baby." He leaned forward a little. "Like I said before, I love you, and I can't bear to see you treated like that."

"So…?"

He scrubbed a hand over his face, unsure of how to word what he had to say. "So, Matt and I took a ride out to Hepworth last night to see what Cartwright planned to do about it."

Her eyes widened. "You spoke to him?"

He quickly shook his head, putting a hand up to calm her. "No, sweetheart. Neither of us spoke to him — or laid a finger on him, for that matter."

She nodded, clearly relieved.

He bit his lip before continuing. "We heard he was planning to wed the senator's niece, so I went up and had a quiet word, that's all."

She frowned. "But you just said…?"

He shook his head. "The quiet word was with the *senator*," he clarified.

"I see."

"He already didn't like Cartwright much. Felt that it was too soon for him to fall in love and propose to his niece when he hadn't been in town five minutes. He didn't want to upset her, though, so I think he was prepared to go through with it."

She nodded.

"I happened to mention that he hadn't paid for his last wedding yet."

She gaped at him, her eyes wide. "You *what*?"

"He was mighty interested in what I told him about all the debt he'd left behind when he skipped town. Last I heard, he was going to have a word with Cartwright this morning when he'd finished partying."

"He had a *word* with him, all right," Rihanna told him. "Told him he had to pay back every penny he owed before he could even *think* about going out with his niece again!"

"Well, that's good, ain't it?" Ace frowned, not sure of himself.

"It's good for me. The senator asked me how much he owed and put the money into my account right away. He's going to get every penny back from Phil but felt it only fair that I didn't have to wait a minute longer, as I was paying interest on the debt. In fact, he paid me even more to cover the interest I'd already paid. Phil's going to be in debt to him for a long time, I reckon."

Ace shrugged. "He can afford it. He's got a good job, by all accounts."

She looked surprised at the revelation but said nothing.

"You don't look all that happy about it?" Ace was still trying to read her, but to no avail. It was almost like she didn't know how she felt herself about what had happened.

"What about that poor girl? She was planning to marry him. How will she feel now?"

"Like she's had a lucky escape, I should think." Ace knew straight away he'd said the wrong thing.

She narrowed her eyes, and he felt his world come crashing down once again.

"Like *I* did, you mean?" she snapped. "So that's all right then, is it?"

"No." He immediately scooted nearer to her, until he could feel her heat against his body. "That's not what I meant. It's just… She was spared everything you went through. And you said yourself, the senator didn't say he could *never* marry her — just that he had to pay off his debts first. I'm sure she knew nothing about any of this and would have been devastated to have married him just to find he was up to his ears in bills he didn't pay from his last relationship, wouldn't she?" He was thinking on his feet, his heart racing, but he tried to keep his voice calm and soft.

Rihanna looked thoughtful for a moment, then shrugged. "But he hadn't been planning to pay any of it back, so he wouldn't have considered himself in debt."

"That doesn't mean he *wasn't,* just because he chose not to acknowledge it," Ace pointed out.

She sighed. "I just hope you haven't ruined that girl's life just to make mine better."

He grabbed her hands. "I haven't. Listen to me. That guy's a senator. He's come into town with his 'honesty is the best policy' mantra and is sticking it to anyone who's not a hundred percent squeaky clean in that office. You can't tell me none of his competitors are gonna be looking to find something on him? And if they did any background checks on his niece's husband

and found all this out, then how the heck would that pan out? Senator Grady would lose face and probably lose his dang job. Where would that leave his niece?"

Rihanna sighed. "I hadn't thought of it that way."

"Like I said, we've done them all a favor, baby."

"That's what *he* said."

"What?" Ace frowned.

"That senator…Grady. He said you were a straight-up guy and he appreciated you alerting him to all this before it was too late." She bit her lip.

He sat up again. "A straight-up guy, hey?"

"You mind that head of yours on the way out the door, cowboy. Something tells me it won't fit like it did on the way in. You might even need to buy a bigger hat." She swatted him playfully with a cushion, making them both laugh.

"Who says I'm going out that door, baby? I reckon you and I have got some celebrating to do tonight." He reached for her and took her soft lips in a kiss that instantly made him rock hard. Dang, that girl had some effect on him!

Rihanna's heart pounded as she allowed Ace to take her hand and lead her to the bedroom. He took her in his arms and kissed the living daylights out of her — not that she was complaining in the slightest.

She put a hand to her swollen lips when he finally released her mouth. She'd never experienced anything like it and hoped there were more where that came from. It was a good thing that he was standing so darn close, as she was sure she might have fallen over otherwise.

He grinned as he slowly unbuttoned her blouse, and she immediately reciprocated with his shirt. Ace was just heeling off his boots when he cursed, shaking his head.

"What is it?" She frowned, suddenly afraid she'd misread his signals.

"I just need to go to the truck," he said, with a sigh, pulling his boots back on.

"Can't it wait?" She couldn't hide her disappointment.

He grimaced. "Nope. It'll only take a minute." He kissed the top of her head, tucking his shirt back in, but didn't bother to fasten the buttons. "You just get comfortable and wait for me."

She watched him go, puzzled. He sure looked disappointed at having to leave, so she surmised she'd done nothing wrong, but it really was lousy timing!

Taking the opportunity to freshen up a little, she combed her hair and sprayed on more perfume. She felt lighter than air now that her debts had gone – and elated that it had been Ace who had made it happen. He must really care about her to do something like that, and she adored him for it.

The door opened again.

"That was quick." She narrowed her eyes at him, still wondering what he was up to.

"That's the only time you'll be saying that tonight," he replied with a grin full of promise.

She gaped at him. "Oh, really?"

He nodded. "Yup. And I thought you were supposed to be getting more comfortable?"

She shook her head. "I didn't think..."

"Good. I don't want you to."

"What?" She frowned.

"Think. Just feel. *Me,* preferably." He winked and pulled her back into the bedroom, already unbuttoning the rest of her blouse, which he threw on the floor before leaning her carefully back onto the bed.

"I think I could manage that," she decided with a salacious grin as she reached for his belt.

He'd already kicked off his boots when she pulled at his zipper and had a tough job pulling it down over the swelling in his pants.

With a deep chuckle, he threw off his shirt then put his hand down to help her out.

She gasped, not just at the size of it but also at the fact that he'd gone commando—a brave move, given his line of work.

"I need to get some laundry done," he confessed with a lopsided grin, clearly reading her mind. "Matt was lucky I had a spare pair of Levi's to put on this morning."

She gaped at him. "Not just Matt—I'll bet the horses were mighty glad, too. They tend to scare easily, don't forget."

"Well, as long as you don't, that's all that matters." His voice was a low growl that did wicked things to her girly parts.

"I must admit it's the biggest one I've ever seen," she admitted, thoughtfully.

"I won't hurt you, baby," he promised, lifting her farther up the bed, so her head lay on the soft pillow. "Trust me."

Gazing into his handsome, flushed face, she nodded. "I do."

"I like the way you said that," he said, stroking her cheek as he lay over her, taking his weight on one elbow. "Maybe you'll say it to me for a different reason one day."

She gaped, realizing what he was suggesting. Her whole body felt hot, and it wasn't just because of his heat that surrounded her. Suddenly, a vision of standing opposite him reciting her marriage vows flashed before her eyes—and it wasn't half as scary as it should have been."

Studying her face, he leaned back slightly. "Sorry, babe. Was that a little presumptuous? I mean, it's probably a little soon, especially after—"

Rihanna shook her head, concerned at the anxiety in his expression. "No, not at all."

He visibly relaxed and his eyes twinkled as he neared her again. "I'm not suggesting rushing into anything. It was just a thought that crossed my mind."

She grinned. "When you realized you'd run out of clean underwear, you mean?"

He let out a loud laugh, his whole body rocking. "Well, now that you mention it..."

She narrowed her eyes at him, playfully. "And you were doing so well, too."

His eyes flashed and he leaned his face over hers. "Was I, now? When I was doing this, you mean?"

Rihanna's whole body melted under his, as his soft kiss smothered her in a haze of happiness.

Ace wasted no time in divesting her of the remainder of her clothes, without even breaking contact with her lips. He continued his sensual assault down her body, where he sucked and pulled at her right nipple, causing her to moan and writhe beneath him.

She reached her arms around his taut back, one hand stroking his hair, while the other ventured farther south as she trailed a finger down his spine. Reaching his ass, she couldn't resist squeezing it hard, delighting at the whimper of arousal that escaped his throat, despite him now having his mouth full of her left breast.

His breath was hot on her body, making her shudder as he ventured farther down, planting wet kisses over her stomach, then down to her throbbing pussy. She hissed as he covered her mound with his mouth and circled her clit, which felt like it would explode at any minute

"Ace," she whispered urgently.

He looked up at her, his fingers replacing his tongue momentarily as he checked her expression. "What is it, baby?"

"I want you." She panted the words out.

"Are you sure?"

"Yess-s."

She heard his deep chuckle as he used one foot to kick his jeans closer then lift them to his hand, before rummaging in the back pocket. Glancing down, she watched him quickly sheath his massive cock.

"You...?" she whispered, her mind whirling.

"Shh-h."

He leaned over her, his face nearing hers again, as she felt his thick cock nudge at her pussy. Any thoughts she might have been having dissipated into thin air at his touch.

With a loud moan, she spread her legs wider to welcome his tremendous girth. His lips once again covered hers, sending electricity thrumming through her body, culminating in her pussy, where she felt every inch of him as he invaded her.

He'd been right about not hurting her, though she felt herself stretch more than ever before. She loved the feel of him and relaxed to allow him to take over completely, her mind full of joyful mush as she lost herself in a wave of euphoria.

As he heaved in and out of her, he nudged her clit, sending delicious shivers that racked her whole body.

She panted for breath, digging her short nails into his shoulders as she rose toward her orgasm.

"That's it, baby. Keep going," he urged, his own voice sounding a little strangled as he was clearly struggling to control his own climax.

"I'm coming," she yelped, as colors danced in front of her eyes.

"Even better." Relief was evident in his voice, as she felt him swell even more before they both tumbled over the edge together, her screaming his name and him letting out a feral roar.

She clung to him as she finally eased back to earth, becoming more aware of his weight and heat as she neared some semblance of normalcy.

His breathing began to slow as he carefully removed himself from her and rolled over before standing up and making for the bathroom.

Rihanna was grateful for a minute to catch her own breath and lie with her eyes closed, still reeling from the amazing experience, which was certainly unlike anything she'd ever felt before.

She opened her eyes upon hearing him return to the room and was surprised at how dark it was, despite the drapes still being pulled back. The bed dipped as he gently lay next to her, toying with her hair, and taking her lips in a soft, lingering kiss.

Something stirred inside her again, and for a second, she wondered if she might be about to come once more. Her arms were wrapped around his neck, and she could feel his body tense slightly.

His deep chuckle told her that he'd read her mind, and he released her mouth.

"You're insatiable, woman."

"Only with you," she admitted, a little shyly.

"Well, that's all right then." He hugged her tight.

"You came prepared," she said, suddenly remembering how he'd cut her off last time she was about to mention it.

He pulled back slightly, stroking her cheek with his thumb.

"I didn't want a repeat of last time," he admitted, "and, besides, I knew you didn't keep any condoms here. I didn't want to be presumptuous, and I never usually carry them around with me anyhow, but I kind of hoped we might get to this point sometime soon, so I bought some and kept them in the truck. Of course, I didn't think for a moment that tonight would be the night, so they were still there when we started getting…close." He tipped her face up and studied it, despite the shadows that fell on them. "I hope that was okay?"

His concerned expression tugged at her heart, and she nodded. "Of course. In fact, it was a good thing you did." She smiled before reaching up to kiss him.

She looked around the room, glad that it was too dark to see the remaining boxes that were stacked in the corner. "I'm sorry we had to be surrounded by all this stuff," she said with a sigh. "I wish I'd left them in storage, but I just couldn't afford to keep paying the bill."

He shrugged. "It's fine. Next time, I hope it'll be *our* wedding things that fill the place, though." His voice was soft with just a hint of humor.

Rihanna gaped at him, not really sure what to think. "Wow, you really *do* want someone to wash your socks for you, don't you?" she quipped back.

"Among other things," he said with a chuckle, before taking her lips in another dangerously searing kiss.

Want to see more from this author? Here's a taster for you to enjoy!

Her Harem:
Romance at Richadam Ranch
Bella Settarra

Excerpt

Charlotte Priestley sighed as she pulled up outside the apartment block she'd called home for the past two years. It was a gray building with not enough windows and looked as bleak as she felt. At two in the morning, she knew she'd have to hurry to bed to have a chance of getting any sleep before her next shift started at six. That meant leaving at a quarter past five at the latest, giving her a full three-and-a-quarter hours of rest if she were lucky. The humidity in the air would usually hinder her efforts to sleep, but she had a feeling that wouldn't be a problem after working a grueling sixteen-hour double-shift.

It was raining as she hauled her tired body out of the car, and she ran full-tilt across the parking lot to get into the dry. Unfortunately, the place wasn't lit, and she tripped on a large stone and hurtled to the pavement with a loud scream. Pain throbbed from her hands and knees, where she'd tried to break her fall, and she quickly scrabbled back to her feet, double-checking that she'd zipped her purse shut so nothing could have fallen out.

As expected, no one came to her aid, despite her yell, but—she had to admit—at this hour no one would be about, and even if they'd heard her, they'd hardly venture out in the dark.

She was well-used to the feeling of dread that enveloped her as she unlocked the door to the apartment and was surprised to find the light still on in the living room. Hurriedly, she pulled off her coat and hung it, with her purse, in the hall, before venturing into the room to see what kind of mood Anthony was in tonight.

The glare on his face spoke volumes, and, as if needed, the whiskey glass in his hand added another few Chapters.

"What time do you call this?" he demanded, a supercilious expression on his face. She used to think that face was really handsome, but just lately, she'd seen past the smarmy façade and had begun to see him for who he really was.

"We're still short-staffed in the kitchen, and I couldn't leave it in a mess," she replied, with a sigh. "And I fell in the car park." She gestured to her knees.

"I think you mean parking lot," he told her, an incredulous sneer now crossing his features.

"Car park was good enough for you in London," she reminded him, crossing the room to reach the kitchen as blood dripped down her legs.

"We're not in London anymore—or hadn't you noticed?" he called after her as she switched on the light and reached for the first-aid kit.

"I'm well aware of that," she assured him, slipping off her shoes and then pulling off her torn tights, which she put straight into the rubbish bin.

"What's that supposed to mean? And what the hell are you doing?" He was craning his neck to see, his curiosity clearly getting the better of him.

"I've just removed my pantyhose and thrown them into the trash," she replied, putting on a very exaggerated American accent.

"Very funny." He sneered again.

She quickly wiped the blood and dirt from her wounds before covering them in a couple of clean dressings, then returned the box to the shelf, switched off the light and went back into the living room.

"I asked you a question," he snapped, stopping her in her tracks as she walked across the room.

She was planning to head straight for bed, but shot back around to face him, shocked at his attitude. She wondered just how many glasses of whiskey he'd had tonight. "What question?" Her brain was almost too tired to think.

"What was that crack about being well aware we're not in London?"

She frowned, annoyed that he wanted to continue talking. "Oh, just...you know. Things are so different here. *You're* much different than how you were back there."

"In what way?" His jaw tensed.

She put a hand to her mouth, covering a yawn. "It doesn't matter. I need to get to bed. I'm on the breakfast shift again tomorrow. Stacey's still off sick, remember?"

"I am aware of the staff situation in my own hotel, yes." His upper lip curled in a snarl, his speech slightly slurred.

"Then I suggest you need to do something about it," she replied, curtly. "I can't keep working all these hours. I'm sure Health and Safety would have a fieldday if they knew I was working all these eighteen-hour shifts, especially as I'm in charge of machinery and all those cooking appliances. And it's certainly not safe for me to be driving home afterward."

"I think you'll find the rules are a bit different over here, love," he replied in a patronizing tone. "Besides, we're advertising for new staff, but we just haven't found the right people yet. And you know what you can do if you're not happy working there."

She raised her eyebrows, staring at him. "You'd want me to leave, would you?"

He shrugged before taking another long sip of his drink. "You didn't *have* to follow me all the way over the Atlantic, begging for a job if you're not happy. It was *your* choice."

"You *asked* me to come to the States with you, Anthony, and you know it. You said the hotel was in need of a decent chef, and you set up my interview with Chris Sempleworth. You said you wanted us to live together over here — and to work together." The words almost got caught in her throat as she fought back the tears. She knew things were a little rocky between them right now, but she'd hoped that would change once he'd settled into his promotion and she'd stopped having to work such long hours.

"Yeah, and you've done nothing but moan since you got here. And lately it's been worse than ever. The apartment's too small, it's too far to travel to and from work, your hours are too long and now — "

"I'm working much longer hours than you and for a lot less money," she reminded him. "And you agreed this place is too small and said yourself it's a lot farther from work than you thought when we moved in here."

"I've never complained about the commute."

"*You* get to stay at the hotel if you have to work a long shift. *I* don't, and I work a lot more back-to-back shifts than you do."

"*You're* not management."

"I was when I was head chef at The Royal Windsor."

"The Royal Windsor Hotel's in London. Things are different here."

"So you keep saying." She sighed, taking another step toward the door. She desperately needed some sleep.

"And you don't *have* to drive all this way. You could walk. It'd do you good."

She glared at him. "It's miles, and you know it. It takes nearly an hour to drive it, for goodness' sake. By the time I walked home, it'd be time to start my next shift."

"Then run. It's about time you took up some decent exercise. It would help you shift a few pounds. And…you really need to, don't you, love?"

Charlotte's whole body began to shake as she fought back more tears and tried to tamp down her anger. He only ever used the term 'love' ironically, to belittle her. "You can be really mean sometimes, d'you know that?"

"The truth always hurts." He shrugged. "You've got to admit you've really piled on the weight since leaving England. You used to be so slim and pretty." He took another swig of his whiskey, clearly oblivious to the tears that flooded her face.

She opened her mouth to defend herself but closed it again when she realized she couldn't speak. The lump in her throat was too big. Instead, she turned and left the room, saving her sobs for her pillow.

* * * *

It seemed like only five minutes later when her alarm invaded her dreams. Although still shattered, she was relieved to be awake. Her thoughts must have been in such turmoil that she'd given herself nightmares — not the sort that you remember when you wake, but the kind that leave you feeling immensely sad and on edge. There were no prizes for guessing what had been on her mind as she'd drifted off. She hadn't even taken the time to undress before flopping onto the bed, and now she felt uncomfortable and irritable.

A hot shower helped wake her a little, and she felt better as she pulled on a clean dress. When she glanced in the mirror, her hand immediately fell to her stomach. It was much bigger than when she'd arrived in the States, but then, she hardly had any time to exercise. Working long shifts meant grabbing food on the go, and that was usually not the healthiest of choices, especially as it was summer and far too hot for a cooked meal. She'd describe herself as plump, nicely rounded — curvaceous even, but not fat. There were many really large people who came to eat at the hotel, and she certainly wasn't as big as they were. She stood tall. Anthony was just being horrid again, and she was determined not to let him upset her anymore.

Noticing the time, she rushed to the kitchen, passing a snoring lump on the couch on her way. She hadn't expected Anthony to join her in the bed last night — he rarely did these days — and he'd clearly drunk himself into a stupor. He was due into work this morning, but not for another couple of hours. If she woke him now, he'd only be nasty to her again, so she left him where he was.

After filling her travel mug with hot coffee, she whizzed out of the apartment and carefully walked over to her car. The sun was rising, and it was already quite warm. Her knees still stung from the previous night's fall, and her hands ached as she clutched the steering wheel. Blue bruises had begun to appear on her fingers where she'd tried to steady herself last night, and she winced, knowing that the pain was bound to plague her all day.

She was right. As she went about her work, her hands throbbed, getting worse every time she lifted a heavy pot or pan. There was no point in moaning about it, though. It had been her own stupid fault for not looking where she was going. With hindsight, she realized she should have used the torch on her phone, but she'd been too tired to think of that at the time.

"Have you and Anthony had another fight?" Kayleigh burst into the kitchen, wide-eyed. She was the head waitress and really good at her job. She wasn't so great in the tact department though, unfortunately.

"I haven't spoken to him all day," Charlotte replied, hoping to deflect the question, which, she noticed, her own staff as well as a couple of waitresses seemed interested to hear the answer to. *Thanks, Kayleigh!*

"Well, something's crawled up his bony ass." Kayleigh rolled her eyes. "He's been in a foul mood all morning!"

"Yeah, bring back Chris," Lucy, another waitress, chimed in. "At least we knew where we stood with him in charge. Anthony's emotions are all over the place. You just don't know what you're going to get whenever he opens his mouth."

"You try living with him." Charlotte hoped a little humor might help the situation. After all, everyone had known from the start that she and Anthony were a couple. It didn't seem to matter when he was the deputy manager, but since his promotion to general manager, it was starting to become more than a little embarrassing. Whenever he made a decision that was unpopular with the staff, they came to her to moan about it—as if she had a say in anything! As Anthony had taken such delight in telling her earlier, she wasn't management there.

She noticed that he hadn't come into the restaurant for a meal today, which was a little unusual. It was common practice for the manager to dine with at least one of his heads of department, using the time to heighten their profile with the guests, as well as discussing any matters that needed their attention. It was deemed a good time-saver, too. After all, everyone had to eat, didn't they? This was supposed to kill two birds with one stone. However, she had noticed that it seemed to just enable Anthony to prolong his lunch break, while enjoying a few too many glasses of wine.

As soon as service was over, she went to find him, just to make sure he was okay. He was often found in the reception area, flaunting his new position in front of the guests, but today he was nowhere to be seen. She went down the corridor to his office and was surprised that Hannah, his PA, called over to her.

"I'm afraid Mr. Mortimer can't be disturbed right now," she informed her, in a tone way too formal for Charlotte's liking.

Why Anthony had suddenly decided the manager needed a PA was a mystery, as it certainly wasn't the norm in any hotel she'd ever worked in. If anything, the reception manager would take on that sort of role, along with their own, but it was hardly considered necessary. And the slim, beautiful blonde he'd chosen for the role was definitely out to make her presence felt.

"He'll see me," Charlotte assured her, stalking past her desk and up to the door.

"He won't see anyone," Hannah insisted, jumping to her feet and heading for the office door herself.

Charlotte shot her a suspicious frown before quickly pouncing on the handle and opening the door. Her jaw dropped, and she felt suddenly very hot as her skin prickled at the sight before her. She'd seen Anthony's arse many times, of course, but not from this angle. His trousers were down around his ankles as he pounded a woman, who was lying — naked, it seemed — across his desk.

"No, you can't — " Hannah wailed, but she was too late.

Anthony must have heard her as he spun his head around and he gave Charlotte a look she'd never seen before. He had clearly been in the throes of passion, as his face was still slightly contorted and red, but his expression was unreadable. *Part guilt, part supercilious*, she decided. It was almost as if he'd wanted to be caught, though he still looked a little shocked.

Charlotte dropped her gaze to the girl on the desk, who was now craning her neck to see why her lover had stopped moving. At least Melanie, the pretty brunette from finance, had the decency to look embarrassed.

Charlotte's instinct was to walk away, but her legs felt like lead, her eyes compelled to keep staring at the couple at the desk. Despite her mouth still being wide open, she couldn't think of a thing to say. It was like a scene from a movie, when suddenly everything seemed to start happening in slow motion.

Anthony's expression turned into a familiar sneer, and she felt him laughing at her. Melanie began pulling her clothes over herself, while Hannah quickly became quite animated in her attempts to remove Charlotte from the doorway.

"Come on." Hannah tugged at her arm, but Charlotte was still unable to move. "You need to leave," the PA insisted.

"Unless you want to join us?" Anthony jeered, raising one eyebrow in question.

That was the point when Charlotte came to her senses. "How could you?" she murmured, before turning on her heel and walking away.

She marched back to the kitchen, dazed, which was just as well, as she knew the tears she was fighting back would fall all too soon, and she wasn't prepared to show her feelings in front of the staff. She hurried into the staff changing room and pulled off her chef's whites before hauling on her dress, emptying all her belongings from her locker into a bag and heading out to her car.

Even then, the floodgates didn't open, as she stared at the road ahead and put her foot down, hardly noticing the journey as she zoomed back to the apartment. It wasn't until she was packing up all her things into her suitcase that she felt the familiar thud in her stomach, and she collapsed on the bed in a fit of hot tears. It was over. She was alone in a foreign country with no home and no job.

What the hell am I supposed to do now?

About the Author

Bella Settarra is a British Erotic Romance author and lives in the beautiful English countryside.

She has several published novels to date, with subject matter including cowboys, BDSM and Myth/Fantasy. She has also written short stories for anthologies and has even had some raunchy poems published.

She likes to keep busy, cramming as much into each day as she possibly can, while battling—and is determined to win—against breast cancer. She loves to hear from her readers, so please get in touch!

Bella loves to hear from readers. You can find her contact information, website details and author profile page at https://www.totallybound.com

Home of Erotic Romance

Sign up for our newsletter and find out about all our romance book releases, eBook sales and promotions, sneak peeks and FREE romance books!